ROBIN HULL was a general practitioner near Stratford-upon-Avon in Warwickshire before becoming a peripatetic academic teaching General Practice to medical students visiting all the continents and teaching on five of them. He has published several medical books and many articles in the medical press. He founded the General Practitioners Writers Association and for some years was its President. In addition he visited many of the islands of the West Coast of Scotland, sometimes teaching on courses, doing locums or just holidaying with a fishing rod, climbing boots and binoculars. He retired from medicine in 1991 to fish, to garden to watch, and to write, about birds. In 2001 his *Scottish Birds: Culture and Tradition* was published, and he is currently working on *Birds of the Old Statistical Account*.

He lives in Perthshire and is married to Gillian, a tourist guide, who also writes articles in *The Scots Magazine*, *The Lady* and other periodicals. He has three daughters and six grandchildren.

Ravens over the Hill
Scottish Birds: Culture and Tradition
Just a GP: a Biography of Professor Sir Michael Drury

The HEALING ISLAND

ROBIN HULL

Steve Savage
LONDON AND EDINBURGH

Steve Savage Publishers Ltd
The Old Truman Brewery
91 Brick Lane
LONDON
E1 6QL

www.savagepublishers.com

Published in Great Britain by Steve Savage Publishers Ltd 2004
The Healing Island first appeared in an abridged form in
The Scots Magazine under the title *The Seudaig Saga*

ISBN 1-904246-10-9

British Library Cataloguing in Publication Data
A catalogue entry for this book is available from the British Library

Cover illustration:

Typeset by Steve Savage Publishers Ltd
Printed and bound by The Cromwell Press Ltd

In memory of my mother
Charlotte Maxwell Chalmers
And for her great grandson
George Peter Hull Waters,
who arrived, all 7 lbs 9 oz of him,
while this book was being written.

Preface

It is no good looking for Laigersay in an Atlas, for you will not find it. The reason is simple: it does not exist except in the minds of all who love the west coast of Scotland. It draws a little from almost every island from Arran to Cape Wrath and is the quintessence of them all.

Like all the characters in this story Laigersay is make-believe, as are the 'quotations' about the island purporting to come from *The Old Statistical Account* and the pens of Pennant and Martin Martin.

However the stories told in it are real enough.

Nearly all have occurred, either within the practice of the author or of those of his friends in many different parts of the world.

Robin Hull
Strathtay
January 2002–October 2003

CHAPTER I

Old Squarebottle

There was no doubt about the coming storm. The sky to the west was blackening, and the sea was that familiar dead leaden hue with an ominous swell. I was going to get to the island, but would I be able to return? After nearly twenty-four hours travelling from London, I was tired and could only think of arrival; return was for later.

The little ship gave a toot and drew away from the quay. I left the deck chilled by the rising wind of an early October afternoon and sought the warmth of the small observation saloon. There were few other passengers, but one drew my attention. He was a clerical gentleman, who had a violin case beside him, and, of all things, was reading *Mein Kampf*—in German. He glanced up and, seeing me looking at his book, laughed and said:–

'Don't worry, I have to study evil if only to keep up with my colleagues in the Free Church! Actually I picked it up in a secondhand bookshop on the mainland... you'll be the new doctor I think?'

I was astonished, for as far as I was aware only my family knew why I was on my way to the remote island of Laigersay.

'Hardly that,' I said, 'I am just up for an interview. Do you know I don't even know how to pronounce the name of the island properly? Are you from round here?'

'Aye, I'm the minister at Port Chalmers, have been for ten years. Incidentally, you say it like legacy—you know, what you hope your favourite uncle will leave you—then lengthen the last syllable as in "pray". They say it comes from Norse. I believe *Laege* means doctor, but they didn't have doctors in those days, so it probably means healer. Aye, there you have it, Laigersay, healing island.'

'Laigersay,' I repeated, 'I like that, the island of healing.'

'That's right,' the minister went on. 'I know Dr Hamish Robertson well. He told me last week you were coming today.'

Not for the first time a feeling of irritation at this island doctor stirred me. 'I answered his advertisement in the *British Medical Journal*,' I said, 'and then he sent me this telegram...' I groped in the pocket of my duffel coat and showed the yellow envelope to the minister. Without taking it, he quoted, 'Come on Wednesday next. Will meet boat. Dr Robertson.'

'How did you know?'

'Because I was talking to him when he wrote it, in Port Chalmers Post Office. Hamish told me if you responded to that, you had the job, but if not...' He shrugged.

'I have to be back in London by the weekend.'

The minister glanced up at the storm clouds and shrugged again. 'I must introduce myself. I am Angus Andersen, with an "e", as a residue of former Viking rape and pillage, and an old friend of your new boss. We disagree on many things but for all that he's a great chap. You'll like him; well most of the time, anyway.'

'What's he like?'

'He's a crusty, paternalistic old bachelor, but a great fisher and a piper. But that's not all: he's a sailor and a mountaineer, an expert on wildflowers and birds. He's a writer and he paints a bit. He's a very spiritual man, though he'd fume to hear me say so, for he claims to be agnostic. He's also very fond of whisky and has a fierce temper, but nearly all his patients adore him. He only has about fifteen hundred patients in his practice, but he needs all the time he can get for his non-medical interests. By the way, he is also a hero.'

'How come?'

'A few years back Jason Smith, a crofter from Assilag—that's an island to the south connected to Laigersay by a causeway—went berserk with a shotgun. It was a terrible business; he shot his wife dead and then drove from the south of the island to Port Chalmers. He holed up in my kirk scaring the cleaner out of her wits. She came running to me saying the man wanted me. I was doing a visit up in town when she found me, so I walked to the kirk. As I passed the Co-op who should come out but Hamish Robertson carrying a bag with two bottles of Johnnie Walker whisky... That's how he got his nickname by the way: Old Squarebottle. Anyway he said he'd come with me to the kirk. When we got there all was quiet and we walked in. Jason was up near the pulpit and he loosed off a shot at us and we were down on the floor in a flash. He had it in for me because he thought one of my sermons was directed at him and said he wanted to kill me.

'So there we were lying behind pillars in a darkening church with him shouting abuse at me. Then Hamish started talking. The Smith family had had appalling misfortune; their eldest son was drowned out fishing when he was nineteen, then they lost their ten-year-old daughter with meningitis. Hamish talked about these children. Of course he knew them well, even to the prizes they had won at school. Slowly Jason calmed down and Hamish slid one of the square bottles along the floor of the aisle to where Jason could get it. They each opened a bottle and started drinking. Meanwhile Hamish went on talking. In the end Jason drank so much he just went to sleep. Hamish picked up the shotgun and the police took over. It was quite a sensation at the time, and Hamish got a gong for it... but enough havering, we're not far from Eilean Lach-bhinn: we'd better have a look at the weather.'

On the deck the wind had freshened and there was sleet in it as we turned into Port Chalmers harbour past a small island. The minister repeated, 'That's Eilean Lach-bhinn, you know, the Isle of the Long-tailed Duck; they used to congregate there in winter time, we still see them sometimes.'

'That's not a bird I know, but I've heard of them... we certainly don't see many in London.'

'Well, you're in luck—there's a handsome male just in line with the lighthouse.'

Squinting through the murk I could just see a pale duck with a dark breast and a long, pheasant-like tail.

'*Lach-bhinn* in Gaelic; but they also call them Coal-and-candlelight, partly because of their colour but also because their calls sound like "candley". We get plenty of them round the island later in the winter.'

He paused, turning to the bay of Port Chalmers to scan the harbour with his binoculars. 'And there's your man waiting for you: borrow the glasses.'

So I saw the man who had sent for me so peremptorily. I have to say I did not relish what I saw. He was a tall, heavily built man whose severe face was darkened by a flowing black beard. He had an aggressive stance, suggesting an autocratic personality. Two sitting Labradors, one black and one yellow, flanked him.

The gangway clattered down and Angus Andersen was soon greeting the doctor and introducing me. I bent to greet the Labradors and the first words the doctor uttered were:–

'Don't touch my dogs.'

I apologised, and wondered why I had travelled six hundred miles from London.

The doctor led me to his battered Land Rover and said, 'Take you to the hotel—pick you up for dinner in about half an hour.'

'OK,' I acquiesced, keeping my words as brief as his, and wondering what sort of man had ordered me to this remote island.

But I was tired of travelling, and a shower at the hotel did much to revive me. By the time Old Squarebottle arrived, the storm had worsened and he came with a spare oilskin for me against the now torrential rain.

'Put this on,' he said. 'We're in for a real Hebridean gale... could last a week.'

As I thought of my appointment in London for three days time, I began to feel full of gloom.

His house was warm and comfortable. It was full of books, and an easel stood by the door. A shotgun hung on the wall above a fire where the two Labradors thumped their tails in greeting.

They, at any rate, seemed welcoming.

'Drink?' he asked.

'Thank you.' And a large scotch was thrust into my hand.

'*Slàinte mhath*,' he said, and sipped. Then he warmed slightly and said, 'Well, you're here. I rather wondered if you'd come.'

'I must get back on the Friday ferry... I have to be in London by Sunday.'

'So soon? But then you don't know our Laigersay storms; this wind could last a week, you'd better resign yourself to longer.'

'I have to confess I answered your advertisement largely out of curiosity. It was not very clear what you were offering. I assumed it to be for a short locum.'

My host stared into his drink. 'Not sure. Locum to start with... if I can find the right person, then something more permanent.'

I was embarrassed. 'Oh, I came here on the assumption that it would be for a short time. I have applied for a job in London that will start in a few months time.'

'Hmmm. We'll have to see what transpires. But right now we must attend to dinner.' He smiled enigmatically. 'My housekeeper will be furious if we do not pay it due attention.'

Dinner was excellent. I was aware of the housekeeper moving about in the adjoining room, which I presumed was the kitchen, but we were not introduced. I made a mental note to congratulate her if I got the chance. The grouse was delicious. I had only eaten it once before, when I had found it tough and heathery. The bird in front of me was pink-fleshed tenderness and splendidly gamy. The Chambertin served with it was a great wine. It seemed that my host was more of a *bon viveur* than was apparent at first sight. Clearly the housekeeper was a talented cook. I hoped I might have another chance to sample her skills.

Over dinner he relaxed and began to speak of the island where he had settled sixteen years before, after service in the RAMC in Italy and Normandy. I commented that I had done three years as a naval doctor but not until long after the war. He clearly loved Laigersay, particularly its wildness and the fine cliffs to the south. He had written a great deal about the island, particularly its climbing, natural history and fishing. As he spoke of it, his gruffness softened, one of the dogs settled by him with its head on his knee and a moment later the other one sat by me.

'You know about dogs?' he asked.

'We bred Labradors at home for years.'

'You did... good. Sorry I told you not to touch them, but I dislike people I don't know fondling my dogs... Florin seems to have taken to you.'

'Florin?'

'Aye. All my dogs have been named after money; the black one is Florin and this one is Siller: she was almost white as a pup.' Slowly he seemed to be mellowing and doubtless would have talked about dogs for hours had the phone not rung. He listened for a moment and then said:–

'We'll not get her away tonight... let me think a moment.' He put down the phone and stared into space, then he said to the caller, 'Tell you what, I've got another doctor with me tonight. I'll send him over to see you and bring her up here. Put all your lights on so he can find you. I'll go to the hospital now and get ready... we'll see you all right, and don't worry, we'll get her sorted.'

He put the phone down and turned to me. 'It's young Thomasina, daughter of Helen and Thomas Chalmers of Pitchroich... sounds like an appendix. By the way, are you a surgeon?'

'A very inexperienced one... I'm certainly no gas-man.'

'I'll do that. Where's the map... I'll show you where the farm is. There... it's about seven miles out of town down the coast road; you cross the Pitchroich Burn there and the farm is on the right. You won't miss it; they will have lots of light showing. Have a look at her and then bring her back to the Cottage Hospital—that's just there on the map, just south of your hotel. Take the Land Rover and I'll see you later.'

He bundled me back into oilskins and took me to his car. Before I knew what was happening I was driving through the gale to the coast. It was not difficult to find the farm for, once clear of Port Chalmers, there was nothing to see but a few storm-battered sheep. There was a group of crofts huddled together against the wind with a burn, rumbling in spate, beyond them. Then to the right I saw the glimmer of lights round the farm.

Thomasina was an attractive child, but she looked apprehensive as I entered her room. She had had tummy ache the night before and had thought little of it, but now the pain was worse, had moved to her right side and she had been sick. Sure enough, she was very tender in the right lower quadrant of her abdomen, and I had little doubt that she had acute appendicitis.

Her mother wrapped her up in a blanket with an oilskin outside it, and I carried her out to the Land Rover. As we drove back, Mrs Chalmers told me her husband was away to the mainland for tractor parts, and wasn't it always when the man was away that these things happened? Then she said, 'Doctor, I don't even know your name.'

'It's the same as yours, I'm a Chalmers too.'

'Och, we're two a penny in this island. Do you come from round here?'

'No, my father came from Dunoon, but he lived in England all his life, that's where I went to school and grew up... looks as though we're here... is this the hospital?'

'Aye. This is where Thomasina was born.' Suddenly the self-controlled mother's voice faltered, and I guessed she was asking herself if the life that had begun here might end here too.

'She'll be fine,' I said, with what I hoped was a reassuring tone. But a sudden snatch of fear touched me, like a cold shiver. Was I really up to this? I remembered my surgical teachers saying that a straightforward appendicectomy was simple, but rare. A competent surgeon had to be able to cope with unexpected developments.

Somehow, even after such brief acquaintance, I seemed to know Thomasina and her mother in a more personal way than the clinical, distant, contact I had had with hospital patients. This added a new dimension to responsibility.

I was not sure what to expect of this cottage hospital in such a remote island and was agreeably surprised to find an adequate if simple theatre. It was certainly as good as the ship's sick bay where I had carried out my last appendicectomy.

Dr Robertson had been busy with the night staff preparing for surgery. He introduced me to Kirsty Stewart, who was matron of the hospital and acting as theatre sister. When he examined Thomasina it was immediately noticeable how at peace the child seemed to be with this gruff monosyllabic man. She had a sedative as premedication. As I scrubbed, Dr Robertson asked Helen Chalmers to hold Thomasina's hand while a needle slipped into a vein, and the child was asleep.

The operation was straightforward: the girl was slim and fit and the muscle layers parted easily under my scalpel to reveal the peritoneum. As soon as this was opened the appendix was visible, grossly engorged with an abscess at its tip. The organ was tied off, divided and its stump buried in the wall of the caecum. The whole job took about half an hour.

I took off my mask and gloves and, glancing at the theatre clock, realised I had not been in bed for over thirty-six hours. After seeing my young patient settle, I went back to the hotel. I felt very tired, but as I drifted into sleep I felt that I was probably going to stay in Laigersay.

CHAPTER 2

The Island

The long, sleep-deprived journey from London to Laigersay, culminating in my strange meeting with Dr Robertson and the emergency appendicectomy, had left me exhausted. As soon as Thomasina Chalmers was settled for the night, I returned to the hotel to sleep for twelve hours.

In the light of the next day, stormy though it was, I reviewed and reversed my late-night decision to stay on in the island. On the face of it such a decision would be crazy; I loved the idea of working in the wilderness, but was equally certain I could not work with a colleague of such bizarre personality as Hamish Robertson. However for the time being such considerations were academic; a glance out of the hotel window told me that I was going nowhere for the foreseeable future. Outside the rain fell almost horizontally, driven by a fierce gale.

I found I had left my toothpaste behind so, struggling into the oilskins Dr Robertson had lent me the night before, I braved the weather, and was dodging between what few patches of cover the main street of Port Chalmers had to offer, when a particularly savage squall thrust me into a bus shelter already occupied by an elderly man. He greeted me as I joined him and for a moment I thought he said, 'Good morning, Doctor,' but then decided the fury of the storm was confusing me.

A few minutes later I reached the Co-op and went in to get out of the weather. Shaking myself and throwing off the hood of the oilskins, I found a middle-aged woman smiling before me.

'It's a dreich day, is it no, Doctor?'

'Yes,' I replied, 'but how do you know I am a doctor?'

'Och, the whole place kens fine who ye are. Dr Hamish has been singing the praises of his new assistant. So has Helen Chalmers.'

A man in a dripping mackintosh added, 'Aye, it was a fine job you did last night, Doctor, and we're right glad you're stopping with us.'

As I reeled under these pleasant but unwanted greetings, I heard a soft, educated, Scottish voice behind me say, 'May I add my welcome too?'

I turned to find a most unexpected person. He was obviously a Sikh, from his turban and immaculate beard, but here, in a remote island, and speaking with a Scots accent?

He saw my surprise and bowed, with his elegant fingers pressed together in the gesture of *namaste* I had so often seen in India, when my ship had called there en route from the Persian Gulf to Fremantle in Western Australia.

'Do not be surprised, I was brought up in Scotland and have learnt the ways of the country. I am, however, as you have observed, still a Sikh. But I have a question for you. Did you enjoy your dinner last night? I like cooking game.'

My mind went back to the night before. This elegant Indian gentleman must have been the 'housekeeper' whose unobtrusive movements I had heard in Dr Robertson's kitchen.

Seeing that I was still puzzled, the Sikh added, 'I am Tetrabal Singh: Doctor Hamish and I are old friends. Actually he saved my life once, and, as I love nothing better than to cook, I now work for him. One day, perhaps, I will tell you what a fine man he is. But now I must hurry back with what the doctor calls "the messages".' He bowed, made *namaste* again, and left.

The man in the wet coat said: 'My, if you've sampled Tet's cooking you're a verra lucky man. They say it's fabulous. And he's a verra decent chap. Mind, we all wondered when he came here. We're not as used to these furriners as they are in Lewis.'

Confused, I bought a few things but found they had no toothpaste. I was directed to the chemist's shop along the street. Over the door I read: 'Port Chalmers Pharmacy. David Ross MPS'. It was the same there, for the pharmacist greeted me like a long-lost friend and added his congratulations on my new post. Everyone, it seemed, knew that I was the new doctor in town, except me.

The chemist's shop had several customers and soon I was the target of much curiosity. Where was I from? Was my wife with me? And, with the name of Chalmers, did I have relatives in the island? I confessed to having come from London but shook my head at wife and relatives. The man in the wet mackintosh seemed to have followed me from the Co-op; he obviously knew the pharmacist well and commented:–

'It'll be nice to have a new face in the surgery. There's nothing wrong wi' Doctor Hamish, mind... But he's no verra talkative.'

He turned to the white coated man behind the counter. 'David, d'ye mind when Archie Campbell had that bit stushie wi' Doctor Hamish?'

There was a stir of laughter in the shop and the man turned back to me. 'I'm Peter McKay, by the way, I farm out by Thomas and Helen Chalmers at Pitchroich—that's how I heard all about last night. But I was telling you about Archie Campbell. Archie is one of those people who never seem to be well, and he's often down at the doctor's. I think Doctor Hamish gets fed up wi' him. Anyroad this time he had a wee bit sore throat. He told the doc who grunted and then told him "open wide" and shone a light in his mouth and then he grunted again. Archie didnae think he was getting value for his NHS stamp so he told the doctor "and my piles are killing me". This time Doctor Hamish spoke a bit more. "Trousers off," he said, "up on the couch." Then he looked at Archie's rear end and he grunted again and said, "Give you something," and he marched off to his dispensary at the back of the surgery and counted out some penicillin lozenges for Archie's throat. He wrote instructions—"one to be held in the cheek until dissolved"—and gave them to Archie and that was his consultation done. A week later Archie was back wi' an awfu' rash on his bum. He was indignant and said to the doctor, "I have to stand still for bloody hours to get those things to dissolve!"'

Joining the general laughter in the shop, I beat a retreat back to the hotel. Here was a pretty state of things; I had reversed my decision of the night before, but everyone in the island seemed to know who I was and that I was staying as the new doctor. I tried to remember if I had said anything the night before that Doctor Hamish, as they all seemed to call him, might have taken as acceptance. Puzzled and confused, I decided to go over to the cottage hospital to see how Thomasina was after her operation.

As I entered the hospital, an unknown nurse greeted me by name. She introduced herself as Morag Finlayson and said: 'You'll be wanting to see Thomasina. You did a good job there; normally all our emergencies are flown to the mainland, but that was not possible in yesterday's storm. The wee girl's fine today. Her mother's with her just now.'

It is strangely unreal to be in a situation where everybody greets one by name and yet everyone is unknown. It was a relief to see Helen Chalmers; at least I had met her before.

'Thank you for what you did last night, Doctor. It was a terrible night, and we'd never have got her to the mainland. By the way, I was so glad when Doctor Hamish said you were staying on to work here; it's not a big community, but we really need two doctors. I managed to get Tom, my husband, on the phone. He was very grateful and he wanted to know if you were a fisher... we've got a stretch of water on the burn below the farm and the sea trout are running well and there's still a few days left of the season.'

'To tell the truth, I don't know what I'm doing. Last night I thought I might stay, but this morning I felt the sooner I got back down south the better. Now everyone I meet tells me I'm staying. I don't know... I have a feeling of unreality... everybody knows me and I know nobody.'

Then I found myself telling her about an embarrassing happening in a practice down south where I had been a locum for a short time. I was sent to see a 17-year-old girl with a nasty quinsy. She needed penicillin and I injected her behind every day for six days after which she was improving. I told her to wait a day or two and then to come and see me in the surgery. When she came in she was well, she was dressed and she was made up. I failed to recognise her until she told me who she was. In my embarrassment I blurted out, 'Sorry but whenever I meet a girl in bed I never know her again.'

Helen was laughing. 'You could have phrased that better!'

'Yes indeed, and the story about the doctor's memory was round that practice in no time. I shall have to be careful here.'

'So you are staying. That's good.'

'Looks as though I shall have to, at least until this gale blows itself out. Anyway Thomasina's on the mend. If I do stay I might take your husband up on the offer of fishing. If I can borrow some tackle.'

'I'm sure we can fix that.'

And with the promise of a bit of late season fishing, I went back to the hotel in a better mood, to telephone my family in the south.

There was a message for me that Dr Robertson was busy, but he hoped I would join him for dinner, and would I like to borrow the car for a bit of a spin round the island? It was by the surgery and the keys were in it. Having come all this way, it certainly seemed a good idea to explore. The Land Rover was pretty battered but in good working order, and I was soon retracing my route of the night before, southwards out of Port Chalmers towards Pitchroich. At first the landscape, viewed through rain and the stroboscope of the wipers, was open moorland, but at the bridge over the Pitchroich burn it began to get higher. I stopped at the burn and, pulling my waterproofs round me, jumped out to look at the stream. It was in high spate, peaty brown and roaring, just the sort of torrent to bring the sea trout up. As I watched, a fish of about three pounds jumped clear of the water below me. There is nothing like the sight of a good fish to stir an angler's heart and I thought again of Tom Chalmers' offer of fishing.

But, with the rain lashing my face, this was no day to hang about watching fish.

Past Pitchroich farm, in the storm's gloom, I could only sense the mountains rising to my right. The road climbed too and I realised the sea was a hundred feet below me. A few scattered crofts appeared to be uninhabited apart from collies that barked damply at me. As I rounded the southern end of the island the full fury of the southwesterly hit me and I could feel the vehicle lurching in the gale. The sea below me was an angry, boiling mass of white, and spume reached even up the hundred feet to the road. I stopped the Land Rover and found Squarebottle's much used map, and could see I had reached the southern tip of the island and was looking over the skerries of Ranneach Bay, with the island of Sgarbh an Sgumain to my left.

Today it was a wild scene and it enthralled me. I longed to see it on a clear day in spring when the cliffs would be thronged with breeding seabirds. Perhaps there would be golden eagles in the towering walls that I saw disappearing upwards into the murk; there might even be sea eagles here and a few peregrines as well. Then I came to, suddenly remembering that I had an interview soon for a prestigious job in London, which might be the opening of the door to my long cherished ambition of a surgical career. It was beginning to look as though I would not get back in time.

I stared into the storm marvelling at the sheer wildness of the place and wondered if I really wanted to go back to the rat race of the teaching hospitals of the south. In an agony of indecision, I turned back the way I had come. The map showed a side turning just after Pitchroich which crossed to the west of the island. I turned into this, driving slowly through worsening rain, which the wipers barely kept up with. Suddenly a speeding Jaguar filled the narrow road. It braked, skidded on the wet road and was in the ditch.

I stopped the car and ran to help the driver. He was unhurt, but very angry.

'What the hell do you think you're doing?' he shouted, 'Look what you've done to my car!'

Keeping my temper with this man, whose own driving had been entirely responsible for his plight, I enquired if he was all right. But he was still angry and demanded the details of my insurance company. I suggested that there was little point in standing in the rain and, since his car was not movable, could I take him anywhere?

'Yes, drive me to the castle.' And he pointed the way he had come.

I began to feel I had met an islander I liked even less than Old Squarebottle. It transpired that he owned Tom Bacadh Castle. In the hallway to the gloomy old castle, I explained that the car I was driving was not mine but belonged to Dr Robertson. In chilly formality I learned that the other driver was Major Thistlethwaite, who noted my full name and address. Here at any rate was one person in the island who did not know who I was.

Fortunately the borrowed Land Rover was undamaged, and I returned to the surgery. Doctor Hamish was home, and I told him of the mishap.

'So you've met the wee lairdie o' Tombaca,' he laughed.

'I thought it was Tom Bacadh...'

'So it is, laddie, it means the "hill of obstruction". They say that comes from an old battlefield where the Vikings were blocked when they were crossing the island. Nowadays everybody calls it *tombaca*, which means tobacco: that's where Major Thistlethwaite is said to have made his wealth... Nobody likes him here, and he likes nobody... including you, it seems.'

'Not a pleasant fellow, it seems. What's he doing here?'

'He bought the castle and the shooting rights for the whole of the south of the island from the real laird of Castle Chalmers two years ago and has been a pain in the arse ever since. Fortunately he's only here a bit of the time and the laird never parted with the fishing rights. James Chalmers, the laird, is a very different man, but he's getting on a bit now. I'll take you up to meet him some day.'

'Aren't you making a bit of an assumption? I probably won't be here.'

He gave me a long searching look: 'You'll be here, laddie, I can see already that the place has got under your skin, just like me. When I first came here, I could not wait to leave... after a day or two, I decided to give it a month... and I'm still here all these years later.'

I told him about the job opportunity in London, and he gave me the same searching stare.

'Angus Andersen told me you are interested in birds, and that when he showed you the long-tailed duck you said that you didn't get many of them in London.' He grinned. 'You have to make a choice... my guess is I know how you'll decide.'

CHAPTER 3

The Laird

My third day in the island was the worst of the storm. The wind was so fierce I could hardly stand against it. One of the hotel staff told me it was so bad that he had had to hold his wife down when they walked along the street. I could well believe it, for there were reports of structural damage all over the island. Much of the day I remained in the hotel, watching the steady drum of rain as it lashed against the windows. The prospect of getting off the island in time to make my interview in London grew bleaker by the hour. I pondered my eventful visit to the island. In three days I had encountered many people who seemed to know all about me, I had formed an uneasy relationship with Dr Hamish Robertson, Old Squarebottle, as he was known to his patients after his encounter with a shotgun toting lunatic in the Kirk. Then I had carried out emergency surgery on an island child and been involved in the wreck of Major Thistlethwaite's Jaguar.

In the afternoon Doctor Hamish phoned. He had been talking to the laird, Vice-Admiral Sir James Chalmers, and we were invited up to Castle Chalmers for an informal drink that evening.

'You'll get on with the laird, he's a great fellow … had a very distinguished war, and won the VC for destroying a German submarine base. He was taken prisoner, but managed to escape the Nazis and got back to Scotland. He's a bit "old school" in his ways, but a charming man and a dear friend.'

Hamish arranged to pick me up and show me part of the island on the way to the castle. By now thoroughly sick of the hotel and its outdated newspapers, I was glad of the break.

Hamish drove me west from Port Chalmers and I followed the route on his map. At first the road ran through forest, not the dreary monoculture of sitka spruce that has blighted so much of Scotland, but a lovely mixture of Scots pine, oak and birch such as might have cloaked the primeval land. Here they were bent and stunted by recurring winter gales, a good habitat for birds, I thought.

As if knowing my thoughts, Dr Robertson spoke of the birds: 'We get a huge number of species here including a number of vagrants after a storm like this. In the spring these woods are full of warblers. On the moors there are red and black grouse. The machair is alive with waders and the mountains have harriers, eagles and falcons … there are ptarmigan and even dotterel up there. Then by the shore there are otters and seals, pine martens and red squirrels in the woods and the hills hold many red deer and hordes of blue hares. The place is a natural historian's paradise… and that's before you start on my speciality, the wild flowers. I have listed over four hundred on the island, including many rarities. It's a wonderful place.'

I noticed that he was more communicative about his beloved island than anything else. He chuckled and added, 'It's not a bit like London!'

Leaving the woods, we turned past a huge expanse of gleaming sands. 'That's Cockle Beach where Jennie—she runs the surgery—likes to come for cockles. The village here is called after them in Gaelic: Coilleag. This is a good place for birds, especially just as the tide is coming: it's too far out just now.'

The road curved south after Coilleag; to the right was moorland stretching away to barely visible low hills covered with soggy heather. On the right the short grass of the machair, mown for countless years by sheep and rabbits, stretched to the sea like a rich man's manicured lawn. Two more tiny villages, Feadag Mhor and Feadag Bheag, led to another large burn marked as Allt Feadag on the map. Here Hamish stopped the car.

'This is one of my favourite fishing spots,' he said. 'At high tide at this time of year, there's a good run of sea trout in the lower stretch below the bridge. They're best at night... I had a six-pounder there last summer. The salmon don't come up here much... you want the Allt Bradan for that... that's getting damned expensive now, but the laird usually lets me have a day or two up there. They're big fish for an island fishery, the best I've had would be about twelve pounds. Upstream there is Loch Bradan itself; that's difficult to get on to for salmon but the brownies are good.

'The hills to the north are calcareous, unlike the volcanic basalt of the mountains in the south. There were once three volcanoes there that make up the Three Witches—our biggest hills—the highest is just 2,735 feet. You can still make out the dykes left by the lava flows when the volcanoes erupted. The major flow was to the south, creating the islands and skerries there, but some lava came northwards. There is basic rock to the north and west of Bradan, so the Loch is slightly alkaline. That makes for good insect life and the trout run big. The machair on the right, between the road and the sea, is also less acid because of the shell sand. It's marvellous for wildflowers, with carpets of yellow flags and thrift, and the place is a mass of breeding waders and a host of little birds in spring. People like to camp there in summer but they only stay one night: they can't sleep for midges and corncrakes.

'The next village is Lutheran, with the most sheltered beach in the island. You get a lot of great northern divers there in winter and of course both red and black-throats breed on the hill lochs... not many of them in London either. Then there are the long-tailed ducks. We get plenty round the island later in the winter.'

Beyond Lutheran we came to high cliffs broken by a winding track down to the causeway leading to the small island of Assilag. The main road ended there above the rocky Assilag Bay which was surrounded by cliffs apart from the way down to the causeway.

'You can drive across to Assilag at low tide but not in weather like this. They get cut off regularly. I got stuck there years ago when I went to a confinement at Tuilleag Farm. There was nothing to do but ceilidh and drink whisky. I managed, though.'

Then, saying that we had better not keep the laird waiting, he reversed and we retraced our route. Near Feadag Mhor, another Land Rover turned from a side road and Hamish pulled into a passing place. The other driver passed in a hurry without acknowledgement.

'Your friend,' said Hamish. 'That's the major all over... thinks the road is his and never gives a wave if you pull over for him. Anyway, he's driving again.'

The route lay through the woods north of Port Chalmers. A woodcock took off from the side of the road and Squarebottle said: 'We get a lot at this time of year— they fly in from Scandinavia—they are the best eating of them all. Tetrabal Singh does them to perfection. They are lovely creatures. Did you know they carry their chicks between their thighs when they fly?'

I realised that I had a lot to learn about the denizens of Laigersay, but right now it was the turn of the laird. Castle Chalmers dated from the late fifteenth century and, like Tom Bacadh Castle, looked forbidding as we approached, but inside it was warm and still despite the battering gale outside. Sir James Chalmers met us at the entry to the castle, which was guarded by an ancient yett of interlaced wrought iron. The laird led us into a sitting room with a huge fire before which a wolfhound raised his head and wagged his tail in drowsy greeting. The admiral was an old man, dressed in tweeds which looked as though they had been made aeons before, and his white hair gave him a benignly venerable air. Unlike the owner of the other castle he was most welcoming.

'Hamish, it's good to see you. My family are away and I'm all by myself. So this is the protégé you were telling me about. It's good to meet you, young man.' And he shook my hand warmly. 'I gather you're a Chalmers too.'

I agreed, and explained about my father leaving Clydeside for work in England and my upbringing there.

'I notice you are James Chalmers,' I added. 'We had a relative of that name we were repeatedly told about as children. The poor chap got eaten by cannibals.'

'Yes, that would be James Chalmers, the missionary, who was killed—in Samoa, I think it was—interesting that he was a relative of yours... but let me get you a dram; you need that on a night like this.'

The old man left us and I studied the room. It was furnished as a library, and walled with shelves of beautiful old leatherbound volumes. There was a haphazard pile of books and papers completely covering a full sized billiard table. By the fireplace there were occasional tables with family photographs.

Hamish pointed at an elderly woman 'That was Lady Chalmers—a wonderful person—she died three years ago; massive cerebral haemorrhage. James has been something of a recluse since. He spends his time writing about naval history, hence the jumble of documents... those are the children... Murdoch, the heir, is working in London as a publisher, he's in his early thirties now.' Picking up another picture of a teenage girl in riding clothes: 'This is

Fiona. She finished at Glasgow University last summer; she got a first-class honours degree in zoology. Gosh, how she's changed, she used to be a plain little thing; she's a real beauty now.'

The laird came back bearing a tray with a cut-glass jug of water and a decanter. He nodded at the piles on the billiard table. 'Please forgive the mess, I'm afraid my in-tray is a bit full at present. I do hope you like this whisky. I found it during the first war, when I was driving a destroyer in Orkney; I've never drunk anything else. It's "Scapa".' Turning to me he added, 'Hamish tells me you were in the Royal Navy too?'

'Only for a little while, I am afraid, sir. I was a Surgeon Lieutenant in the Persian Gulf. I left the service last spring.'

'Ah yes I remember the Gulf well. I was SNOPG a few years before I retired. Sorry, Hamish, that's Senior Naval Officer Persian Gulf. A very warm posting, but I liked the Gulf.'

Inevitably conversation turned on naval matters, and I found myself warming to this grand old man who was such a contrast to the angry major I had met the day before.

He spoke of Dubai and I told him of a visit I had made there. I had promised to buy some pearls for my mother and called at a lapidary's shop in the suq at Dubai. The shop did not look very prepossessing but I went in and said I was interested in seeing some pearls. The Indian shopkeeper led me upstairs and a huge Arab in a dishdasha followed and stood at the doorway. It did not take much to make me realise this was 'Security'.

I was invited to sit, and the merchant opened a wall safe and drew out a canvas bag and a series of metal dishes rather like colanders. Each of these had holes of differing diameter. The merchant poured pearls from the sack into the colander with the largest holes and shook it until most of the pearls fell into the next colander below. By repeating this he sorted his pearls by size and gave me a price for each size. I made a selection of four pearls and the merchant asked what I intended doing with them

I told him they were for my mother but I did not know what I would do with them back home. He suggested putting a coloured stone with them and asked if I would like to see some. He opened the safe again and from an interior drawer took out a number of tissue paper parcels. Each contained different gemstones; it was as if I were in Aladdin's cave. I ran sapphires, rubies and emeralds through my fingers and felt like Croesus. Tentatively I asked prices, and was surprised at how low they were. In the end I bought a sapphire for my mother and a beautiful quarter-carat emerald.

'For memsahib?' The merchant enquired.

I shook my head. 'I have no memsahib... but perhaps one day.'

The admiral chuckled. 'There is still no memsahib?'

'That's right: a wife tends to inhibit a career in medicine; but I still have the emerald. I carry it with me; I never know when it might come in useful.' I pulled out the little box and showed him the gem.

'Lucky girl,' he said. 'I always liked having a doctor on board,' he continued, changing the subject. 'They not only gave an air of security but they brought a new angle into a ship, a marked change from the tradition of the service. But I always wondered what happened if the doctor himself got sick?'

'That happened to me, sir. I was quite ill in the Gulf with a high fever. Nobody knew what was the matter with me and they thought I was dying... the Chief Boatswain even went so far as to make a canvas bag for me.'

'But you obviously did not need burial at sea... do you know where the last stitch in the bag went?' I knew, but guessing he wanted to tell me, I shook my head. 'It went through the dead man's nose; it was his last chance, if he didn't squeal then he went over the side!'

'We did have one bizarre thing happen. One ship's doctor went very odd in the intense heat. His captain signalled us that the fellow believed himself to be Jesus Christ and demanded that he take over command of the ship. We rendezvoused with the other frigate and I took a look at my colleague. Frankly, he was a severe schizophrenic and completely confused. The intense heat of the Gulf seemed to have precipitated his illness. I stayed in his ship and sedated him, and eventually we got to an RAF hospital in Aden, by which time he was much better. We arrived there in the heat of the day when every one was at siesta. I couldn't find anyone to hand him over to and we both walked round the hospital looking for someone. Eventually I ran into an RAF sergeant who said, 'We have been expecting you, sir, come this way.' I followed and my mad colleague dawdled after us. Suddenly the sergeant opened a door and ushered me in. The door slammed behind me and I found myself in a padded cell. I shouted out, 'It's not me, it's the other chap,' and I heard the sergeant's voice through the door saying, 'That, sir, is what they all say!'

The admiral chuckled. ' How long did you stay there?'

'Not very long, but the authorities took some convincing.'

So a very pleasant interlude continued, with the laird capping each naval anecdote with one of his own, and then he asked me what I planned for my future now I was out of the service. I told him I intended to become a consultant surgeon.

'So why are you here in Laigersay?'

'A good question. I answered Dr Robertson's advertisement for a locum on impulse. I love Scotland and part of me has always wanted to live here. But, medically speaking, this is the back of beyond. I'd never achieve anything here. All the same, I have to say I'm fed up with the rat race down south. Part of me longs for the peace and wilderness I find here. Right now I'm torn by indecision. I have an interview for a very good job in London next week.'

'Difficult for you. I know how you feel. As a young man I travelled all over the world, yet I always remembered my boyhood in Laigersay. When my father died, just after the war, I faced the same sort of choice you have. I was offered an ambassadorial post after I left the service; it was that or return to Laigersay as the new laird. I chose the latter. If it helps you, I have never regretted it.'

Hamish was glancing at his watch. 'I still have patients to see, James, so I think we should slip away. Thanks for the dram. I think you'll be seeing more of Dr Robert Chalmers.'

'Hamish, I have an inkling you may be right.'

As we left, I wondered why everything seemed to conspire to make me decide the wrong way. We drove back to Port Chalmers in silence. Hamish suddenly stopped the car. There in the road ahead of us was the round-headed, sleek form of an otter. Rather than run, he stood erect and gazed at us with curiosity, his whiskers gleaming in the headlights. Then, deciding that we meant him no harm, he turned and slipped away into the woods. He was the first otter I had ever seen,

'Damn,' I said. 'Damn it all, why do even the wild creatures here try to make me stay against my better judgement?'

Beside me, Hamish chuckled to himself.

CHAPTER 4

Home Visits

Much as I like smoked fish, I was getting rather tired of the hotel breakfast menu. Finnan haddock on a daily basis becomes tedious. The waiter regretted the lack of choice, explaining that the steamer had been unable to call during the storm. As it had for the past three days, the rain, blown horizontally by the force of the gale, was lashing the windows. I was pondering a further damp exploration of the island when I was called to the phone.

I immediately recognised Dr Robertson's voice. 'Laddie, I'm a bit busy this morning. Could you help me out with a couple of visits? They are both regulars I see once in a while, and I promised them today, but something has cropped up. If you come over to the surgery when convenient, I'll leave the car for you and Jennie Churches will tell you all you need to know.'

This seemed fun, and would give me a chance to explore a bit more. I readily agreed, commenting that it was time I saw the surgery anyway. Finishing my haddock and having a third cup of coffee to wash away some of its salt, I donned Old Squarebottle's oilskins and fought my way the few hundred yards against the wind to the surgery. The low red sandstone building was quite an eye-opener. There were two doors; one marked 'Boys', the other 'Girls'. Obviously it had served as the primary school for Port Chalmers until a new school had been built just after the war. Inside the old familiar smells of chalk dust and drying ink mingled with those of ether and carbolic. The old assembly room, though it was now the waiting room, looked as though it had hardly changed. An ancient leather tawse hung threateningly from a hook on the wall. The wall blackboard was still in use, with chalked messages asking patients to bring a SPECIMEN when attending surgery. A list of the days when the doctor visited various parts of the Island hung there. I looked to see what Saturday had logged against it, and saw that Doctor Hamish visited Lutheran and Assilag that day. I remembered that was near one of his favourite fishing spots, and suspected a combination of business and pleasure.

'Good morning, Doctor.' A voice behind startled me. 'Another terrible day, but I've got the coffee made. I'm

Jennie Churches, by the way, for my sins I have to try to organise Dr Hamish. That's an uphill task, I can tell you. He'd completely forgotten that there's a committee meeting at the new school today and he's chairing it. Then I discovered he'd promised a visit to Maggie McPhee up by Loch Bradan. Anyone else and I would have phoned to cancel, but I can't do that for Maggie. Anyway come and have your coffee, and I'll explain.'

Jennie led the way into one of the smallest consulting rooms I had ever seen. It was crammed with books, instruments and unopened journals. A fishing rod in its case and a landing net were close by the door, an old fashioned botanist's tin vasculum lay among correspondence and drug advertisements littered on the huge roll-top desk, which dominated the room. A well-used swivel chair showed evidence of years of polish from the Harris-tweeded bottom of the doctor. Beside it a lesser chair was set for his patients. There seemed to be no examination couch.

Jennie burst out laughing at my face. 'You wouldn't believe what a marvellous doctor he is. But even his greatest admirer would never accuse him of being well organised. I am not allowed to touch anything in here. I shudder to think what has become of what was my office when I was head teacher here. He says he knows where everything is. I will say this for him: he's got a wonderful memory. Knows everything about everyone since the day they were born.'

'But there's nowhere to examine patients!' I burst out.

'We had an examination couch once, but it got so rickety Dr Hamish threw it out. Here in the island they don't expect to get examined very often. If they're that sick, Dr Hamish sends them home to bed and examines them there... now, mind, if you are coming to work here you're not to be so untidy.'

'Um,' I began, when for a moment she paused to draw breath, 'I'm not at all sure I will be... coming to work,

I mean. I'm only here this morning to help with some visits...'

'Ah yes. I'll tell you about them in a minute, but here's your coffee: drink it while it's hot. By the way, I made the shortbread myself. The doctor says it's the best in the world.'

So saying, she made a little space on the cluttered desk, and set a large cup of freshly brewed, aromatic coffee before me. I sat at the desk, bumping my knee on a half-open, completely jammed drawer, and nibbled her shortbread. It was excellent and she beamed when I told her so.

'Now,' she said, 'I'm bursting to know all about you, though I have hardly forgiven you for not coming to see me before. I know you're single, your father came from Dunoon, you're reluctant to accept the doctor's offer of a job, you have an interview for a surgical registrar's job at your old teaching hospital and you're an accomplished surgeon who has completely stolen young Thomasina Chalmers' heart, as well as her appendix—and Admiral Chalmers' heart too, by the sound o't. What have I missed?'

Now it was my turn to laugh at this energetic, septuagenarian 'dragon-at-the-gate', as so many doctors' receptionists were called. 'You seem to know it all, though some of it is rather exaggerated. You are right, I don't think I shall stay in Laigersay: the job in London beckons. But I have to say I love it here, apart from the weather.'

'Ah! You should see it in May. It doesn't always blow, and the spring is wonderful, when the sea is calm and the birds are breeding. The machair is pink with thrift and the woods a blue haze of hyacinths against the fresh green of the trees. It's a time for lovers and loving and even my old bones stop aching. If you saw it then you'd never want your smoky, smelly old London ever again.'

I could see the Scottish poetic tradition lived on in Jennie. In fact she would have gone on talking forever had I not reminded her of the visits Dr Robertson had asked me to do. Then she became businesslike, brought out an

Ordnance Survey map and gave me precise six-figure references for the three houses I was to visit. 'I'll show you my own map in a moment, but for the time being we'll make do with the shop map.'

Two of the visits were close together, set on a small track turning of the main road south of Lutheran. 'It's not a bad road,' she said, 'for it leads up to Loch Bradan Lodge where the Sinclairs live. They're well to do and keep the road in good order. The second house on the left is where Archie McPhee lives and his sister Maggie is in the next on the right. Hers is a black hoose, I think you are in for a surprise if you've never seen one before. But then Maggie will surprise you too. She is completely blind and deaf and has lived alone there as long as I can remember. She's in her eighties now and as indomitable as ever. She's a right old *cailleach*, if ever there was one...

'What's that?'

'A *cailleach*? Well literally it means an old woman but it is often used as a witch. Maggie is the kindest creature alive, but she does have her peculiarities... you'll discover that for yourself. I couldn't put her off today because there is no means of contacting her, and she loves her visit from the doctor. Before that, in the other house, lives her brother. Archie is a mere boy of 75 or so, but as spry as ever, though the gout catches him sometimes. He keeps an eye on his sister and does little jobs for her. Doctor Hamish always looks in when he's by.

'The other call is for Hettie Simpson. Hettie is one of two valetudinarian elderly spinster sisters who live with their pets in Lutheran village. While you're away, I will be making up the medicine Doctor Hamish always gives her; just tell her the postbus will bring it on Monday.' She paused and added, 'Oh, I should explain: this is a dispensing practice for all the patients who live more than a mile from David Ross's pharmacy. Most of the medicines are made up here by the doctor or me and they are delivered with the post.'

'But how do you know what Miss Simpson will need?'

'If she doesn't need her usual bottle, it will be the first time these last ten years. Now, here's the map I made of the island. I used to use this when I was teaching and I put in the house of every boy and girl who came to the school over all the time I was there. It's a wee bitty out o' date now, but is still quite useful to show visiting doctors like you where to go. There are a few houses missing; a few homes hadna a pupil of mine and one or two have been built since I retired. I have copies of this, so you keep it.'

Jennie showed me on her map the places I was to visit. 'I suggest you do the McPhees first, then the tide will be about right for you to see the great northern divers in Lutheran Bay. Then, when you've had your fill of them, go and see Hettie. One of the few good pubs in the island is near Cockle bay, you'll get your lunch there and be sure to tell Mhairi, who runs the Charmer Inn, that I'll be over as usual next week.' She explained that her name was spelled 'Mhairi' but started with a V sound.

'You might see some interesting birds in Cockle Bay too; it's a bit sheltered on the north there. Cockle Bay is one of my very favourite places and it's well named. I've gathered bucketfuls of them there. Not everyone likes cockles but I love them, especially in omelettes. When you've done, bring the car back here and let me know if there's anything I need to tell the doctor.'

She thought for a moment, looking at the map in front of us. 'If you wanted to see more of the island you could go across the moor.' She grinned at me. 'You've been on a bit of that road before, for that's where you put the Galloping Major in the ditch. The road is good and goes by the top of Loch Bradan, past the fishing lodge, to Feadag Bheag, just above Lutheran.'

Wishing me good luck, she bundled me into the car and returned to her knitting at the fireside in the dispensary-cum-office. I had a certainty that every single one of the few words that I had uttered was under careful scrutiny. Despite my intention to leave Laigersay as soon as possible, I could not help hoping that I had passed my interview with Jennie.

I took her advice and drove south through the rain to turn off towards Tom Bacadh. This time there was no speeding major, and I soon found myself passing the woods surrounding his gloomy castle. Loch Bradan, from its upper end, was bigger than I expected, but grey and brooding in the storm. There was a wooden structure that looked like a boathouse, with a small jetty beside it. The rain had lessened and I could see birds on the loch's white-horsed surface. Hamish had left his binoculars in the Land Rover and I identified several tufted duck and goldeneye. Further away were a group of swans whose long straight necks and yellow lores (as the part between the eyes and the base of the bill is known) pronounced them to be whoopers. These must have come south from their breeding grounds in Iceland and Scandinavia, where the weather must now be even worse than that of Laigersay. As I looked down the length of the loch, I realised I was only about ten miles away from my destination at Maggie McPhee's black house.

Thanks to Jennie's precise directions, the journey was easy, but it was at least fifteen miles by road. In Lutheran, I passed the side road over the hill towards the southern end of Loch Bradan, and I marvelled at the solitude. After a single house at the turning, there was nothing but desolate, drenched, moorland covered in heather. Occasional green areas showed parallel ridges of ancient lazy beds. Erstwhile peoples had cultivated potatoes before the clearances, showing that the land had once been productive. By the River Bradan, furious and boiling in spate, a small turning to the left seemed to correspond with Jennie's map. After about half a mile there was a small, whitewashed cottage by the road. That too was productive. A neatly dug vegetable patch with a pile of rotting kelp for manure showed that even this barren looking land could produce food. A neat peat-stack stood by the garden wall and smoke curled from the chimney filling the air with the acrid smell of a turf fire.

Archie, a bright-eyed little wisp of a man, was expecting me. He bustled to the door in greeting. 'You'll be the new doctor. Postie was telling me all about you. Come in to the fire and get warm.'

'It's a remote place that you live, Mr McPhee, especially since you're not so young. Still, I suppose you have neighbours just down the road.'

Archie looked surprised. 'I havena spoken to thae for thirty years and I'm never lonely. Haven't I my sister next door?' At that the old man peered out of the window and added, 'And I see she is well the day.'

I must have looked my astonishment, for there was nothing to see but a solitary Ayrshire cow ambling placidly along the road. He laughed, and added: 'You see, every morning at exactly twenty to eleven she lets the coo out. If she doesna pass my door by a quarter to, then I need to go and see my sister's all right. But she always is, she's all steel and leather that woman.'

I asked after his own health.

'Och, I am always well, except when the gout troubles me,' he said. 'I'm far too busy to be else. Mind you, I'm better in health than temper. My sister is a big responsibility. She shouldna live there all alone, but she's thrawn, like all the McPhees. But though she's blind, she has the sight, and that means she will know when it is time to leave. Meanwhile I keep the garden going for vegetables for us both, there's fish in the loch—when the laird's no looking—and I get rabbits and a bit game off the hill. Then the postbus comes most days on the way up to the Lodge to the Sinclairs, there's butcher meat delivered on Thursday and the bread twice a week. I tell you it's all go here, never a moment's peace. Will you take a dram? The old doctor usually does.'

I shook my head. 'That's kind, but I need a clear head to find my way in the island.' He chatted on about his work in the garden and poaching in the Allt Bradan. I allowed my mind to wander and considered the role of a country doctor in a place like this. It seemed a long way from the medicine I had been taught in medical school. I liked its easy camaraderie, and knew I would never find such a relationship with my patients in London. I was also puzzled by his sister 'having the sight' and wondered what I was going to find on my next house call.

Archie's lifestyle was dictated by the seasons, by tides, by sunup and sundown. He gathered kelp with a pony and trap from near the Assilag causeway, and hauled it home to fertilise his vegetable patch. He grew enough cabbages and carrots, peas and potatoes to feed himself and his sister and to win most of the prizes at the annual Lutheran show. His produce, preserved in ancient Kilner jars and as pickles and chutneys, fed them all winter. His main complaint was of the old laird, his former landlord. He seemed unaware that the old laird had died years before. He spoke, as of yesterday, of being summonsed for poaching salmon from Loch Bradan and fined ten pounds. 'It's not as if the laird put the fish in the loch. It was God put them there for the likes o' his people, me f'r instance.'

I wondered how Major Thistlethwaite would react to such philosophy. At length I apologised, saying I must go and see his sister. Archie pressed a jar of honey into my hand, adding, 'the heather was bountiful last summer and my bees were busy.'

CHAPTER 5

More Visiting

For once the rain had eased; there was even a faint hint of blue sky to the west as I drove the short distance to Maggie's home. As Jennie had warned, both the house and its owner were very surprising. I had heard of black houses but had little idea of how primitive they were. The building was a long, low shack built of rough-hewn stone with rounded corners and no windows. It appeared to have two entrances. One was clearly for the cow I had seen earlier; its doorstep showed all the evidence of a byre. The other entrance led into a black interior smelling of peat smoke. The thatch was composed of a mixture of bracken and heather from which sprouted innumerable weeds and a good growth of green grass. A mesh of ropes, each weighted with a rock hanging down the walls, anchored this complex garden of a roof. After the winds I had experienced the last few days, I could see that such lashing must be essential and I guessed that was why the corners of the building were rounded.

Hearing the noise of sticks being cut, I walked round behind the house. Maggie was outside, splitting kindling for her fire. I hesitated, watching this bent old woman, whom I knew to be both blind and almost totally deaf, wielding an axe. I could see, as the wood split before it, that the blade was razor sharp. How could I let her know I was there? A false move and she might injure herself, or me. She was remarkably accurate, cutting the wood with precision based only on touch. She was thin and obviously very strong for her eighty odd years. I could see why her brother described her as made of steel and leather. Suddenly she put down the axe, scrabbled the kindling together with her foot and turned to me. I saw, above a nutcracker jaw, the opaque eyes turned on me and noticed the deep wrinkles of her face engraved with the soot of her peat fire. No wonder they said she was a witch.

'Is it the laird?' she asked loudly.

'No, no,' I answered, forgetting she could not hear, 'just the doctor.'

Then, remembering, I placed my stethoscope in her hand. She felt it and spoke again: 'I ken fine who ye are and who you will be. The laird has come. I saw that Dr Hamish couldna come the day and I'm glad it's you. I know the troubles of your mind at present but dinna fash yersel, time will sort everything. You shall yet be laird. Follow me.'

With that she led her way into the dark recesses of her house. I began to feel I had inadvertently walked into a scene from Macbeth, as a line learnt at school flashed into my head: 'Great Glamis, Worthy Cawdor, Greater than both by the all-hail hereafter'. The unreality of the situation was incredible and my inability to communicate with her was as bizarre as her utterances. I followed her into the house and for a moment, even after the poor light outside, I could see nothing.

'My fire went out in the night,' she said. 'I maun start it again. Sit by the hearth so I don't fall over you and we'll soon be warm again.'

She was right: within a few moments the kindling was ablaze, and she added a few lumps of coal. 'I don't use coal much but it's quicker than turf and we both need our tea.'

In the firelight I looked at the house. It reeked of cow and of peat smoke and everything was black. For decades the smoke of the fire had circulated round the unhewn trees which formed the cruck and rafters of the house. Cobwebs, ages old, hung festooned with soot from the roof. Other things hung there too: a haunch of ham, tools and utensils. A sleepy hen contemplated me from an old fish box suspended from a beam. It would not have surprised me to see a stuffed alligator, or other evidence of necromancy.

The old blind woman moved about her home, precisely avoiding many hazards which, even with vision, would have tripped me. In a corner was a bucket of water, presumably from a nearby burn. She dipped water from it and filled the iron kettle suspended over the fire. It seemed to boil immediately and she took up a teapot and spooned tea into it. Then she did something I had never seen before. Steam billowed fiercely from the spout of the boiling kettle. She held it, her hand enveloping the iron spout, and tilting it towards her poured boiling water through her hand into the teapot. I shuddered, expecting to see a serious burn on her palm, but then I realised this was her habit and that her hands were so calloused she could hold such intense heat. She set the teapot down and spoke again.

'Now let it draw while I find out about you.' She moved close to my chair and held her hands up in front of me. By the dancing light of the fire I could see they were horny with calluses. But she caressed my face lightly, muttering as she did so, 'Young, not yet thirty, and good looking. You will be hurt soon, do take care... for you will nearly die, but survive you will... for you will be laird. Now drink your tea while it's hot.'

Then she sat on the opposite side of the fire and started to speak like a society hostess. 'Now that I know you better, young man, we should deal with why you have come to me. Tell Doctor Hamish I did not care for his medicine. My little trouble settled with a mixture of amanita and butterwort and I am now quite well again. But though I always enjoy his visits, ask him to send you in future. When you know me better, you will understand my ways. I know you find it difficult to make contact with me, but I know more about what you want to say to me than you are aware. Thank you for the care and respect you show to what I know you must judge to be an extremely eccentric old woman. Now, if you have finished your tea, I have work to do. I shall look forward to your next visit. I am glad you have studied Shakespeare, but I assure you I am not a witch.'

After what was the most bizarre encounter with a patient I had ever experienced, I did what I was told and stumbled out of the black house. For some time I sat in the car and thought about Maggie McPhee. A feeling of *déjà vu* at the Shakespearean prophecy, recalling Macbeth's rise to the crown of Scotland, haunted me. How could she have known what I was thinking, and what did she mean by her repeated reference to the lairdship? Finally, how did she sense the extraordinary feeling of respect and admiration, almost of love, that I felt for this indomitable old woman as she mothered me with tea? Jennie had been right; Maggie had certainly surprised me.

I started the car and drove back down the hill to Lutheran. It was raining steadily. In the bay a great northern diver was fishing near the shore. I had seen these primitive birds occasionally in winter off the south coast, but this bird seemed quite unconcerned by me, and allowed me to study its beautiful black and white plumage and strange serpentine shape. It dived repeatedly; often submerging for so long I thought it must drown. Somehow this atavistic bird, unchanged for millennia, fitted well with my feelings after my encounter with Maggie McPhee.

It was easy to find the Simpson house. In contrast to the black house, it was an extremely ordinary semi-detached villa in the main street of Lutheran village. I was greeted on the doorstep by an effusive hearthrug of a mongrel dog. This beast jumped at me, smearing mud and worse on my trousers. As if to add insult to injury, it then clasped my leg in mock copulation. I raised my hand to restrain it and rapidly changed the motion from a blow to that of a pat as the door was opened. A well-dressed elderly lady looked at me suspiciously and the dog bolted inside the house.

'I am Dr Chalmers. Dr Robertson asked me to call on you,' I told her.

'Oh yes, it is for my sister Hetty. Do come in.'

I was ushered into a chintzy sitting room adorned with an aspidistra and flights of china ducks. The mongrel had preceded me and was noisily routing two corpulent and aged cats. My patient introduced herself, raising her voice to a shout above the barking.

'I'm Miss Hetty and this is my sister Miss Hermione.' Looking anxiously at the dog, which had cocked its leg against the sofa, Miss Hetty explained her symptoms. The account of recurring dizziness and palpitations sounded like the problems of boredom rather than serious disease. I suggested that she went to her bedroom so that I could examine her chest and heart. This she did and her dog went too. After a few moments discussing the storm with Miss Hermione I followed my patient upstairs. She was lying in bed covered modestly with a sheet. Her pulse was normal. I withdrew the sheet and applied my stethoscope. To my intense irritation, the dog leapt onto the bed and started licking the lady's exposed bosom. I pushed it away somewhat roughly and then, remembering how Jennie had said they were attached to their pets, apologised and resumed my examination. I was not surprised to find nothing wrong. I reassured the lady by saying there was nothing amiss that some of Dr Robertson's usual medicine would not put right.

I went downstairs and made my farewells to the other Miss Simpson, and left. Perhaps, in contrast to Maggie MacPhee, I was unjust to the two ladies, but I was smarting at the behaviour of their dog and it was clear there was little physical cause for Miss Hetty's symptoms.

I eased my irritation by seizing the opportunity to explore Cockle Bay. I drove down a track from the road that took me across the machair. The rain had let up. I could see that the tide was on the make and was about an hour from full. At first I thought there was little to see in the bay, which was sheltered by a basalt dyke on each side.

Looking at this, I could visualise the volcanic eruption, which, in some earlier millennium, had spilled magma across the land. The lava flow must have run through clefts in the bedrock and solidified. Over the years the surrounding rock had eroded away, leaving the dykes as great walls which ran into the sea on either side of the bay. The hard rock, now weathered by the sea, remained as two arms embracing the wide strand of Cockle Bay between them.

I saw movement among the rocks and walked over to them. There were turnstones and purple sandpipers feeding there. In the bay itself red-breasted mergansers, eider, scoter and a few long-tailed duck were bobbing on the swell. I noticed a number of smaller birds flying low over the waves. I thought them house martins till I remembered the season. Then it dawned on me I was looking at storm petrels, named after St Peter because they appear to walk upon the sea. I had read about these birds, but had never seen them. Always excited at seeing the first of a new species, I watched the erratic flight of these little birds as they picked up invisible goodies from the sea. One of them seemed to have a forked tail. With growing excitement I watched until I was certain that as well as the British storm petrel there were Leach's petrels here as well. The forked tail and less conspicuous white on the rump distinguished the 'forkies', as I knew them to be called in the Hebrides. To see two new, closely related species together was extremely gratifying. At the sight of these birds blown in from the open ocean, my irritation at the Misses Simpson and their beastly pets dissipated.

Hunger called and I sought out the Charmer Inn to see what was to be had. There were two cars parked outside and on entering I was surprised to find the Reverend Angus Andersen and an unknown man sharing beer and sandwiches. Angus greeted me like an old friend and introduced his companion Peter McTavish, the local undertaker.

'Actually', Angus added, 'we were over here for a very sad funeral. Do you know Peter and his team were the only people there apart from me? The deceased was something of a recluse, but it's sad when nobody at all turns up for a funeral. So we looked in here to see what Mhairi could do to cheer us up. If you're looking for lunch may I recommend what I call M'hairi's M'haggis. It's always very good. What brings you to Coilleag?'

I told them about the storm petrels and Angus confirmed that both species were sometimes inshore at this time of year especially after a westerly gale.

'Did you come here just to see them?' he asked.

'No, I was doing a visit for Dr Robertson.'

'Don't tell, me let me guess,' said Angus. 'I bet it was one of the Miss Simpsons.'

I grinned and told them about the dog.

'So they've got a dog now, have they?' Peter cut in. 'I had awful trouble with their cats some years ago. One of them—I always find it hard to remember which is Hetty and which Hermione—rang me up to ask for my professional services. I went round there and one of them opened the door. So I guessed it was the other that had died. But I was wrong: it was one of their cats. They were most upset, and asked me to build a casket for poor pussy. They were most insistent that it should be lined with beige satin. Apparently that was the pussy's favourite colour. Well it was good business, so I did it. I made a small coffin out o' mahogany, took it round and helped to lay pussy in it. They were delighted and insisted on settling my account forthwith, and without raising an eyebrow at its size. Then they treated me to the wretched animal's biography, and I thought I'd never get away. I earned more than my fee by listening, I can tell you. They followed me out to the car, still eulogising the cat. I got in and started the engine, but still they talked. Finally, I just couldn't stay any longer. I let in the clutch and that's when it happened...'

'What?'

'I ran over another ruddy cat!'

Angus was right about the haggis. On a cold October day the delicious savoury spicy Scottish sausage with its accompanying neeps and tatties was splendid. But what really surprised me was the beer. It was brewed on the premises from a secret ancient recipe, alleged to include heather. It was strong, aromatic and excellent. Mhairi, a big busty widow, was—as she put it—past the bloom of youth. Both daughter and then widow of previous owners of the inn, she had strong views on the publican's service to the community. She had renamed the house as a pun on

Chalmers because charm was what she sought for her clientele. The pub was always open (though in those days you had to be a bona fide traveller on the Sabbath) and everyone but the unruly was welcome. As Angus commented pointedly, the Charmer Inn was, in itself, a good reason for living in Laigersay. I remembered to give Mhairi Jennie's message, and recalled that I had promised to report back to Jennie. The heavens had blackened again when I took to the road again, but the wind had lessened and I began to feel the storm had done its worst.

Back at the surgery, Jennie was speaking on the phone in the tiny dispensary where she ruled. Unlike Hamish's consulting room, this was immaculate, with rows of Winchesters, each with their concentrated galenical medicines. There were rows of tincture bottles whose labels suggested a garden of foxglove, valerian, gentian, scillas and autumn crocus. There were eastern spices such as cardamom, clove oil, ginger, pepper and asafoetida, but apart from a few modern antibiotics and sulphonamides, there was hardly a real drug amongst them. But there was enough poison in the form of strychnine, arsenic and cyanide to kill off the whole island. When Jennie replaced the phone, I asked her about the poisons.

'Och well, they were all used on the farms for various forms of vermin. I remember the cyanide was used for wasp bikes. Then it got stored in a shed until someone decided the doctor ought to look after it for safety. It's accumulated over the years. We never bother about it. Now, tell me how you got on.'

When I told her about the McPhees and her prophecy, Jennie looked serious and thoughtful, but when I recounted my visit to Hetty Simpson and her awful dog, she burst out laughing.

'That explains their telephone call,' she exclaimed, rocking with laughter.

'You might share the joke!' I muttered with some irritation.

'They rang to say the new doctor was very nice but, next time he called, would he please not bring his dog!'

CHAPTER 6

The Big Fish

The storm which had stopped all communication between Laigersay and the rest of the world abated slowly. It was still too rough for the ferry but at least the telephone was working again. I managed to call my parents in Sussex and reassure them that I was still alive. Then I phoned the consultant who was to interview me and explained the situation. He told me that the other contender for the surgical job had also been stormbound in another part of the country and that the interview was being postponed for a week.

As I put the phone down I began to reckon my chances; they had clearly narrowed the short-list down to two candidates; I had an even chance of being awarded one of the most prestigious junior jobs in surgery, with a clear week for the weather to allow travel. The chances looked extremely promising. At the moment, since I could not leave the island, I might just as well make the best of it for a day or two more and see if the fishing was really as good as Old Squarebottle and Helen Chalmers said it was. The rain was no longer falling in great grey swathes, like ghosts marching up a glen, so this seemed a good time for a few casts. I had fished for sea trout in other islands after a spate and had caught a number of small fish, but nothing approaching the six-pounder Dr Robertson had caught.

I phoned Helen, and asked after Thomasina. The little girl was well, up and about in the cottage hospital and eating heartily. Then Helen asked, 'What about the fishing? The burn's in spate, but there are only a few more days of the season... Tom can't get back yet, but you might as well try; his rod is all made up and hanging in the steading. Why don't I bring you back on my way home from the hospital?'

This seemed an excellent arrangement and Helen met me at the hotel a couple of hours later. She was keen to know how I had been filling my time. I told her about my visit to Castle Chalmers.

'Isn't the laird great?' she interjected. 'He's always so charming and he'd do anything to help anyone from the island. He's always the first person to support any charity "do" we put on. Angus Andersen—have you met him?'

I nodded.

'That's another marvellous person; he thinks the world of the laird. Not like that man.' She gestured towards the side turning leading to Tom Bacadh Castle. 'He's well named, that man, for he's as prickly as a thistle! Do you know what the "laird of Tombaca" did last year? He threatened my Tom with a solicitor's letter because he said our sheep had strayed into his garden. They weren't ours at all—in fact they turned out to be his own all the time.'

'I had a little contretemps with him the other day. He ran off the road and narrowly missed me. I reckon he was driving without due care and attention.'

'Nobody likes him here, but he's more bark than bite. How are you getting on with Doctor Hamish?'

That was a difficult question. I did not want to criticise a colleague to one of his patients. I evaded it by talking about the splendid dinner I had had at Squarebottle's house.

'So you've met the indomitable Tetrabal Singh?'

'Yes. What a chef that man is. But I was surprised to meet a Sikh here.'

'You shouldn't be. There are lots of people from India and Pakistan in the islands generally. When they started coming to Britain, the Outer Isles was one of the places they arrived first. They settled in well there, and in some cases they are into the third generation. Some of them now speak the Gaelic better than the natives. But, going back to Tet, he's a splendid chap but he keeps to himself a lot. You know, he was distantly related to the Maharajah Duleep Singh.'

'Sorry, who's he?'

'My fault, no reason why you should know. He was famous among the shooting fraternity and my Tom often speaks of him. He holds the record for grouse bagged in a day. It was at Grandtully in Perthshire, in 1871, I believe. He shot two hundred and twenty brace all by himself.'

'That's some shooting, but I can't say I admire it. I don't mind killing the occasional bird for the pot but I hate that sort of wholesale slaughter.'

'Oh, I agree entirely. But Tet's very well educated, Cambridge I believe. He had a promising career before the war, but he was very badly wounded in France after D-day. The story goes that Doctor Hamish saved his life. He's a self-taught Gaelic speaker too and, believe it or not, he's an authority on Burns.'

Helen burst out laughing. 'It was very funny. He was at a ceilidh a year or two back when one or two of the lads had had a dram too many. They were trying to recite Burns but they only knew the first line or two of each poem. Tet finished each one for them. As a result of that we try to get him to perform at ceilidhs. For the most part he refuses. But you should hear his "Scots Wha Hae" and he melts every lassie's heart with his "Red, Red Rose".'

With that she swept into the drive at Pitchroich farm and stopped by an outhouse.

'Here we are. I'll just show you Tom's rod. He keeps it hanging up on a couple of nails in the steading roof.'

I was soon flexing her husband's rod in my hand. The storm had lulled and the rain had eased to a drizzle.

'Tom usually uses a small "Teal, Blue and Silver" as a single fly. See, he's left one on... use that, but I'll give you some spare flies as well.'

'You know all about it... do you fish too?'

'We all grow up fishing here. But I rarely have a cast now... women's work, you know! Just go up the road a bit, about a hundred yards or so, to the bridge, and then follow the path down behind the sheep fank. It's a bit of a scramble getting down the cliff but it's not too bad. It's best fished from this side, so cross by the footbridge and fish down after the trees. The best place is the large pool near the sea. That should hold some good fish after all this rain.'

Feeling like a small boy released from school, I followed the path down the broken cliff by an enclosure for sheep. I could hear the stream in full spate tumbling in a succession of small falls and soon the path crossed it by a wooden bridge, nearly submerged in the peat-stained torrent. High up, the Pitchroich burn was flanked by alders and almost impossible to fish but, below, I could see the pool. At high tide it was very full and surprisingly calm, as pressures of tide and spate balanced each other. As I watched, a large fish leapt clear of the water, quickening my pulse. The pool was clear of trees, and even casting with an unfamiliar rod was not difficult.

Soon Tom's 'Teal, Blue and Silver' was curving out over the pool. The rocks at the edge of the pool were extremely slippery and I had to keep checking that my feet were firmly placed. Thus distracted, I missed a good hard take from a fish near the seaward end of the pool. But that was encouraging, for it showed I was doing the right thing. I fished more seriously after that, concentrating as the fly neared the end of its run, though I kept a wary eye on my foothold. Nothing happened for an hour, and it began to rain heavily again.

'Three more casts,' I said to myself and sent the fly over the spot where the fish had taken earlier. The line went dead and heavy and I thought I was stuck on the bottom. I tried to free it and I realised this was no snag, as the reel screeched and the sort of fish I dreamed of rushed seawards. Then it jumped clear of the water, a larger sea trout than I had ever seen, and I smartly lowered the rod tip to prevent the biggest fish of my life from breaking the cast. It ran back towards me and I hand-lined in as fast as I could, stumbling backwards and falling on my back. Scrambling up, I found that the fish was still on and reeled spare line in as hard as I could. Then he ran again, tearing yards of line off in a determined effort to reach the sea. Then, when the last of Tom's backing was showing on the drum of the reel, he turned again and had me frantically coping with yards of spare line as I fought to keep tension on.

But the fish was still on. 'I must have hooked him well,' I thought to myself.

The fight must have gone on half an hour, until the fish came towards me on its side, ready for the net. Only then did I realise that, in my enthusiasm, I had forgotten the landing net. If I was to get this fish at all it meant taking it in by hand. There was nowhere that I could beach it, but I manipulated the fish alongside a large flat rock, where I might just be able to hand it out. I knelt down and drew the great fish towards me. It was exhausted and lay within grasp. I lunged at the fish and my knees slipped, and in the instant I was in the turbulent stream. I was bowled head over heels and then there was an awful pain in my head.

A bearded face came slowly into focus and I was aware of awful painful pressure on my chest.

'Aye, laddie, I thought ye were gone. Sit up and cough.'

I tried to obey, but the searing pain in my chest prevented either sitting or coughing. I also had a severely aching head.

'Man, man that was a braw fush ye lost. I was watching from the brig and just as well... if yous'd been in there longer ye'd've drooned. As it was I had a job to make ye breathe.'

I looked at the huge man who was kneeling beside me. Then I realised he had been carrying out cardio-pulmonary resuscitation on me... no wonder my chest ached. The man threw his coat over me, but even then I found myself wondering that, in this remote place, a passer-by would have such skill.

'Now then... stay where ye are, laddie, and dinna go for another swim. I'm away up to the farm for help.' Cold and wet though I was, I lay still to ease my chest pain and breathed uncomfortably.

Soon Helen arrived, and fussed over me with some hot soup, and told me they had sent for more help. The soup helped to warm me, but it was ages before the island's ambulance came, and carried me back to the hospital at Port Chalmers. There, Hamish was waiting for me with sarcastic comment diluted with concern.

'Well, if ye will get resuscitated by the Scottish caber-tossing record holder ye must expect a little pain in your chest.'

He was right, for an x-ray revealed two fractured ribs. But, I reflected, I would rather be undrowned and fractured than feeding the fish in the Pitchroich burn. Then, drowsing comfortably after a needleful of pain relief, I thought back over the incident. I must have hit my head on an underwater rock as I fell, and after that it would have only been a little while before I drowned. But I was sorry to lose that fish, and just as I was beginning to dream of another big sea trout I became aware of a pair of large, solemn brown eyes regarding me.

'I came to say get well soon and thank you for curing me.' It was Thomasina, whom I had operated on... was it only three days ago?

I thanked her and she continued, 'Are you going to stay here? You see, I don't like Old Squarebottle very much.'

I tried to laugh, but was stopped by a stab of pain. The child looked concerned, and stammered, 'Sorry,' and was gone.

Later on I woke to find two letters, addressed to me at the hotel, on my bedside locker. The first was from Major Thistlethwaite's solicitor, informing me that his client held me responsible for the damage to his car. The second was from Admiral Chalmers, the laird, who had been looking up family records. He wrote that if James Chalmers, the celebrated missionary, really was a relative of mine then I must also be distantly related to him. Ever interested in genealogy, he wanted details of my father's family in Dunoon and said he would like to chat with me again. How different was the real Laird from the nouveau riche major!

Then another visitor disturbed my somnolence. The man was so big he seemed to darken the room as he entered.

A now familiar voice said, 'I'm Erchie Thomson, come to apologise for busting your ribs. Sorry I got a bit enthusiastic... but it's no often I have a chance to practise the trick Doctor Hamish taught me.'

He explained that the island doctor, concerned at so many deaths from drowning occurring in the island, had instituted a programme of education, including the wearing of life-jackets and training in artificial respiration for the near drowned. Apparently I was the first successful resuscitation, which was small consolation for the pain I felt on coughing!

Erchie explained again that that he had been watching me play the fish and had seen my ham-handed attempt to land it without a net. When I fell in he was down the hill in an instant, and I was fortunate in having this immensely strong man as my rescuer; few others could have extracted me from that pool in spate. Erchie, having told his tale and offered his apology, seized my hand, making me wince again.

'But man, it was a braw fush... I'll help you get as good a one again!'

Enforced rest in bed encourages thought, and still there was my unresolved problem. The job that possibly awaited me in London was the first step on what could be a distinguished career. After my accident it now seemed remote. Here, in the island, there was respect, love almost; from a community that wanted me, and which offered me the wilderness that my Scottish blood desired. Had the accident, I wondered, decided between London and Laigersay for me? With the dilemma as unresolved as ever, I slept and dreamt of storm petrels.

CHAPTER 7

The Way South

After my accident I almost gave up hope of the job in London. Certainly I was not fit for the long journey. But I had not bargained on Squarebottle's intervention. Soon after my accident he visited me in the cottage hospital and wheedled out details of my proposed interview. Then he was on the phone to London explaining to the secretary that I was not fit to attend and insisting that the interview was rescheduled. The secretary was doubtful, but Hamish told her it really ought to be! She caved in and said she would talk to her boss and phone him back.

'Laddie,' he said, 'they must want you. She phoned back within the hour and they've postponed the date for two weeks—can't be longer—his nibs is going to America. I have to say I don't want you to get this job but I'll do everything I can, so you dinna blame me if ye don't.'

With nothing to do but think while my ribs knitted together, I mulled over my chances. I did not know who else might be up for the job but, as Hamish had said, I must be in with a chance if they were prepared to be so accommodating.

Not that time hung heavily, for I had many visitors. Hamish looked in professionally each day and Helen combined visits to Thomasina with calling on me. One day she brought her husband Thomas. He was a born and bred islander who had taken over his father's farm at Pitchroich. He wanted to hear in full detail my story of the one that got away.

'I know some good fish come up the burn. Any idea how big it was?'

'Might have been eight or nine pounds.'

'Losh, that's a great fish. Today's the last day—I'll have to have a go at them. Where did you do your fishing?'

'Mostly down south in reservoirs, after rainbows.'

Tom pulled a face. 'Ach, they're nothing but vermin. It's a good thing we don't have them here. They ruin the brown trout fishing.'

'I have had a good few of those too. I remember some good ones in Lewis a few years back. I was there on holiday.'

Thomas had brought me a number of fishing books and these helped to pass time as, slowly, my ribs knitted together. But it all took much longer than I wished. I was not used to being out of action and began to realise for the first time in my life why the sick and injured were referred to as 'patients'. But inactivity did not suit me. I began to worry about how I would cope on the long journey to my interview. But Hamish was at work again.

'I've to send a couple of patients to Glasgow for more sophisticated x-rays than we can do here—the air ambulance is taking them next week—all patients have to be accompanied by a nurse or a doctor—so you go— that'll speed up your journey.'

'How do I go on from Glasgow?'

'By train—there's one about two-thirty—gets to London in the evening—I'll get a friend to meet you and see you to the train in Glasgow—and another will meet you and give you a bed near the hospital in London.'

So it was fixed. By the time the day came, I could move a bit more easily, though there was still pain, and coughing or sneezing made me feel I was being torn apart. Hamish drove me to the little landing strip on the machair near Camus Coilleag. He introduced me to my fellow passengers, both from Port Chalmers.

'He's here to look after you two,' he told them, 'but you're fitter than he is. You look after him.'

A brisk young man came to collect us and take us to the single-engined monoplane. He introduced himself to me. 'I'm George MacPherson, your pilot today. I gather you're here both as official escort and patient. You'd better come and sit beside me: that's where I usually put the doctor.'

He helped me with an uncomfortable climb into the co-pilot's seat, settled beside me and handed me earphones. 'Put these cans on, then we can talk to each other once we're clear of the island.'

With the other two patients comfortable at the back, George busied himself with pre-flight checks, conversing softly with a distant radio station whose replies I could not hear. All this reminded me of a day out with the Australian Flying Doctor Service that I had managed to wangle when my ship had visited Fremantle.

The little aircraft vibrated enthusiastically and we were soon speeding along the runway. Almost immediately we were airborne and wheeling above the island. Laigersay seemed to fall away beneath us. I recognised the vast expanse of the sands of Camus Coilleag exposed at low tide. As we banked, I had a clear view of the ancient turrets of Castle Chalmers a few hundred feet below. The aircraft levelled and turned south, with Port Chalmers on the port wing. I could see the road I had driven to Pitchroich and soon the farm and even the pool, where I had lost my fish and nearly drowned, were clear below me. To the south, the volcanic peaks of the three witches, Ranneach Mhor, Ranneach Bheag and Sgarbh an Sgumain, loomed ahead. Then suddenly we were over the sea and Laigersay was out of sight. Suddenly I felt an appalling oppressive sadness. Would I ever see the island again?

My reverie was broken by a voice in my ear.

'Now we're clear of the island, I can talk to you,' said George. 'Have you ever flown like this before?'

I told him about my day with the Royal Australian Flying Doctor Service.

'Interesting. I'd love to go there. I expect it's a bit different being with the original Flying Doctors.'

'There's nothing to see in Western Australia but desert for enormous distances. Till you get down to the far south, where there are forests of great trees. But it is a marvellous service and often quite life saving.'

'Aye, so is this. But the terrain is different. Here it's the sea that makes it so remote. For example, you see that island over to the southeast there? That's Solsay. It's an interesting place. It has a doctor, an ornithologist of some repute, who has built an energy saving house complete with a little windmill that drives a generator. I'll just fly over it so you can see it.'

With a slight detour, the little island was beneath me. It seemed completely surrounded by a long wall. George told me this dyke was to keep out the unusual breed of seaweed-eating sheep that came from Orkney. Below us was a superb but isolated modern house. Building it must have been a major project for this doctor in one of the smallest general practices in Britain.

'I like coming here, but landing is hairy. In the winter there are hundreds of geese, barnacle mostly, and in spring there are squadrons of oystercatchers, redshanks and dunlins breeding all over the machair. I try to avoid the nests on the landing strip. It's not always easy at seventy miles an hour.'

George spoke of his job, which, he said, was much more interesting than most commercial flying. 'The chaps who fly big airline planes get the fame, but I do more take-offs and landings in a day than they may do in a fortnight. It can be dodgy here in the winter and sometimes I have to discuss flight safety with the doctors. We have to balance risk to the patient against hazardous flying conditions. We rarely get ice up here but once, further south, I ran into bad ice; the wings were covered in it and I wondered if I was going to make it. Bad visibility and wind are the difficulties here.'

'Do you ever have any difficulties with the patients?' I asked.

'Very rarely, but I don't like psychiatric cases.'

'That's what the pilot in Australia told me. They often get very disturbed in the air.'

'That's why we always have to have a doctor or a nurse with us now. We used not to, but had a co-pilot instead. Once I had to fly a chap in from Orkney to Inverness. He became very violent on board and actually managed to kick the door out. It was hairy, I can tell you.'

'What did you do?'

'Well, we carry an emergency bag. It's got morphine in it. My co-pilot managed to inject a huge dose into the fellow's bum, through his trousers an' all. It quietened him well, but we got a blast for it. Apparently the dose was so big it nearly killed him. But my co-pilot wasn't taking any chances. Anyway, we landed safely, but it was very dangerous, and very draughty without the door.'

Below us I could see more islands, and could just make out the shape of Islay with the Paps of Jura beyond.

'That's the place for barnacle geese,' I commented.

'Aye. Have you been there?'

'Yes. It's about the last place you can guarantee to see red-billed choughs in Britain, I came up just to see them. That,' I asked, pointing ahead, 'presumably is the Mull of Kintyre?'

'Aye, and you can see the hills of Arran behind there slightly to the south. We won't be long now. There's the Clyde coming into view beyond the Mull. Glasgow airport is about twenty miles ahead. I'll have to start business now.'

With that George began his mumbled conversation with a distant control tower and didn't speak to me again until we were on the ground. Landing was surprisingly quick and easy. One moment the tarmac of the airport seemed to be rushing at us at alarming speed; the next, with hardly a bump, we were down, and slowed to a gentle taxi almost immediately.

An ambulance car whisked the two patients off to the hospital. The organisation was superb. Flying patients are given priority; they would have their x-rays and be back at the airport for their return flight to the island within an hour or two. Hamish, with his genius for organisation, had arranged for a district nurse on holiday from Laigersay to accompany them on their return journey.

I waited for a few minutes in the airport lounge, noting, with growing anxiety, a nagging pain in my chest. George said goodbye, as he had other business to transact before his return flight to Laigersay.

'Are you Dr Robert Chalmers?' asked a red-faced, kilted gentleman.

I nodded.

'I'm Peter Kidd, a friend of Hamish Robertson's, he asked me to meet you. He told me to get you on the afternoon train down south. I gather you have a reservation. You've got several hours to wait, so come home with me for a bit.'

In no time we were driving from the airport into the grimy city. I had never liked Glasgow since visiting it as a very small child just before the war. It had frightened me then and it frightened me now. I had a clear memory of a very old woman dressed in ragged black eating from a dustbin. I cannot have been much more than four when this happened but the episode, which epitomised the poverty and squalor of the city before the war, returned vividly to me colouring, perhaps unfairly, my adult view of Glasgow. Though the city was infinitely better than it had been in earlier centuries, Glasgow was still renowned for crime, poverty and deprivation.

Peter Kidd, it transpired, had known Hamish in the army and, like the doctor's Sikh manservant, had been wounded shortly after D-day. He had been a patient of Hamish's, who had treated him for severe head injuries.

'If it hadn't been for Hamish I wouldn't be here. He's a great doctor. Have you met Tetrabal Singh?'

I was feeling a dragging pain starting in my chest and was not keen on talking. Indeed just breathing was bad enough. I nodded in answer to his question.

'There's another great character; he should be dead too. He and I landed at Sword beachhead. We got to a place called Lion-sur-Mer when we ran into trouble with the 21st Panzers. He was hit by a mortar bomb and lay with a couple of dead tommies in a ruined house for two days. Hamish was up among the action with a stretcher party, where, as a doctor, he had no business to be. It was he who found Tet. He got him back under fire and saved his life. He got a mention in despatches for it. We all thought it should have been a VC.'

'Interesting,' I managed to say through gritted teeth.

Peter turned to look at me. 'Here, are you all right?'

'Just a bit of pain. The flight seems to have upset me.'

'We're nearly there. I've got something that'll make you feel better.'

A few minutes later Peter drove me into a quiet side turning beside a high tenement block.

'Here we are. This was one of the first areas to be developed after the war. It is part of the old Glasgow but has been converted into some very pleasant flats. It's even got a lift.'

I was glad of that, for I don't think I could have climbed the four flights of stairs to Peter's flat. Though not really feeling up to appreciating his home, I was surprised at the conversion of the tenement into a pleasant bachelor flat. He led me to a bedroom and made me lie down. A few minutes later he was back with a large glass of whisky.

'Here, try this, it's a single malt from Islay, guaranteed to ease all pain.' He raised his own glass. 'Here's tae us, wha's like us? De'il a yin, they're a' deid.'

'Anything you say, cheers.'

The delicious amber dram, redolent of the west coast's salty peat, did help. 'Interesting,' I commented, 'I must have flown over the distillery where this was made.'

'Aye, you would. You look better already,' said my host, who had tossed his drink down in one. 'Here, drink up and let me get you another.'

I sipped my whisky and marvelled at the swiftness of its pain-relieving effect.

'Well, thank you, just a little one.'

'You'd be too young for the war,' Peter reverted to his former topic. 'It changed a lot of lives. Tet, for example, he was my platoon sergeant. Though only an NCO, he'd been at Cambridge before the war. He was quite a scholar and set for a big career. After Hamish put all his bits back together he seemed to lose all ambition. He became a bit of a mystic and he developed his passion for cooking. I remember his curries; they were famous. On special occasions he used to lay on tiffin for some of us who were old India hands.' He took my empty glass and refilled it.

The drink was certainly easing the pain but I began to weary of my hard-drinking host who chatted on and on about his war service.

'After the war Hamish went back to Laigersay. He had spent most of his boyhood holidays in the island before going to Edinburgh to read medicine. He always loved the island. He ran into Tet in Edinburgh by chance when he was down at some medical meeting. The poor man was very sick, very depressed; that's when Hamish invited Tet to the island. Then the Sikh fell under its spell too: you know it's supposed to have a special healing quality, and he stayed there to look after Hamish. He said it was the least he could do after what Hamish had done for him. I think he found the peacefulness of the island suited him. I know he was very upset after the partition of India and very religious. I haven't seen him for years now, but I hear of him from Hamish.'

Peter filled the glasses again. My pain had gone but I began to notice some difficulty in focussing.

'Anyway, it seems to have worked well. Hamish and Tet have been together for some years now. Hamish is much respected in Laigersay, but they all seem to love Tet.'

So an hour or more passed, with Peter prattling on. Between us we managed to finish the bottle and I felt ever so much better.

'My goodness,' exclaimed Peter, 'we must get you to St Enoch's, or you'll miss your train.'

I got up from the bed where I had been resting. The pain was quite gone but I felt a little giddy.

'Let me help you,' said Peter as we negotiated the lift.

I don't seem to remember much of the journey to the station; I think I dozed. Even Peter was quiet and seemed to be concentrating hard on driving. At the station he consulted the indicator, muttered 'platform six' and hurried me to the train.

Then a strange thing happened. A young woman came running up to the barrier, dropped her suitcase and fumbled for her ticket. 'Is this the London train?' she asked.

The ticket inspector punched her ticket, 'Aye,' he replied, 'but you'd best hurry. It's due away in another minute.'

With some difficulty I focussed on her luggage and read the label.

It said 'Fiona Chalmers, Castle Chalmers, Laigersay.' I looked again at the very beautiful girl. In that moment, drunk as I was, I decided I was going to marry her.

CHAPTER 8

Fiona

Fortunately the train was lightly loaded. A soon as I stepped into the coach, the train gave a slight shudder and was moving. We had been only just in time. I was delighted to find my booked seat was in an empty compartment. I kicked my shoes off, lay down on the seat and was instantly asleep.

My sleep was full of dreams. I was a tiny child again travelling to Scotland with my parents. Father had lifted me on to the luggage rack. Between the wars the luggage racks were wider and made good beds for sleepy children on the long journey north. We used to travel to Arran during the school holidays when father could get away from his teaching post in Sussex. His parents were alive then, living on the Ayrshire coast, which made a good stop for us before sailing via Brodick to Lamlash. Though father always seemed happy enough as a housemaster at the school, he longed for his native Scotland, and returned whenever he could. It was these early experiences of the islands of the west coast that had started my fascination for remote places.

The train gave a sudden jerk and I was falling from the luggage rack. I woke with a start and found the train had stopped at a station. Looking out I saw we were at Carlisle. While asleep I had travelled over a hundred miles. I sat up, rubbed my eyes and found myself again thinking about my parents, whom I seemed to see so rarely now. Mother was longing to return to Scotland but Father, now past retirement age, was hanging on at the school which had been his life for so long. It was he who had taught me to observe and to enjoy nature, both at home in Sussex and on our annual Scottish holidays in Arran and the Clyde coast. I thought how much they would adore Laigersay and found myself dreaming of showing them the island. Father particularly would love the wildness of the hills and machair. I had spoken to him about it on the phone when reporting my accident and my convalescence. However I always had a pang of guilt that I saw so little of him and mother.

Shaking myself free of guilty sentimentality I realised that I was terribly thirsty and went in search of a restaurant car in the hope of tea. The corridor was empty and so was almost every compartment. I remembered that on the long journeys of my childhood I stopped to look at the pictures of Scotland that hung below the luggage racks. It was a game with my parents to see how many we could recognise. I was delighted that this train was still using old rolling stock. There were rumours of a great reorganisation of the railways; a man called Beeching was supposed to be making a report on the whole network and, it was rumoured, scrapping much of the permanent way in rural areas of Scotland. I might not be able to see these old, somewhat faded, photographs ever again.

I found the restaurant car and asked about tea. It was too early for a traditional Scottish high tea but the attendant said he could find me a cup. He added, 'It looks as though you could do with it. Find a seat and I'll bring it to you.'

With this gratuitous information about my appearance I lurched along the central aisle. Suddenly I saw her sitting alone at a table.

'Excuse me, but it is Fiona Chalmers isn't it?'

She looked up in surprise 'Ah! The tipsy man from the ticket barrier. Yes, I'm Fiona Chalmers. Who are you?'

'Robert Chalmers; I think we're related. I mean very distant cousins or something.'

'Wait a minute, are you the doctor chap my father told me about on the phone? Have you just come from the island?'

'Yes, that's me. I had a drink with your father at the castle a week or two ago.'

A voice behind me announced the arrival of my tea. I thanked the attendant and, turning back to Fiona, I gestured at the empty seat at her table and asked, 'May I join you?'

'Of course,' she said, but I could have wished there was more enthusiasm in her voice.

I settled in the seat groaning slightly as the pain in my chest stirred.

'Are you all right?' she asked. 'Father told me you had an accident while fishing.'

Sipping my welcome, re-hydrating tea, I found myself telling her about the lost sea trout.

'I have had some good days on that burn. It's one of my favourite spots on the island,' she said. 'And the Thomases are such nice people. I loved Tom's parents. We used to go there a lot when we were children. Old Mrs Thomas was a darling and she knew how to feed hungry children. My brother caught big sea trout there too. I only had little ones, though my best was nearly two pounds.'

I had to be careful not to stare at Fiona; she was so beautiful, with long blonde hair surrounding a long, rather triangular face like her father's. From my glimpse of her at the station I knew her to be tall with a stunning figure. Her name suited her. I knew from the smattering of Gaelic that I had picked up from mountain names that *fionn* had several meanings, including fair, sincere and fine. I guessed she was all of these.

She interrupted my thoughts by asking about my accident. I recounted the tale of my near drowning and rescue by Erchie Thomson.

'If Erchie was on your chest it's no wonder you hurt. The man's a gorilla... but a nice one, if you know what I mean. He's a tremendous character. But let me give you a word of warning: never drink with him.' She paused, giving me an amused look. 'The man's got hollow legs and, what's more, it's rumoured he has some very special whisky he distils himself up in the hills.' She paused and added: 'There was the famous episode of the funeral.'

'The funeral?'

Fiona adopted an expression of mock seriousness, but her eyes laughed at me. 'Yes, it was poor old Lizzie Work; she came from Orkney and was schoolmistress in Port Chalmers, before Jennie Churches—where Dr Robertson has his surgery now. She started nearly all the island's children at the primary school, including Murdo, but being eight years younger Mrs Churches was my teacher. Miss Work was a terror with the tawse, but everyone adored her despite it. She was one of the fattest women I ever knew. She used to call herself "a guid Scots dumpie". She had a standing order at the sweetie shop by the harbour for a half-pound box of Black Magic every day. She said she couldn't read our essays without the solace of chocolate!

'Anyway, poor soul, she had cancer and went down to nothing. When she died practically the whole island went to pay respect. Erchie Thomson turned up with a wee barrel. He said he'd been saving it for such an occasion. The men all had a dram to show respect. That was the beginning. Dram followed dram out of Erchie's barrel. The party went on for days, with the men sleeping where they fell.

'Eventually it was time to take the coffin to the kirkyard. Erchie organised the six most sober men to take it on their shoulders, so it held them all together as one piece, and they lurched off to the kirk. Erchie commented it was a good thing Lizzie had lost weight or they would never have managed.

'They got the coffin into the grave and helped to fill it in. Then they went back to the party. Meanwhile one of the girls had sneaked into Lizzie's bedroom, and found she was still in bed.'

I burst out laughing, and had to clutch my ribs. 'They'd buried an empty coffin?'

'Yes. They had to dig it up and start all over again. It sobered them up very quickly. But everyone agreed that

Lizzie would have split herself laughing and told them she always knew they were all good-for-nothings. My teacher, Jennie Churches, was very different. She's a lovely person. She was married to a fisherman who was drowned not long after she married him and so she had no children. She made the school her life and we were all her children. When she finally retired, she took on organising Dr Robertson. She once told me it was like having another schoolboy to look after.'

I told Fiona how I had met Jennie and then I found myself telling her about the interview I was going to. It was so easy to talk to this beautiful, intelligent girl that my guard slipped and I found myself talking openly about my life and ambition to be a leading surgeon in London. I told her about my Scottish father and how he brought us to his homeland on holiday. I told her how I had been thinking that he would have adored Laigersay and how I should love to show it to him. But now it seemed unlikely that I would ever see the island again.

We talked of her family and her childhood at Castle Chalmers.

'Daddy is getting on now. I hate to think what may happen when he goes. Murdoch, my brother, is heir but I can't see how we could keep the estate on. I should hate to see it sold to someone like Major Thistlethwaite. That's what happened when old Colonel Johnson died. He used to own Tom Bacadh Castle.'

The attendant was hovering beside us. 'Excuse me, sir, we have to set for High Tea.'

'Of course,' said Fiona. 'Anyway, I must get some work done. I'm staying with my brother in town and have some documents to put in order for him. I will tell him all about you. By the way, here's his telephone number. Do let us know the result of your interview.'

She paused, looking seriously at me. 'I have to tell you my father said it would be a good thing if they turn you down; then you might come back to Laigersay. The island needs another doctor.' With that she let me pay the small bill and walked along the corridor in the opposite way from my seat.

I returned to my own compartment in thoughtful mood. Of course I had thought about my first reaction on seeing this girl at the platform barrier. There I had had the sudden conviction that Fiona would one day be my wife. On the face of it this seemed a crazy effect of two much whisky on an empty stomach. How could one make so momentous a decision on the spur of a moment's casual encounter? I had heard people speak of love at first sight and never really believed in it. Anyway I was not in love, unless a very basic sexual attraction was love. But, on reflection, there was more to it than that.

Perhaps there comes a time in a man's life when casual flirtation is not enough (there had been plenty in the life of a medical student and a bachelor naval officer). Maybe it was that I was ready to settle down, and that I recognised in Fiona someone with whom I could share my life. If that were love, then maybe I was in it. However there was little room for marriage in the life of a surgical registrar in a teaching hospital. I had to resign myself to the bleak fact that, attractive as matrimony was, it could not be part of my career plans for a long time to come.

So, as the train lurched Londonwards, I turned my thoughts to the forthcoming interview and rehearsed the sort of questions that the board might put to me. I really felt reasonably confident because they had been so accommodating in rescheduling the meeting. As the grimy outskirts of London passed the compartment window, I began to think of what life here might be like. The post I so coveted was extremely prestigious but also extremely poorly paid. I should have to find accommodation near the hospital because I could not be more than a few minutes away. That meant living in one of the dreariest and least salubrious parts of the city. What a far cry from the pure air and open vistas of Laigersay. With that thought, I remembered Fiona quoting her father's hope that the interview board would turn me down.

Practicality brought me back to earth. Hamish had arranged for another friend of his to meet me at St Pancras, give me a bed for the night and see me to the interview. I just hoped this new friend of Squarebottle's was not so alcoholic as Peter Kidd. I rummaged in my bag and found the note that Hamish had given me. This new friend's name was Stanley Johnson, another army associate of the strange doctor of Port Chalmers. Hamish said I would recognise him immediately, as he was very tall.

Sure enough, there at the barrier was a man who must have been nearly six foot eight. I saw him raise his hat to Fiona, who walked ahead of me down the platform without turning to look for me.

A moment later he was greeting me: 'Dr Chalmers, I presume? I am Stanley Johnson, a friend of Hamish Robertson.'

I laughed. 'You seem well named by the way you greet me! But I saw you raise your hat to Fiona Chalmers just now. Do you know her?'

'Ah, was that who she was? I thought I knew her! But I haven't seen her for some time. I probably met her when I took the fishing at Loch Bradan in Laigersay. She's a very pretty girl.'

I thought to myself, I shall get on with this man: he was a fisherman, he knew Laigersay and he admired Fiona.

He ushered me to a taxi while making solicitous enquiry about my health and journey. 'I confess I was a little anxious,' he added, 'when Hamish told me you were seeing Peter Kidd in Glasgow. He has a reputation for over-generous hospitality.'

'Don't remind me,' I said. 'My head's still aching, but at least my chest has stopped hurting.'

We travelled west along Euston Road and turned into Bayswater where I knew, in the light of morning, we would overlook Hyde Park.

'Hamish Robertson asked me to put you up, because I'm quite close to the hospital where your interview is tomorrow.'

'Yes, Hamish would not let me travel till the last moment.' I told Stanley about my accident. He, too, seemed to know the very pool where it had happened.

'I've had some good fish there myself.'

After dinner, at a nearby Italian restaurant, my host took me home for coffee and a nightcap. We reminisced about Laigersay, and I spoke of the laird and his beautiful daughter. Stanley was clearly well to do, but he seemed rather secretive about himself. His flat was expensive and he could afford to rent the best fishing in the island by the season. Suddenly he surprised me by asking, 'Do you, by any chance, know a man called John Thistlethwaite there? He moved there about a couple of years ago.'

Warily I confessed that I had met him briefly.

'Rum bloke. I knew him in the City. There was a bit of a cloud over him when he went north.'

'He doesn't seem very popular in Laigersay.'

'Hmmm, that fits. But I mustn't keep the convalescent up. You've got an important day tomorrow.' Getting to his feet, he ushered me to my bedroom to wrestle with recurring dreams about Fiona.

CHAPTER 9

Mixed Feelings

I was prepared for a grilling interview for one of the most prestigious surgical jobs in Britain, but instead the questions were all about my ambitions for the future. In particular they asked if I had plans for marriage. Wedded hospital registrars, they reminded me, were unacceptable, as there was no time for the distractions of married life. The interviewing board seemed more interested in Laigersay than in my surgical skill and knowledge. When I expressed surprise, a consultant anaesthetist said, 'We know all about your abilities; we want to know what will you be like to work with. I know the island slightly, having sailed round it.' Then he asked me about the fishing in Laigersay. The board enjoyed my tale of the lost sea trout and laughed at my cardio-pulmonary resuscitation at the hands of the champion caber-tosser.

So the interview was quite enjoyable, but when I was called back to hear I had been awarded the job, there was a terrible feeling of anticlimax. I had to tell someone, but this was no time to ring home—both my parents would be teaching. I hurried back to Stanley's flat. He was out, but I let myself in with the key he had lent me. Remembering that Fiona had asked me to let her know, I phoned the number of her brother's flat, but the phone rang in an empty home. In this vast city, I had no one with whom to share my news and celebrate. I felt quite desolate, a sensation I had never felt in the remoteness of Laigersay.

I walked to the park. Here, at least I could feel a fresher air, less tainted with exhaust fumes, and enjoy green space. The sudden flight of a kestrel near the Serpentine reminded me of the country. On the lake there were coots and mallard recalling the massed rafts of eider, scoter and the lovely long tailed ducks of Port Chalmers Bay. Again the doubts that had been assailing me since I answered Hamish Robertson's strange summons to Laigersay returned. Did I really want to live in this teeming city of loneliness? Of course, as a registrar in one of the busiest surgical firms in the country, I would have little time for loneliness... except at night, in my solitary, celibate bed.

I thought again of Fiona. She was lovely, and physical longing burned within me. But this was more than sexual attraction. Subconsciously, I must have compiled a list of criteria for a future wife. I had never even been aware of this until, more than half drunk, I saw Fiona at the ticket barrier at St Enoch's station in Glasgow. Instantly I recognised the embodiment of my subconscious criteria. Perhaps this was the 'love at first sight' beloved of novelists. I wanted desperately to be a surgeon but I also wanted the fresh air and nature of an outdoor rural lifestyle. More than anything I wanted Fiona.

In this state of unhappy indecision I found my way back to Stanley Johnson's flat. He was still out, but this time when I phoned, Murdoch Chalmer's number answered.

'Chalmers,' a voice said.

'Chalmers here too,' I replied. 'I met your sister on the train yesterday.'

'Ah yes. You will be the doctor chappie. Fiona told me all about you... in fact she has spoken of little else. She said you might ring. Father says you are probably a cousin or something. I am afraid she's out, but why don't you come over for a drink? She should be back about six. What about half past?'

I accepted immediately, aware that my depression was banished in a second: life was suddenly very much brighter. That Fiona had been talking about me seemed hopeful. But then I remembered the comment of the waiter in the train that I looked as though I needed tea. Had the state I was in been so obvious? Perhaps she thought I was always getting drunk. The more I thought, the more I worried that she spoke of me as a drunken stranger who had chatted her up in the train.

Stanley Johnson returned, in desperate need of tea. While he was brewing up he asked about the interview.

'I got the job.'

He looked at me over his spectacles. 'You don't sound pleased. I thought you'd set your heart on it?'

'I am confused, and troubled. I really wish I'd never heard of Laigersay. It seems to have bewitched me.

Honestly the thought of living here in London horrifies me. It's so impersonal here. I can see myself having nothing in life except work. You see, something changed in the last few days. I am not sure I want that job after all.'

'Something changed?' He again gave me a searching look. 'That sounds like a woman to me. It wouldn't have anything to do with the fair Fiona, would it?'

'What makes you think that?'

'My dear chap, you spoke of her all the time when you got here last night. Tea?'

Not caring for this line of enquiry, I accepted the cup and changed the subject. 'Have you had a good day? You never told me what you do.'

'Oh, this and that. My mother describes me as "something in the City", that's good enough. But, yes thank you, my day has been reasonably productive. But I'd much rather talk about Fiona and your love life!'

He was beginning to irritate me and, saying I had to meet a man for a drink, I finished my tea and escaped. Squarebottle did seem to have some odd friends. First there was the persuasive alcoholic in Glasgow and now this enigmatic giant who seemed so interested in me and at the same time so secretive about himself.

A taxi dropped me at Murdoch Chalmers' flat. The door opened at my first ring, and there was Fiona standing in front of me. I stared at her, thinking her the loveliest girl I had ever seen. I must have looked odd.

'Don't tell me you're drunk again,' she said. 'You'd better come in. Murdo wants to meet you.'

'I'm terribly sorry... about yesterday, I mean. Actually, I can explain everything. I'm not usually like that.'

'Murdo, here's the chap who says he's our cousin.' She introduced me to a tall athletic young man a little older than myself. He looked incredibly like the admiral, his father. He shook me warmly by the hand. 'I'm sorry,' he said, 'I forgot to ask on the phone. Did you get the job?'

'Yes.'

'Is that all you've got to say about it?' asked Fiona. 'You seemed dead set on it yesterday.'

'Well, I've been thinking. Things have changed since then.'

She looked puzzled 'In what way?'

'Well, the major difference is that I have met you.'

Murdoch burst out laughing. 'Fiona, there seems to be more to your medical friend than I reckoned on. You told me he was drunk, not smitten; but perhaps he's both!'

'All right. I know I'd had too much Islay malt yesterday. Maybe it was that made me decide I was going to marry your sister.'

'Hey, do I get a say in this?' burst in Fiona. 'Anyway, I have never heard anything so ridiculous. We only met yesterday.'

'Yes,' agreed Murdoch. 'It does seem precipitate. At the risk of encouraging further complication, I think I'd better offer you a drink. Come and help me, little sister.'

Alone in the elegant sitting room I found myself calmer than I had been all this extraordinarily emotional day. Suddenly, on the doorstep, when I had seen Fiona again I had known exactly what I wanted. I studied a watercolour of Port Chalmers above the mantelpiece and felt an almost unbearable nostalgia for the island.

Murdoch and Fiona came back bearing a drinks tray and some smoked salmon which, they told me, also hailed from Laigersay.

Murdo said, 'Doc, if you're serious about all this, I'd better know something about you. Some of Fiona's boy friends have been badly smitten but nobody has ever talked of marriage before.'

'Murdo, will you stop it. I am not planning marriage, certainly not to a man I don't know. Anyway, Dr Chalmers hasn't even asked me.'

'Well, I'm asking you now, and I shall continue to ask you at five-minute intervals until you say yes.'

She stared at me. 'Yesterday you were drunk. Today you're clearly mad!'

Murdoch was laughing. 'May I take advantage of the five-minute break before the next proposal to get to know you a bit? Father told me on the phone that you'd rather taken Laigersay by storm.'

I told him about the emergency surgery during the gale which had prevented us getting young Thomasina to the mainland, and my operating on her. Next came the tale of the big sea trout and the encounter with Erchie Thomson, who saved my life, and broke my ribs. Then there was Hamish's careful organisation of my journey south, which had led to my alcoholic meeting with Peter Kidd.

'That's why I was tight when I met you, Fiona. But it made no difference. I'd have fallen in love drunk or sober.'

She laughed. 'You are quite impossible. You'd better have some more smoked salmon, before Murdo eats it all.'

'Lovely. And the five minutes is up. Will you marry me?'

'No, I will not. I've only just left university and have quite other plans.'

'But you're laughing, so I shan't give up.' I fumbled in an inside pocket. 'You can have these if you'll just say yes.' And I showed her the emerald and two pearls that I had bought in Dubai, with little thought then to whom I might offer them.

Fiona glanced at the gems, and I repeated the tale I had told her father.

Murdoch cut in with questions about Laigersay. He knew Helen and Thomas Chalmers at Pitchroich well, but could not remember Thomasina. 'They are a lovely couple. I've known Tom all my life. We used to fish that pool as kids. I've had some lovely fish out of it too. And then you met that lovable old rascal Erchie Thomson. You certainly filled your time in the island. I hear you also had a run in with Thistlethwaite; that's not unusual;

nobody likes him. I've heard of Peter Kidd's reputation but haven't actually met him. Where are you staying in London?'

I told him about Stanley Johnson.

'Ah, I do know him. He booked the fishing at Loch Bradan for a whole season last year. A strange chap; he wasn't in the island all the season, just kept coming and going. I seem to remember he did well at the fishing. I got the impression he was doing some sort of research on birds or something; he was often out with maps and a telescope. Father told me you were in the navy.'

'Yes. I spent a year in the Persian Gulf.'

'That would make the old man happy. No wonder he liked you. Father never really forgave me for doing my National Service in the RAF but, you see, I love flying. I have my own plane: that's how I travel to and fro to Laigersay.'

It was encouraging to hear that the admiral had approved of me, and Murdo seemed warm. Despite Fiona's protestation, the portents looked promising. They pressed me to stay for supper. There was no more talk of marriage, despite my five-minute threat. We talked more of the island and its people. Fiona and her brother were planning to be with their father for Christmas and Hogmanay, and I thought how nice it would be to be back there too.

I returned to the flat, where Stanley was still out. With a sudden pang of conscience, I telephoned my father.

In a moment his calm voice plunged me into a gloom of guilt.

'Ah Rob, I am so glad you've phoned. I haven't been able to get in touch with you. I have bad news, I am afraid. Your mother is in hospital; she had a stroke last night. She has not recovered consciousness.'

A cold hand wrenched at my heart, but father's calm reassured me for a moment, until he added, 'I think you'd better get down here. The doctors seem unhopeful.'

For a moment we discussed ways and means, and I promised to get to the hospital as soon as possible. I scribbled a brief note of explanation to Stanley Johnson. A second phone call told me there was just time to catch the last train to Sussex.

The journey was dreadful: the slow train crawling from stop to stop while I wrestled with my guilt at having seen so little of my mother these last few years. She had always told me to get on with my life, a life which had taken me away from her so much. Now it was too late.

I went straight to the hospital and arrived barely half an hour before she died. I held her hand and thought there might just have been recognition, as I was sure I felt the answering squeeze of her dying fingers.

Then it was over. My father, calm as ever, took me in his arms and hugged me twice, adding, 'The second hug is from her.'

For some weeks I stayed in Sussex, supporting and being supported by father during and after the funeral. Every day I spoke to Fiona on the phone. Though I repeated my proposal, she did not accept, but she was sympathetic about my mother and shared in my grief by remembering the loss of her own mother.

Father and I talked all the time, about mother and my childhood and our Scottish holidays together. He asked about my future, and I told him of my confusion, and how I was torn between Laigersay and surgery.

His eyes twinkled as I spoke of the island. 'You speak like a man in love. Your island seems to have enchanted you. Do you remember J.M. Barrie's play "Mary Rose" about the "Island that loved to be loved"? The child, Mary Rose, was enchanted and finally was spirited away by the island's fairies and she never came back.'

'Yes. I have this strange recurring feeling that Laigersay is unreal; it doesn't exist unless I am actually there myself. I seem to dream about it every night. The island is full of peculiar people like blind Maggie McPhee who sees the future and the minister who reads *Mein Kampf* and plays the fiddle.'

My father quoted softly: '"The isle is full of noises, sounds and sweet airs, that give delight and hurt not". Laigersay sounds enchanting, like Prospero's island in "The Tempest". I look forward to seeing it.'

My dream became tangible when, in a kind letter from Castle Chalmers, the laird wrote with condolence on the loss of my mother. He also mentioned his genealogical research and his conclusion that he and my father were definitely, if distantly, related. He expressed the hope that they might meet. I showed this to father and then I told him about Fiona.

'Ah,' he said, 'I was right, you are in love. Your mother would have been happy.'

Perhaps it was these words of his that convinced me, for soon after I wrote a letter to the hospital declining the registrarship, and sent a telegram of acceptance to 'Old Squarebottle'. I went to bed feeling I had made a momentous and absolutely correct decision. Next day an answering telegram read:–

'GOOD. I'M TIRED OF BEING ASKED WHEN YOU ARE COMING BACK. START JAN 1ST. ROBERTSON.'

The die was cast. Again I phoned Fiona to tell her I was returning to the island. For the first time, she sounded enthusiastic, and reminded me of the Hogmanay party at Castle Chalmers. She made me promise to come, but told me I must wear a kilt and behave myself. My father had an Ericht Cameron kilt, so I promised to be there. Life suddenly had sunshine in it again.

Chapter 10

Return to Laigersay

On New Year's Eve the crossing to the island was calm but bitterly cold. The ferry was practically deserted and I leant on the rail watching the approaching lights of Port Chalmers. Before four o'clock it was already nearly dark, but I felt that I was coming home. Hamish had found me a little flat attached to the cottage hospital, but Fiona had invited me to the Castle to join her family for Hogmanay. It had been a difficult time after my mother's funeral; father had been marvellous, but was clearly very lonely. He had offered his resignation to the school, and was planning to come and see Laigersay and the remote island I had chosen to practise in. Like the admiral, he was intrigued by the possibility of our families being related.

As the ferry docked I could see a small crowd, all wearing Highland dress. Squarebottle was talking to the laird and Angus Andersen. Nearby Murdoch and Fiona were chatting with Tom and Helen Chalmers from Pitchroich. I was surprised at so many people waiting to greet the ferry, as there were so few passengers. There was even Erchie Thomson, magnificent in kilt with pipes on his shoulder. Suddenly it dawned on me: they were all there to welcome me back to the island. The moment the gangway was down, Erchie's pipes skirled and I shouldered my bag and was down among them.

First Hamish gave me a gruff handshake; Angus muttered a blessing; Tom and Helen greeted me as old friends, and young Thomasina, shy as ever, said she was glad I was back. Fiona smiled a greeting, adding, 'Rob, it's good to see you back.' Then the laird whisked me away with Murdoch and Fiona to his waiting Land Rover.

They took me back to the castle, where I was to stay for the party. The laird and Murdoch seemed delighted that I was back; Fiona seemed subdued and reflective.

At the castle I had my first opportunity to be alone with her for weeks. She seemed shy, and suddenly I felt embarrassed.

She broke the ice by saying, 'Sorry about your mother.'

'Yes, it was a shock, and Dad needed a lot of support; but I can't tell you how glad I am to be back.' I paused, studying her. 'Fiona, I know I have made a joke of it, but I really do love you. I have thought of little else since I last saw you. I really want to marry you.'

'Rob, you're quite incorrigible, and you must not rush me. Please remember, I have just finished at university. I have been offered a research fellowship there. I have to think. I will give you an answer, but not yet, meanwhile here's a little kiss.' With that she gave me a chaste peck on the cheek and fled, leaving me marvelling that this was the first time we had even touched each other.

Murdoch bustled in, took me to a room in a castle turret and told me to get changed for the party, adding, 'If you're wise, you'll tie a string to the doorknob of your room—it's not easy to find your way back. The Minotaur's labyrinth had nothing on Castle Chalmers!'

I changed quickly into my father's kilt, still reeling from Fiona's sisterly kiss and followed the sound of pipes down to the great hall of the castle. To my astonishment, I was alone, apart from Erchie Thomson, who was warming up his pipes.

'Erchie, that's a horrible noise you're making!'

'Och, my drones are a wee bit oot o' tune wi' ma chanter.' He grinned at me. 'But you're right, there's only one thing worse than tuning pipes, and that's *not* tuning them. Man, it's great that ye're back. And it's a great honour to be here at the laird's Hogmanay party.' He glanced round the great hall. 'This place has seen a few sair heids ower the centuries. And more, forbye, there have been a few bloody deeds round Castle Chalmers, and one or two murders to boot. But are ye well and mended since I gied ye the kiss o' life?'

'Yes, Erchie, I'm quite recovered, but I hope there'll be no bloodshed tonight.'

'Ach, no, that's just haverin'. But have ye heard about Major Pomposo, as Doctor Hamish calls him?'

'You mean Thistlethwaite?'

'Aye, himself. There has been a slight aftermath of your accident wi' him. A letter came from his solicitor addressed to you care o' Doctor Hamish, and he opened it.'

'Oh Lord, I'd forgotten about that...'

'And so you should, laddie, so you should.' And Erchie explained how Squarebottle had silenced the major. Apparently Hamish served as police surgeon and Erchie was a special constable. A year or so before there had been a special police conference attended by the Chief Constable from the mainland. Everyone connected with what Erchie called 'the Polis' had to be there. Hamish was returning from the final dinner with Erchie who was in uniform. Major Thistlethwaite had been dining elsewhere, rather too well, and he drove into Hamish's car. The major was, as usual, very abusive but he was also obviously drunk.

Winking at Erchie, Hamish said they would have to take official notice of the incident and that he and Special Constable Thomson insisted on taking the major to the police station for an examination. Hamish pronounced him too drunk to drive and, though the law did not then require it, said he must have a blood sample.

The major, full of brandy and bravado, said, 'You can only take it from my John Thomas.'

'Very well,' said Hamish, 'put it on the table.' He then ostentatiously put on his spectacles and contemplated the member. 'No,' he said, 'it's too small and, what's more, I shall say so in court.'

Apparently the major's sleeve was up in no time. Both Hamish and Erchie chose to forget about the whole affair, for they were neither of them quite sober. However the major had not forgotten, and when Hamish phoned the solicitor about my accident, all he had to do was to ask the solicitor to remind his client about the blood sample and before long the complaint was withdrawn. 'The man's both a fool and a coward,' added Erchie, 'but I don't think you'll hear any more about your little accident.'

By the time Erchie had finished his tale the company had begun to gather. All the people from the reception at the jetty came in. Each man was in full highland evening dress, making me feel underdressed in father's kilt and sporran, but I was pleased to note that the tartan was the same as many others present. The ladies were all in stunning dresses with Cameron sashes. Fiona was ravishing, and it was difficult to take my eyes off her.

The first tray of generous drams came round and I recognised the admiral's favourite—Scapa whisky. Then the dancing started with alternately Angus playing his fiddle and Erchie on the pipes. We stripped the willow, were gay with the Gordons and revolved giddyingly in the eightsome reel before attempting the local Laigersay Strathspey, which had me hopelessly lost, confused and counting. After that there was a pause for another dram.

Then Angus Andersen gave a rendering of 'Holy Willie's Prayer'. Donning a nightcap he revelled in the mock sanctity of Burns' satirical poem, grinning round at the assembled drinkers and dancers when he came to the lines:–

'O Lord, Thou kens what zeal I bear
When drinkers drink, an' swearers swear,
An' singing here, an' dancing there,
Wi' great and sma';
For I am keepit by Thy fear
Free frae them a'.'

When Fiona sang, '*Bheir mi òro bhan o*,' the haunting 'Eriskay Love Lilt', I was almost in tears. In contrast, the laird, who loved Gilbert and Sullivan, sang, 'I am the Captain of the *Pinafore*', to which all replied, 'and a right good Captain too'. Clearly this was his party piece, everyone knew the chorus and joined in. As more whisky came round, even Hamish growled a bit of the 'Skye Boat Song'.

Then there was a general shout for Erchie to perform. The big man handed his pipes to Angus and became rather coy.

'Och, I'm awfu' shy,' he protested unconvincingly. He seized a decanter half full of the laird's special whisky and poured most of its contents down his throat. Then he took two swords from a display on the wall, placed them on the floor, tightened his belt and nodded to Angus.

The minister launched into a fast reel. Erchie sprang to the swords and, with immaculate and astonishingly fast footwork, performed the finest sword dance I had ever seen. Faster and faster moved the minister's bow, and Erchie's dancing grew more frantic; his kilt and sporran swirling until decency nearly drew its last breath. Then, with a final flourish, piper and dancer finished together. Erchie gathered a sword in each hand and, with a low bow, laid them at the feet of the admiral, his Chief. Erchie's gesture epitomised centuries of highland history with the clan's total allegiance to its chief.

It was only then that it started to dawn on me that at a ceilidh like this everyone had to contribute in some way. My courage drained at the thought and, as one after each other the guests came forward with a song or a story, I searched my memory.

Then suddenly there was a cry for the new doctor. Fiona led the call and as I turned to her, Heaven came to my help, as I suddenly remembered lines my father had taught me. I drained my dram and, without taking my eyes from Fiona, I recited:–

> O my luve is like a red, red rose.
> That's newly sprung in June:
> O my luve is like a melodie,
> That's sweetly played in tune.

As fair art thou my bonnie lass,
So deep in luve am I;
And I will luve thee still, my dear,
Till a' the seas gang dry.

Till a' the seas gang dry, my dear,
And the rocks melt wi' the sun
And I will luve thee still, my dear,
While the sands o' life shall run.

As I finished there was silence for a moment and then a cheer. Someone said: 'Not bad for someone brought up in the South, but there's another verse.'

Still looking at Fiona, I replied: 'Aye, but that mentions parting. I've found my lass and will not speak of parting.'

The pipes started again and I saw Fiona leave the hall. Following her, I saw her enter the study where the laird had entertained me on my first visit to the castle, now seemingly aeons before. She had slipped a shoe off and stood staring into the fire caressing the admiral's sleepy wolfhound with her stockinged foot. She heard me enter and, turning, said: 'You did that beautifully, Rob, but you do wear your heart on your sleeve.'

'Maybe, but it's an honest heart.'

She put her hand on my shoulder and said, 'Rob, I don't know what to think but part of me is beginning to want you.'

Slipping my arms around her I drew her to me and we had our first real kiss.

A moment later, I added: 'Considering how many times I have asked you to marry me, it's about time we did that!' As she laughed, the door opened and the admiral came into the study.

He stood on the threshold staring at us, then he spoke.

'See here, young man, I don't want Fiona hurt. I suggest you take things a bit more slowly. Murdoch seems very amused by your attitude to my daughter, but I should remind the pair of you that you hardly know each other.

I don't want the whole island jumping to conclusions. Now get back to the ceilidh, if you please.' With that the admiral held the door open for us to pass.

I was a bit abashed at this heavy father act, but Fiona slipped her hand into mine and whispered, 'Don't worry, he can be a bit of a bear sometimes, he's very much "old school", but I know he's very fond of you.'

Despite the laird's caution, we danced together for most of the rest of the evening, pausing to hear others contribute to the ceilidh and to sip the lovely Orcadian malt whisky. Midnight came with 'Auld Lang Syne', and I found myself wondering and hoping about what the New Year would bring. The old year had ended in confusion following my mother's death, with a short—and clearly displeased—note from the Professor of Surgery who might have been my new boss. In the New Year there was Laigersay, Hamish Robertson and, if all went well, Fiona.

Eventually it was time to say goodnight. One by one the guests departed. Hamish took me aside to warn me that there was a full surgery booked for me on January 2nd, and also said that he had left his car at the castle for me. I suddenly remembered that I was in the island to work.

I tried to get Fiona by herself, but the laird shepherded her away, however not so closely as to prevent a blown kiss as she turned at the turret stair to an upper floor.

Then I was suddenly alone apart from the great wolfhound, who came to me and nuzzled me. Then, with a slight jump, he put his forepaws on my shoulder and licked my face. Here at any rate was an inhabitant of Castle Chalmers who accepted me. I turned round in the great hall of the castle and realised I had no idea which of the many doors led to my room. Each one opened onto an unfamiliar room or passage. Soon I had tried them all, but as Murdoch had warned, the castle was a labyrinth. Eventually a passage seemed familiar and I wandered along a dimly lit corridor of ancestors feeling as though I was in a scene from 'Ruddigore' where, at any moment, the pictures might come to life. Just as I realised I was lost, the lights went out and I was in complete darkness. Something touched me in the dark and I started in fear, only to realise that the wolfhound had followed me and was nudging me slightly. Grasping the dog's collar at my waist level, I sensed the animal knew where he was, and he slowly led me through the darkness. Once I bumped into a suit of armour and I thought the resulting clang must wake the house, but the dog walked on calmly. Then my foot struck stone and I found myself climbing a spiral staircase with one hand on the outer wall and the other holding the dog's collar. The wolfhound stopped, and I realised the stair ended in a passage extending left and right. The dog seemed to want to move to the right and as I followed I soon bumped into a door, which flew open, and before me stood a white apparition.

I thought I was seeing a ghost until the admiral, clad in a nightshirt, shone a light in my face.

'What the hell are you doing walking round the castle at this time of night?' he thundered, and then he added: 'Don't tell me, I can guess. You'd better go back to your room immediately.'

'But I don't know where it is. I am sorry, Sir, but I am completely lost. If it hadn't been for the dog I wouldn't be here.'

The laird turned his torch on the wolfhound at my side.

'All right,' he said, 'I can see what happened. Cuhlan found you when the generator stopped for the night and brought you to me.' Then he laughed. 'That dog knows this castle better than I do; but you were lucky. He sometimes takes people to the oubliette. If you fell in there it would be quite a job to get you out. Come on, I'll show you to your bed. And no more wandering about, no matter how much you love her.' The old man gave a gruff chuckle and added, 'You know, as laird, I still have right of Pit and Gallows, though I must say I don't use it very often.' And with that he led me to my room.

At the door he paused, then he shook me by the hand. 'I'm not saying you won't do for her, just take your time, laddie. However, it's a mark in your favour that Cuhlan likes you. I think that dog has the second sight, like the old witch in the hills that bred him.'

And with that, he gave me a spare torch and firmly shut the door behind me. A cold shiver ran down my back. I was certain he was referring to old Maggie McPhee, whose Macbeth-like prophesy I had been trying to forget since I met her at her home on my last visit to the island.

The next day, breakfast at the castle was not served until midday. I was embarrassed at meeting the admiral over the kedgeree and devilled kidneys which appeared along with porridge. Breakfast was a substantial meal on New Year's Day. Several years in a naval mess had instilled in me a belief that speaking at breakfast was likely to lead to keelhauling. For once I was grateful for silence. The admiral rustled his newspaper but did not give me so much as a glance, and nobody else appeared. Since he had obviously attributed my night time wanderings as a threat to his daughter's honour, I was glad to be ignored. Eventually the laird got up, poured himself another cup of coffee and shuffled off in his bedroom slippers into an adjacent room.

A few minutes later I was summoned by a bellow: 'Dr Chalmers, I need your help!'

I jumped up and hurried into the sitting room, half expecting that the old man had taken ill. He was hidden in a huge easy chair with *The Times* clutched in his hand.

'I've finished it all but one corner. The clue is "It's to let, but don't set your heart on it the rent may take your breath away". It's eight letters.'

I counted on my fingers. 'It's an anagram, sir... try "stiletto".'

'Brilliant! Of course it is. Now why didn't I see that?' The old man scribbled rapidly, muttering as he did so, 'Five down is "trust", six is "lieutenant", seven down "truthful" and, the last one, eight down is "objective". Finished it.'

'Well done, sir! And, if I may say so, "trust—lieutenant—truthful—objective" is apt. I rather think you misinterpreted my wandering about in the castle last night.'

For a moment the old man glared at me, then he burst out laughing. 'All right, you'll do. Just take things easily. I'm not saying no to your obvious intentions but I repeat, I do not want Fiona upset. She hasn't a mother to turn to and I keep asking myself what my wife would have to say about the precipitate proposal of marriage that Murdo told me about.' The admiral paused, and his eyes twinkled. 'I have to say I think she would probably have liked you. Hamish told me you are not on duty in the practice until tomorrow. I suggest you stay another night. We usually have a quiet day on New Year's Day—we have a rough pheasant shoot in the afternoon. I gather you don't shoot but you'd be welcome to come and watch. Now, however, if you will excuse me, I have business to attend to.'

He heaved himself out of the chair and ambled off to his study.

A few minutes later, Fiona appeared and I told her I had found favour with her father over a crossword clue, and had been invited to stay on. She laughed. 'He likes things like that. You could not have chosen a better way to impress him. Come and talk to me while I have breakfast.'

She led me back into the dining room and I had more coffee as she tucked in to a substantial breakfast. 'There probably won't be anything until dinner, so it is just as well to stoke up. Have some more, the kidneys are traditional here after Hogmanay, and I love them.'

As I helped myself to a second breakfast, she asked, 'What did you think of the ceilidh?'

'It was great. I specially enjoyed Erchie Thomson's sword dance and the minister's fiddling.'

'They are two of the nicest people, but so very different. You did quite well yourself, even if you were somewhat transparent.' She looked towards the door as Murdoch came in and asked, 'How's the head?'

'Needing coffee,' her brother answered, looking askance at her plate. 'God, how can you eat that lot?'

'Never mind, a good walk with your gun will soon set you up.'

So it was that early in the afternoon I set out with the admiral and Murdo walking round the castle policies, acting as ghillie and collecting several dead pheasants and a couple of brown hares. The light began to go at about three thirty, and as we walked back to the castle the laird asked me why I did not shoot.

'I used to a bit, but I decided I did not like killing birds. It's not that I'm anti field sports, because I love fishing. My father brought me up as a natural historian and rather put me off shooting. Now I'm quite happy watching better shots than I making a good job of it when I would only maim.'

'I look forward to meeting your father some time.'

'You'd like him sir, he is an old friend of Ximenes, who used to compose the hardest crossword in the country.'

'Ah! In *The Observer* on Sunday. I remember Ximenes: he succeeded Torquemada as confessor to Queen Isabella of Spain. That crossword was fiendishly difficult. Did you ever complete it?'

'Only once or twice: a friend and I used to spend duty Sundays in hospital wrestling with it. My father did it regularly. It was composed by a classics master at the school where he teaches.'

'Your father sounds a man after my heart, does he play bridge too?'

'I am afraid so, sir!' I feared that this line of questioning would lose me any credit I had managed to earn with the laird.

'Why afraid?'

'Because I was expected to be as good as he is, and I'm not!'

'We must have a rubber after dinner! D'ye hear that, Murdo? The young fella plays bridge.'

So it was that—with some trepidation—I partnered the admiral against Murdo and Fiona in what they called 'family bridge'. 'Family' or no, the laird took it desperately seriously. In the third rubber, when the score was pretty even, I picked up the sort of hand one dreams about. I opened the bidding confidently, and my host replied enthusiastically.

'Four no trumps,' I said.

'Hrrumph. I hope you know what you are doing, boy,' said my partner. 'Five clubs.'

I could only see one loser. 'Six no trumps.'

The admiral drew a deep breath, but did not speak.

Murdo lead the ace of hearts, the single loser I had anticipated. The admiral laid his cards out and got up and stood behind me watching my play, and for once I did not regret the hours wasted at bridge as a student.

I made the contract, and the old man was jubilant. I could see that cunning at crosswords and success at cards had increased my chance of luck in love.

CHAPTER 9

Work

The alarm shrilled in my ear and I woke with a groan. It was January 2nd. I groped for my watch and saw I had half an hour to get to my first consulting session in Laigersay's General Practice. With luck it would be simple, after all there would be none of the complicated medical problems I was used to dealing with in hospital. I shaved and threw my clothes on as quickly as possible and ran down the spiral stair to the ground floor. There was no sign of life anywhere, except for the thump of Cuhlan's enormous tail. 'Say thank you for me,' I said and, remembering the dog's guidance two nights before, I added, 'and thanks for not putting me in the oubliette. Give Fiona my love.'

The tail thumped twice as if in acquiescence, and I ran for the car which Hamish had left for me. Driving to the surgery, I passed along the edge of the wood near the Castle Chalmers policies. Turning a corner, I was delighted to see a beautiful male hen harrier quartering the moor. As I watched, there was a shot and the lovely bird collapsed in a tangle of blood and grey and black feathers into the heather. I was furious, but there was nobody in sight who could have killed the bird. Knowing I was short of time I drove on, fuming to myself. Then I came across a parked pick-up van. A huge man was putting a shotgun into the vehicle. I drew up in a screech of brakes.

'Did you shoot that harrier?' I demanded.

The man turned to look at me with a single eye. 'Who wants to know?' he asked, in a strange accent.

'Don't you know they are a protected species?'

'I suggest you mind your own business. I am a keeper; my business is destroying vermin.' So saying, he stared arrogantly at me for a moment, slammed the door of his motor and drove off, leaving me shaking with anger.

As a result I was late for the surgery. Jennie was already fussing. 'It doesnae do to be late unless there's some good medical reason... you see, they'll always know if there has been a real emergency.'

I told her about my encounter with the one-eyed keeper.

'Oh aye, that'll be the new man at Tom Bacadh. Erchie Thomson calls him "Oleg the 'Orrible". He's from Finland, I've heard tell. Anyway, you've a full house for your first surgery. I'll send the first one in, it's Angusina McDuff, and her mother says she's got a cold.'

'Okay,' I said as I slid into Squarebottle's well-polished chair. 'Where are the notes?'

Jennie looked at me in astonishment. 'What notes? Doctor Hamish doesnae make notes, he can remember everything.'

'Do you mean I have to see all these people with no indication of who they are and what illnesses they may have?' I asked, feeling that this was the start of a nightmare.

'Och, I'll just be outside if you have difficulty. I'll send Angusina in just now.'

The child who came in was obviously full of cold. She said she was home from the Mainland for the holiday and suddenly had developed this streaming cold and a sore throat. I felt irritated that her mother should feel it necessary to send her to the doctor. I told her to keep warm and drink plenty. As she was leaving she mentioned there was to be a party that afternoon, and could she go?

'That rather depends on what the other mothers say but, as it's just a cold, I don't see why not.'

I rang the bell and an old man came in for more of his arthritis pills. Panic struck me. I had no way of knowing what any of Hamish's patients might be taking. Apologising, I slipped out to ask Jennie.

'Och, it's all right,' she said. 'I've got old Jock's tablets all ready for him.'

'What do you mean?' I asked.

'Jock comes in on the first Monday of every month and always has the same pills. I put them up yesterday.' She showed me a packet of what I recognised as a proprietary pain-relieving drug.

'Do you know what everyone has?'

'Pretty well, but don't go confusing me with fancy newfangled medicines, Doctor Hamish likes the old ones best. He has a particular penchant for yellow aspirin.'

'Why yellow?'

'Och, he says they're much better than the ordinary white ones. They're just the same really, only the patients don't recognise them—so they work better!'

The surgery progressed very slowly, for with each patient I had to ask Jennie what to do. I began to wonder why there was a need for a new doctor; she seemed quite capable of catering for the medical needs of the island all by herself. She had, after all, known most of the patients since they were children.

At last the surgery came to an end leaving me feeling both inadequate and incompetent. Jennie came to the rescue with coffee and some of her superb shortbread.

'I was thinking,' she said as she stirred her coffee, 'Angusina McDuff: I said she had a cold, but she put me in mind o' the measles... we haven't had that in the island for some years.'

'I have never seen a case of measles; they don't teach us that sort of thing in medical school,' I muttered through a mouthful of shortbread.

Well, if I'm right you may be going to see some now. Anyway, here's your list of visits. Doctor Hamish had to go to the Mainland today for some enquiry. He'll be back tomorrow evening. There's old Mrs McCormick, she'll no be with us long, I fear. She has a morphine injection night and morning; the doctor and the nurse take turn and turn about and nurse did it last night. Poor soul, she has a dreadful cancer. Then there a couple of old biddies in Port Chalmers Old Cottage Hospital that need their ulcers dressed. Like as not Kirsty Stewart—she's in charge there—will want you to see some of the others. That's all at present, but I expect there'll be more as the day wears on, so look in when you're passing in case anything urgent happens.'

So I set off in Hamish's car, thinking that the people I was to see could all be dealt with by a nurse or perhaps Jennie herself. I wondered if I had really made the right decision to return to the island. As I drove the short distance to my first visit on the northern outskirts of Port Chalmers, I heard a strange throbbing engine noise. Glancing up I saw a helicopter flying in from the sea. I stopped the car and got out to watch the strange aircraft. Though I had heard that they were increasingly common since the end of the war, this was the first I had seen, and I was intrigued by it. The aircraft moved steadily on a southwestern course and passed out of sight.

Mrs McCormick lived with her daughter Ruth, who looked almost as haggard as her mother. It was clear that the younger woman could not cope with her dying mother. The only alternative was the cottage hospital, but the old lady steadfastly refused to go there. I gave her the injection and prepared to leave.

'So soon, Doctor?' asked the daughter. 'Dr Robertson usually stays for a cup of tea.'

'That's very kind, but everything takes me so long when I'm new, I really must keep going.'

The old lady spoke from her bed. 'We quite understand, Doctor; when will Dr Robertson be back?'

I explained about him being on the Mainland and, with a vague sense of failure, left for the old people's home. There I dressed the varicose ulcers of two ancient ladies, neither of whom spoke a word. The home was depressing, with a number of old people staring into space apparently waiting for Death to claim them. Kirsty Stewart, the matron, asked me to see two old men who had coughs, but neither had signs of serious infection. Then the matron pointed to an old man sitting by a window staring out at the sea. 'He's been here for three weeks,' she said. 'He comes from South Uist but he hasnae spoken since he came here. I think he's homesick. See if you can get through to him.'

I sat beside the old man and looked at him. He was wearing a peaked sailor's cap and he had the palest of blue eyes that looked as though they had gazed at distant horizons for a lifetime.

'Good morning, Admiral,' I said. He turned his gaze on me, as if asking what I meant by such an address. I don't know what prompted me, but I asked 'Does the name "Politician" mean anything to you?'

Suddenly the old man changed, and he replied: 'Aye, I was there twice,' and with that he began a story he must have told a hundred times. But I was a new listener.

In the early years of the Second World War a steamer by the name of the SS *Politician* was wrecked with a cargo of whisky in Eriskay Sound. The story of the ship was immortalised in Compton Mackenzie's *Whisky Galore*. This old sailor turned out to be the first person I had ever met who had actually been there.

'It was a terrible storm, but I and a pal managed to row out to the wreck. Man there was booze everywhere. We got a couple o' crates into our boat an' a lot o' single bottles. Then it blew so hard we thought we'd never make it to the shore. We had to row awfu' hard but eventually we got back...' He stopped and the glow in his eyes faded. 'Ye ken, I can't remember much after that...'

Though the old sailor had cheered me up a bit, I was still in a state of dejection as I went back to Jennie at the Surgery. She was as bright as ever. 'Don't worry,' she reassured me, 'there are always some black days, but you'll find most people here are fine folk... you've just had a bad day.'

Just how bad that first morning was, I was to learn from Squarebottle a few days later.

'Laddie, you've got a lot to learn. Firstly Angusina McDuff *did* have measles, and she probably infected half the kids in Port Chalmers at the party you allowed her to go to. Then there was Agnes McCormick; she wanted to talk but you were too busy...'

'But,' I stammered, 'there was nothing I could do for her...'

'Never say that; there is always something you can do, the trick is to find it. You're right; of course, conventional medicine has little to offer the terminally ill. But if you take the trouble to sit, hold a hand, maybe, talk a little and listen a lot, you can bring more ease than the morphia you injected.

'Listen, laddie—a few years back I looked after a woman with motor neurone disease—she was completely paralysed and could only speak in whispers—near the end I was by her bedside in the Cottage Hospital, and I said, "If I am ever as you are now, I'm sure boredom will be my worst problem."

'"You're too right," she said. "What are you going to do about it?"

'Then I remembered when I had been ill myself with vertigo—I was fine as long as I lay still with my eyes shut, but as soon as I opened them I vomited—I was going mad with boredom—so I started composing poetry in my head. I said to her, "Write poetry"—her reply was most unladylike—next day I saw her again and asked about the poetry—her reply was even worse this time.

'On the third day she whispered a couplet to me: "The doctor came around again, And said that I should use my pen"—hardly great verse, but I got the hospital secretary to type it up, and showed it to her—she was encouraged to see her work in typescript—there was no stopping her then—she wrote poetry for me and for the nurses—she was able to say things to her husband she had never been able to say before. She died a few days later but she had a smile on her face—I felt I had earned my dram that day. That's what I mean about finding something to do when there is nothing to be done.'

Then he grinned. 'And don't worry about the measles. We are going to be so busy for the next few weeks there won't be time to worry... but next time, look in the lassie's mouth—that's where the spots come first—after the cold symptoms. If it's any consolation, I remember missing my first case of measles.'

I began to realise how inadequate were my years of training for dealing with medicine in a rural community. Hamish, though gruff and monosyllabic, was a splendid and understanding teacher, but I winced every time he called me 'laddie'. And he was right: we were inundated with work. The island had been free of measles for years and soon each of the many non-immune children got the illness. Measles is a nasty disease of upper respiratory misery. But it is the complications of eye, ear and chest infections that really cause the problems. Each child had two, sometimes three, visits, and more when antibiotics were necessary for middle ear infections, and the few cases that developed pneumonia were really demanding.

The epidemic raged for weeks and all survived, apart from a grandfather of nearly ninety whose pneumonia refused to respond to antibiotics. It seemed unjust to die of measles at his age, but it was a reminder that in former days the disease had been a major killer.

If my first day had been depressing, the work involved with the measles epidemic was uplifting. I had never worked so hard, visiting sometimes a score or more of houses in the island's scattered community every day. By then I had my own rather ramshackle car. It was reliable enough, and got me round the island night and day. But travelling took many hours in the day, even in so small an island. I had reason to be thankful for Jennie's sketch map of the houses on Laigersay. I learnt a lot of lessons, especially after my first day, and I began to feel important to the people of the island, who were often worried and who relied upon me. I felt more needed that I had ever felt in my life.

I was able to rehabilitate myself with Agnes McCormick, learning that merely listening and being present may bring more ease to a dying person than opiates can. I learnt about morphia too, that it could be used safely in much larger dosage for those in severe pain than I was ever taught in medical school. Following Hamish's example I began to find some of my most rewarding work was with those patients that specialist colleagues had dismissed as having 'nothing more that could be done'. I also began to learn that many of Hamish's rather bizarre methods of managing his patients seemed to pay dividends.

But it was the island itself that enchanted me. Whenever I could, I would stop the car on the crest of a hill and drink in the views on clear warm late winter days. The island, warmed by the Gulf Stream, seldom had much frost, and soon there were the first hints of spring.

There were always birds to observe along the shore and machair, though the winter moors were lifeless. I got quite familiar with the island's otters and seals. But most of all I adored the wildness of the cliffs at the southern end of the island. There, where the wind whipped past the crags, there were peregrine and an occasional glimpse of an eagle. Sometimes I had to pinch myself to get back to my work, and often I wondered whether it was Laigersay or Fiona I loved the most.

My little flat at the cottage hospital was adequate enough, but I had other plans, and I began to look out for a place of my own. Work was so busy I rarely had time to see Fiona, but as my patients came to know me she heard of my progress in the practice. I remembered the charge placed on me by the laird and went, as I thought, slowly with my wooing of his daughter.

One day, as spring was painting the countryside yellow and white with windflowers and celandines, we walked together by the sea at Cockle Bay. She told me this walk had always been her favourite. Often there were otters here, and the spring brought flotillas of eider duck uttering their amorous cooing calls. The males looked so handsome in spring with their apple-green napes and smart black and white plumage. There were purple sandpipers and ringed plover skittering along the shingle, and turnstones flung pebbles out of their way to feed on sand-hoppers among the weed. Redshanks called and flashed their chiaroscuro wings as they folded them with precision on landing on the shore. As Jennie had promised, in Laigersay the spring was exquisite.

We found the first primroses and together we explored the things we liked, flowers, birds, books and pictures, music and poetry.

'Where did you learn to recite Burns so well, you who were brought up in England?'

'You forget, my father is a Scot, even if he's an English master down south. He always encouraged me to read, especially Shakespeare and Burns, and he is a great natural historian who brought me up to love wild places... just like this. He's retiring at the end of the school year and plans to come here to see my island and to meet the mother of his future grandchildren.'

'I may forget, but you count chickens before they hatch...'

'Not chickens, children. Fiona, please will you marry me? Do you want me to go down on my knees in the mud?

'No, I mean, yes, of course I'll marry you. I think it's the only way to stop the barrage of proposals.'

I was astonished, and for a moment could not take in what she had said, and then we were in each other's arms. We ran most of the way back to the castle to see the laird and to tell him what he had already known for some time. I phoned my father, who was equally unsurprised.

Then we got down to planning. The admiral thought that, as I was still in the Royal Naval Reserve, we might have the ceremony in uniform. 'It would be nice to have a sailor's wedding. I'm sure Angus Andersen would approve.'

The laird went off to consult protocol, to see if it could be arranged, while Fiona and I looked at the calendar and planned our future. Both my loves, Laigersay and Fiona, were mine; I was supremely happy.

CHAPTER 12

A day out with Jennie

Work pressure in the practice was often slack, especially in April when the winter epidemics were subsiding and the visitors had not yet arrived in the island. Hamish was off duty on Tuesday and I had a half-day to myself every

Thursday. Then I would fish or walk in the beautiful hills in the south of Laigersay. In addition the whole practice had its half-day on Wednesday, when Hamish and I took it in turns to be available by phone, and calls to the surgery were switched through to the cottage hospital. Then Kirsty Stewart or Morag Finlayson, whoever was on duty, would relay messages to whichever of us was 'on'. A similar rota covered weekends. This allowed Jennie her weekends and a half-day on Wednesday. Night duty was shared between Hamish and me in a complex rota which gave an easy week of two nights 'on' followed by a hard one of five nights when the duty doctor was responsible for the whole island.

Jennie had been on to me for some time about going cockling with her. One Wednesday the tide suited and she arranged to pick me up, when the morning's work was done, for a picnic and an expedition to Camus Coilleag, Cockle Beach. This proved to be an illuminating day. The day was quiet professionally, and I presented myself at the surgery by 11.30 after my two visits of the day were done. She appeared at the door clad in trousers and walking boots, with various bits of equipment including two buckets, each containing a battered kitchen fork, a huge hamper, and the walking stick which she carried on all her walks. This stick was about five feet of weathered hazel with a thumb notch at its upper end.

'The tide's not fully out for an hour or two, so I thought I might show you some of our flora and fauna,' she said as she loaded her gear into my car. 'On a fine spring day like this there should be plenty to see.'

She directed me south from the village of Port Chalmers, saying she wanted to check out something on Loch Bradan. 'We'll have to mind your friend the galloping major as we go past Tom Bacadh,' she teased me with a wry look. 'Now tell me, how are you liking Laigersay?'

'I just love it... but I get a bit worried about how it likes me.'

'Och, ye needna fash yersel aboot that, ye're doing just fine...'

'I'm not sure the boss thinks so...'

'His bark's worse than his bite. You'll never get praise to your face, but I ken he thinks highly of you, he says so to others, but ye'll no hear it from him yersel'. He is a gruff old stick at times but, mark my words, he's a wise man and a kind one: that's two good qualities in a doctor.'

As we passed the last houses of the village, she directed me across the moors towards Tom Bacadh and continued her monologue.

'Mind, he's been in the island a long time, he was brought up not far away and he came to the island a lot as a boy. He understands our ways, and how the way we have evolved makes us the people we are. We Scots are a mongrel race, especially here in the islands. We have been invaded that many times in the past we're all a right mixture.'

'But that was centuries ago.'

'That's as maybe, but you don't have to dig deep to find the Celt in all of us. Before them were the Picts, then there was a contribution to our genes from Rome, when Agricola brought his legions and fought the battle of Mons Graupius. Tacitus, Agricola's son-in-law, tells us about that. Then came Christianity with St Ninian way down in Wigtownshire; he was before Columba.'

'Ninian?' I asked.

'Och, it was St Ninian who first brought the Christian message to Scotland. He settled in Whithorn over a hundred and fifty years before Columba set up in Iona. He did the hard work and Columba—who was a bit of a rascal—got the credit.'

'Hey, wait a minute. I've never heard of Ninian, and why was Columba a rascal? That sounds like heretical blether!'

Jennie laughed. 'Columba was something of a tearaway as a youngster. He fell out with the Irish King Diarmit, who refused to return a book he had borrowed. In revenge he fought and defeated Diarmit at the bloody battle of Cuildremne at which, it is said, three thousand dead were left on the field. For his part in this battle Columba was threatened with excommunication and sentenced to exile. He sailed on a mission of penance, accompanied by twelve disciples, and found shelter first in Oronsay, but he didnae like it there, for he could still see Ireland, so he headed on to Iona. Between them, Ninian and Columba established Christianity in Scotland, and with their message of peace started the troubles of dissension, war and cruelty which has lasted in Scotland ever since.'

'Gosh, what would Angus Andersen say to hear you?'

'Och, he'd agree,' she replied complacently. 'He's a wise and educated man who kens well that dreadful things have been done in Scotland in the name of religion. Anyway, to continue my potted history, no sooner had the Christian invasion converted the heathen natives than there was a new invasion. The Vikings, mostly Danes, attacked the east coast from Lindisfarne north, while the Norwegian longboats sailed round the north and then all the way down the west coast as far as Arran, raping and pillaging as they went. They settled eventually, married the local girls and farmed; they were there for about three centuries. They left their genes and their culture. They also left their language; until quite recently the Orkney tongue was Norn, a variant of the Norseman's speech. Wherever you go in the west, you come across Viking place names. Why even Laigersay is Norse, it means...'

'I know, Healer's Island. Angus Andersen told me that.'

'Good, ye've learnt something. But that's not all; while the Norsemen were up to no good, there was another invasion, in the eighth century from Ireland, by people calling themselves Scotti. They came from County Meath in Ireland and settled in Argyllshire, calling their new home Dalriada. There they jostled the old inhabitants, the

Celtic and Pictish people, and by devious means of marriage and murder, managed to subdue them. Their leader, Kenneth MacAlpin, was crowned King of Dalriada and King of the Picts and Scots at Scone in 843. He set up his capital at Forteviot in Perthshire. Scotland was united for the first time, as the Kingdom of Alba.

'But invasion was not over yet. After 1066 and all that, the Normans came to Scotland with their feudal organisation and grafted that onto the clan system. Many of the great names in Scotland today date back to the arrival of Normans in the days of King Malcolm Can More and his son David I. Ye see, ye simply have to know all this to understand why we're such a complex and thrawn people. Sorry to go on but, as you may know, I was a teacher before I retired to keep Doctor Hamish in order.'

'Fascinating stuff, Jennie. You know, we're not taught anything at all about Scottish history down south.'

'Well that's England for you!' she said with an expressive sniff. 'You know you need to know this background to keep up wi' that wee wifey o' yours. Fiona was one o' my star pupils, and loved history when she was little. I was chatting to her the other day, and she was talking about her days in my classes. I told her she's got a good brain and she should use it. She told me she was pondering putting some of her zoology together with the history I taught her, to research some of the early mammals of Scotland. You see, Laigersay has not always been an island. Till about eight thousand years ago, Britain was joined to the continent by land bridges and almost all the islands from Ireland to Cape Wrath were united when sea levels were lowered by most of the water being ice. There were all sorts o' strange creatures in Scotland then: mammoths, wolves, lynxes, beavers and aurochs.'

'What on earth is an auroch?'

'It was a primitive coo that was around in the Iron Age... ask Fiona about it.'

'I will indeed.'

'Anyway, here's the end of Loch Bradan. Let's get out and have a look. I am looking for another invader, though strictly speaking he is not really an invader, he's more of a returner. Have you ever seen an osprey?

'I saw one in West Australia, but I've never seen one in Britain.'

'Not surprising, they're believed to have become extinct in Britain in about 1916 due to persecution and egg collection. They did not officially return until the 1950s. However, in a few isolated spots in Scotland it seems they never became completely extinct, and remained in very small numbers in carefully guarded secret places between 1916 and 1954. Loch Bradan was one of those sites. Now in early April they may be back. I thought we'd just sit here for a bit and see what we can see. Nowadays they are protected, and it is a crime to molest them or take their eggs.'

The fishing lodge on Loch Bradan was an idyllic setting on a fine spring morning. As we sat on the jetty by the lodge, there was much to see on the loch. Nearby, pairs of great crested grebes were carrying out their courting ritual.

In turn the birds rose in the water, fluffed out their chestnut tippets and confronted each other bill to bill. Then they turned away and dived, to emerge a moment later each with a piece of waterweed held in their dagger-like bills. This they presented to each other as elegantly as ever a beau presented a bouquet, then they were away chasing each other over the surface in an ecstasy of sexual arousal. Further out, a pair of black throated divers dived for long breathless minutes in pursuit of fish, while overhead a pair of buzzards mewed and sported in the thermals. Suddenly Jennie touched my arm and pointed. A large black and white bird circled the end of the loch, paused, hovered and then plunged with a splash into the water. A moment later, scattering spray in all directions, the osprey emerged, seemingly putting all its strength into heaving free of the loch. In its talons was a trout about fifteen inches long.

'There,' said Jennie. 'They're back and they will be fishing the loch all summer long. The nest-site is about half a mile down the loch on the Tom Bacadh side. It's good to see them back. They always return from Africa about the same day every year. Now we must get on. I have other business before ye get any lunch.'

From the lodge the road turned north westwards over the moor towards Feadag Mhor. A small, single-track, side turning was marked 'Milton of Bacadh'. Jennie told me to take this turn, explaining that in earlier times each community had its own water-powered mill, now often only remembered in the name Milton. 'The mills were usually for grinding corn and some were used in the making of linen from flax. This one, powered by a wee burn, which feeds the Allt Feadag, was a corn mill for the Bacadh estate. It's just a fermtoun now... that's the old name for a farm and its cottage and steadings where the workers lived. In its heyday there may have been as many as twenty souls living here. The weans would have walked over the moor to Feadag for school: two miles there and two miles back.'

She directed me to a passing place with room to pull the car off the road. 'Now we'll see if some other friends have woken up after the winter.' She started searching the ground as she walked over short sheep-nibbled grass among which bluebells were showing colour. 'The hyacinths are coming along,' she commented. 'You probably call them bluebells, but here we keep that name for the campanula that you call harebells. Ah! There we are, there's the sarpint.' She stopped, pointing into taller grass where a snake lay coiled. 'People hate them,' she said, 'but that's because they don't understand them and are frightened of them. This is the adder, some call them vipers, and indeed that is the proper name, for its scientific title is *Viper berus*. This one is female.'

'How can you tell?'

'Colour; do you see? She's a sort of tan colour, almost gold, and the zigzag down her back is brown. Males are usually grey, with intensely black markings. This one is pretty torpid, but it's not as warm as she would like. Do you see the V just behind the head? I always find them about here, and each year I write a report about them for a herpetologist at Glasgow University. I know this group well. I call this one Ziggy.'

I admired the snake from a distance, and found it difficult to share Jennie's enthusiasm. But there was no stopping her.

'They vary in colour a lot. When I was wee I remember all-black adders. I grew up in the village of Sannox in Arran. There were a lot of them there then. My father hated them, especially the black ones, and would kill any he saw. I didn't like that and later made a study of them so I could teach my classes about them. We had a dog, called Corrie, a great favourite of mine, who was always finding them. One day he surprised an adder and it bit him on the nose. I was so frightened for the dog I grabbed the snake and pulled it off him and that's when I got bitten too. The dog nearly died, but after a few weeks recovered completely. They rushed me to the doctor and I was in the cottage hospital at Lamlash for weeks. My hand was swollen and sore for a long time. They got some antivenom sent up from Edinburgh and that nearly killed me. I heard afterwards that deaths from reaction to the anivenom were more common than those from the snake bite itself. I went into some sort of shock; Doctor Hamish calls it anaphylaxis and says I was lucky to survive it. As it was, I probably only had a wee bit of venom: the dog got most of it.'

As she talked, the snake gradually uncoiled and started moving away. 'Look at that,' she said. 'Just watch that beautiful living creature. She can do everything you can do—swim, climb trees—and she hasn't any limbs.'

I still found it hard to like the snake.

'Now I'll show you something, but I want you to promise never to try to do this yourself. Either you or the snake might get hurt.'

So saying, she folded soft foam into the notch on her stick and in a moment the adder was pinned down, held by the forked stick less than an inch behind its head. Jennie stooped and, with finger and thumb, she grasped the creature immediately behind its head. For a moment the snake writhed, its coils encircling the stick.

'Easy now.' She spoke to it, while to me she said, 'You must be careful lifting a snake: the upper cervical vertebrae are easily dislocated.' Dropping her stick, she used her left hand to support the adder's body. 'Now, if you pick up my stick, you'll see it's marked off in centimetres. Just hold it front of me so I can measure Ziggy and see how much she's grown since last year.'

'Do you have names for them all?'

'Some that I have seen before. This one is identifiable by having a bright orange tip to the underside of the tail. She is about seven years old and, as it's mating time, she will be looking for a male. They can live as long as fifteen or so years if people leave them alone. They have a few natural enemies: if she goes for a swim a pike might take her. The hedgehog is the worst: that will creep up on a snake, seize it by the tail and then roll in a ball so the adder can't bite it, and then it eats its way up.'

'Poor snake.'

'Ah, I see you're beginning to like them a bit more. Fortunately we don't have any hedgehogs in the island, so Ziggy is spared that. Her greatest danger is from man.'

'What does she eat?'

'Mostly small mammals, birds, frogs and creatures like that. She captures prey by injecting it with venom, then she follows it until it dies, and then swallows it whole. Adders will only bite for food or in self-defence. All snakes are shy creatures and avoid humans whenever possible. People have little to fear from them if only they leave them alone. The danger of adder bite needs to be kept in perspective. There have been only a few fatalities from adder bite this century, practically all among children. For healthy adults adders pose no serious threat and it is a pity that so many snakes are killed by people for reasons of hysterical prejudice.'

With a bit of manipulation Jennie managed to measure Ziggy. 'She's grown a good deal since last year: she's now 63 centimetres. The females are always bigger, and I have seen one of over 80 centimetres, but that is unusual, though I believe they can get to nearly a metre. Now for the tricky bit: in my rucksack you'll find a little muslin bag and a spring balance. Hold the bag so the mouth is open—that's right—and in Ziggy goes where she cannot hurt anyone and I can weigh her.' Placing the bag on the ground, Jennie made a few notes in her field book, recording the reptile's weight and length. Then carefully she loosened the neck of the bag, and the snake slithered out and made off into the grass.

'Awa' ye go and find your boyfriend,' was Jennie's parting admonition.

We spent another hour hunting snakes, finding two more females and a couple of males. Each was carefully weighed and measured. As I watched I began to lose the atavistic fear I had of serpents in general and began to understand Jennie's fascination.

'It's odd how people seem to divide creation into the good and the bad,' Jennie went on. 'That distinction is so subjective and based on vested interest. If you are a farmer or a gamekeeper certain animals are bad and regarded as vermin. Myself, I think all God's creatures are good if you take the trouble to understand them. Mind, I can think of a few humans who are exceptions to that rule. If Man were not here, all these creatures, preying or preyed upon, would reach a balance. It's Man with his blind prejudice that upsets that balance.'

I pondered that for a moment. 'In general I agree with you, but I am not sure I can extend your argument to the smallpox virus or the plague bacillus.'

At that moment we heard the now easily recognised throbbing engine of the helicopter I had seen before. I commented on it, saying it was the first I had seen.

'Aye,' said Jennie, 'I think we could do without such new-fangled machines, though it must be a good way of crossing to the mainland. I believe it belongs to one o' the people at Tom Bacadh. I've seen it several times over there.'

But it was time for a late lunch by the shore at Camus Coilleag. When Jennie unpacked her hamper I was reminded of Ratty's picnic in *The Wind and the Willows*. It seemed to have everything in it. The lobster sandwiches were particularly delicious and there was even a glass of chilled Chablis to wash them down.

'The bottle is something of an indulgence,' said Jennie 'But lobster is so good, and it's so cheap here, I like a glass of wine with it, and this Chablis is a favourite of mine.'

Lunch over, Jennie studied the wide expanse of Cockle Bay between the two points where ancient boiling basalt had run from the erupting volcano into the sea to encircle the bay. 'The tide's just right. It'll no take long to fill our pails.' She gathered the remains of our meal together and picked up the two buckets. 'Come and I'll show you what to do.'

We walked across the firm wet sand scattering flights of ringed plover, which were feeding on invertebrates left by the tide. Jennie studied the sand and then she stopped.

'Now, do you see that little dimple in the sand just at my foot? It was left by the cockle when it buried itself. It will be about an inch or so down, and all you have to do is to howk it out with your fork. There.' And she showed the neat round shape of the shell. 'Actually that's too small, so we'll try again.'

So we walked the half mile out to the tide line, howking cockles all the way. In half an hour my pail was full and heavy to carry. I went back to where Jennie was washing her catch in the fresh water of a burn running down to the sea.

'I love it here,' she said. 'It appeals to the hunter-gatherer in me. That has been handed down since the Mesolithic, when these beasties must have been an important food source. But look at that sea. Isn't it just a wonderful colour, and there's a pair of arctic skuas harrying the gulls. My! But it's good to be alive in the spring in Laigersay.'

CHAPTER 13

A Tale o' Twa Dogs

My life has been well and truly dogged by Labradors. As I told Hamish when first I met him, my parents bred them at the school where my father was housemaster. As a child I looked forward to the arrival of those splendid families of golden and black whelps. I had to work hard with them, for the raising of a large Labrador family meant much labour for all their human owners. But I still remember the warm love given by those squirming pups, with their hot wet tongues, the sleek velvet of their coats and that strange milky smell that young creatures have. Many of our Labs found a home in what, as a child, I always called the Blind Dogs for the Guides.

In Laigersay, dogs were part of everyone's life. There was hardly a house without them (apart from the two sisters Miss Hetty and Miss Hermione, who preferred cats). Most were hard-working collies, but there were also many Labradors like Florin and Siller, Hamish's bitches, and a few other recognised breeds such as the laird's Irish wolfhound. You could almost guess a man's job by the dog at his heel. The farmers all had collies with perhaps a terrier or two to keep vermin down round the steadings. The keepers and sportsman had Labradors or springer spaniels. Major Thistlethwaite had a Doberman pinscher and a Rottweiler.

Very early one morning at the beginning of May, I was coming home from a call in the far south of the island where I had been welcomed by a King Charles spaniel and a border terrier. The call had seemed serious, but turned out to be tonsillitis in a six-year-old boy. I had penicillin in my bag and dealt with the problem quickly. Over the tea that followed I talked of dogs to my patient's parents in their kitchen. The King Charles, all proptosis and affection, wagged the plume of his tail and stared at me with his protruding eyes, demanding attention and, when it was not immediately forthcoming, gave a single sharp bark to remind me of my lack of due respect. The border terrier looked on from his basket under the kitchen table. His wise whiskery face seemed to say that petting was all very well but he was in the business of working for his living. When I commented on the difference between them, the man said, 'Aye, ye should see yon terrier after a rat!'

It was a beautiful morning, and I took my time driving home, taking a rough track off the main road above the cliffs near Camus Lutheran. I was watching the sea for birds and pondering on the island dogs and thinking about what breed Fiona and I should get, once we were married and had settled into a home of our own. She, I knew, loved Cuhlan, her father's enormous shaggy wolfhound. To me there was something eerie and detached about the dog, which made me doubt that the personality of the breed would ever jell with mine.

With that, my thoughts changed to the man with whom I was invited to dinner that evening. I had met Douglas White, the island veterinary surgeon, a short time before on the bank of the Allt Feadag burn, where we had both been unsuccessfully trying to catch trout on a bright summer day. We had sat together on the bank to discuss life, fishing and other important questions. Douglas had been in his practice for about five years, having taken over from Archie Smith, a vet who, like Hamish, was a legend in the Island. We spoke of the problems of following such dominating personalities and it soon became obvious that Douglas was quite a personality in his own right; he certainly had strong views about some of the island farmers.

'Most of them are fine chaps, but there are one or two I'd like to drum out o' the place. They treat their stock that badly. There is one guy not far from here who is appalling. He keeps sheep in dreadful conditions and never calls on veterinary help in case it costs him money. Even his dogs are badly treated. One of these days I'll find a way of dealing with O'Flynn.'

He had paused then shaken his head. 'Sorry, I had a bit of a stushie with the man this morning about his sheep, that's why I'm fishing on a day as warm and bright as this, when nobody in his right mind would put a fly on the water. Casting soothes my temper.'

I was looking forward to the evening and hearing more of Douglas, whose professional life held such parallels with my own. At that moment something on a beach far below the cliff caught my eye. Stopping the car I focussed my binoculars and felt my heart sink.

Just above the tidemark there was a pile of clothes; slacks and shirt were neatly folded and weighed down by a well-polished pair of brown shoes with socks tucked into them. Most alarming of all was an envelope held down by one of the shoes. Depression is common in northern latitudes and more than one island life had ended in a lonely swim out to sea. Often, when a person took his own life, a note was left for the family, or perhaps the Procurator Fiscal, whose task it was to enquire into such unnatural deaths. I parked the car and soon found a well-used path down the cliff to the sand of the beach. In the dry sand any tracks were indecipherable, but when I reached sand still wet from the ebbing tide I saw the prints of what I took to be the shoes I had seen. To my surprise they were accompanied by paw marks. Whoever had come here to end it all had had a dog with him.

When I reached the pile of clothes the mystery deepened. Beside the clothes was a harness, which I recognised as that worn by a guide dog. I picked up the letter and saw it was addressed, by means of an official label, to the laird's Estate Office in Port Chalmers. Of the dog and the man there was no sign. I searched out to sea, where the next land was in America, but nothing stirred the gentle swell. Then, through binoculars, I saw a seal with another close behind it. They came towards me and as they approached I realised I had found my man and his dog. They were swimming towards me. I watched them with relief and was amazed to see the dog swim first on one side of the man and then the other. With each change of the dog's position the man altered course slightly, and I realised that the dog was guiding his blind master back to where he had left his clothes.

A few minutes later the naked man stood up in the sea and walked towards me. He was laughing and the golden Labrador beside was laughing too, as only dogs can.

I must have given voice to my relief, for the man stopped and said: 'Good morning, Doctor. I trust you will forgive my state of dress. At this time of day we usually have the beach to ourselves.' He shook himself dry and made himself respectable. I sat on the sand waiting for him to dress.

'You had me worried. I thought you had drowned yourself and left a letter for the procurator.'

'Sorry about that, but a man does not need a dog to kill himself—did you not see the harness? And the letter is the rent of my cottage, left with my clothes so I don't forget to post it on my way home. But what brings you to a deserted beach at six o'clock in the morning?'

I explained about my call.

'Ah,' he said, 'that'll be the Stewarts. Is their wee Johnnie ill?'

'Nothing too bad, he's on antibiotics and he'll soon be better. But tell me about yourself. Do you often swim like this—isn't it very cold?'

'No, it's not too bad, the Gulf Stream keeps the chill off and I'm used to it. We come here every morning in the summer. I think Galla would like me to come in winter too, she loves swimming, don't you, girl?' The dog's tail thumped on the sand when she knew she was being spoken about.

'Forgive me, but isn't what you are doing rather dangerous?'

'Depends what you mean by dangerous. I don't need to tell a doctor that life is full of danger. Why even eating and breathing is fraught with risk, but it would be foolish to give them up! It all depends on how much danger you can tolerate. Life would be dull if one never took a risk. But I mustn't waste your time philosophising. I am Jack Gillespie, by the way: I live in the cottage up on the cliff. You, I know, are Dr Chalmers, about whom I hear so much, and whose voice I have heard in the Co-op. Once I have identified a man by his speech I never forget him.'

'I have heard blind men have very acute hearing.'

Jack picked up a small pebble and lobbed it at me, and it struck me lightly in the middle of my chest.

'Did I get you?' he asked. 'I can usually place a sound accurately enough to throw a stone at it. My sense of smell is pretty good too. For example, my eyes are lying beside you, where she has just farted—that's her only fault— otherwise she's a canine miracle.'

I laughed, remembering the Labrador's tendency to blow off at random, and added, 'I was watching her bring you in, she seemed to be steering you. How long have you been swimming together?'

The blind man sat on the sand beside me. 'If you are not in a hurry, I'll tell you. I lost my sight in an accident as a teenager. Before that I was pretty good at swimming, won all the school prizes and that sort of thing. I had to give it up when I went blind; people said it was too dangerous. Then I met Galla. She is the most remarkable dog I have ever known. Right now, she knows she is off duty because her harness is off, but you'll see her change when I put it on. I got her when she was two years old, about six years ago, and I soon realised what a very intelligent creature she is. The first thing I did was to teach her a number of words. They all had simple syllables, were associated with a strong smell and represented my needs. Words like "beer", "bread", "baccy" and "news". Then all I had to do was to put on Galla's harness on and say the word. She would lead me to the appropriate shop and all I had to do was hold out my hand and ask for my Braille newspaper, twenty Players, a pint of beer or what you will.

'Then one summer day I went to a party where there was a swimming pool. My host asked me if I would like to swim, and I told him I had promised my folks not to. But he persuaded me, saying he would be with me as a guard. So I stripped and went to the edge of the pool and dived in. It was wonderful to be in the water again, but I realised that my dog had dived in too. It was then that we learned that the one thing we both loved to do was to swim. Since then we've never looked back. When we came here I hesitated at first, after all this is the Atlantic and it's pretty big, but Galla is magnificent. I expect you saw how she guides me back to exactly where I leave my clothes. You're wonderful, aren't you, girl?' And again the tail thumped in the sand.

Jack picked up the harness and at once the dog came and stood by him while he fastened it on to her. 'Back to work, girl, but we'll be here again tomorrow.' He grinned at me. 'I talk to her all the time; I reckon I'm only mad when I hear her talk back to me! Well, it's good to have met you properly, Doctor, but I hope I never meet you professionally. No offence, but I prefer to keep away from the doctors. Now it's time to give my eyes some breakfast. Home, Galla.'

And with that, two remarkable creatures walked briskly over the sand and climbed the cliff out of sight. With much to think about, I followed slowly and pottered back home for my own breakfast.

Morning surgery was routine except for Angus McLellan, who was giving me some problems. He was an old retired keeper, whose diabetes had suddenly gone out of control and was proving difficult to put right. He was still spilling sugar in his urine and I was worried about him. At his age, his sight was at risk and I had had enough experience of blindness for one day.

When the surgery was over I spent a few minutes with the textbooks, wondering what I had missed in Angus's case. Hamish looked in from his rounds to get coffee and some of Janet's shortbread, to which he was clearly addicted. I told him about my encounter with Jack Gillespie. Hamish dunked his shortbread and regarded me over his spectacles. 'Jack's a fine man, and very well educated. He was born here, and came back a few years ago; I tell you this... he never comes near the surgery... if you ever get a call from him, no matter how trivial it sounds, treat it as very urgent.'

Then, as if he knew what I had been doing when he came in, he asked, 'How are you getting on with old Angus McLellan? I saw him in town and he spoke highly of you, but I thought he didn't look well.'

'Interesting that you should ask. I'm having difficulty controlling his diabetes. It seems to be a straightforward late onset form, but it's suddenly gone haywire. I was just checking the biochemistry when you came in.'

'You mean all that dreadful Krebs Cycle stuff they drummed into us at medical school? I wouldn't worry yourself about that. You told me you knew about dogs, have you asked Angus about his?'

I looked at my boss in astonishment. Here was a relatively straightforward biochemical problem, a metabolism that required a bit of juggling with sugar intake and drugs, and Hamish was wittering on about the man's dog. He must have guessed what I was thinking.

'Ye've got a lot to learn, laddie, and don't think those clever chaps at the medical school have all the answers. Let me tell you about Angus. I've known him since I first came here. He used to be the laird's head keeper. What he doesnae know about the island isn't worth knowing. His wife died a while back. At the time his dog, an old black Labrador, prevented him from developing a full-blown bereavement syndrome. I had spotted his diabetes a couple of years before his wife went. As you say, a mild late onset type, which I controlled with diet alone.

'Angus was always an active man and he used to walk with his dog to town every day to the Co-op. There he could buy a bit of steak for himself and his dog's favourite tinned food. Then a couple of months ago the dog died in his sleep. Poor old Angus was shattered. He suddenly had a double dose of bereavement, both his wife and his dog. He got depressed... no longer walked into town, but went to the little shop by his house. It's a nice enough shop, but the only food they sell is bread, cakes, biscuits and sweeties. Angus wouldnae tell you all this... he'd no see it as relevant. But that's why you cannot control his problem. His level of exercise has changed and his diet has suddenly altered from one high in protein to one high in carbohydrate. Laddie, you don't need biochemistry. What you need is another dog.'

Hamish finished his coffee and was gone.

Of course he was right, and I was left wondering why the professors in my medical school put so much more stress on the science of disease than on the understanding of people. Once again Hamish had taught me more practical medicine in a few minutes than I had ever learnt at university.

That evening I drove to the little village of Feadag Mhor. Douglas White and his wife Joanna lived in the house of his predecessor, the one-eyed Archie Smith, since they had taken over his veterinary practice. I had heard something of the former indestructible vet of Laigersay. Archie was a tremendous source of country knowledge and a shrewd businessman who served on many government committees. He was immensely strong and the stories of his encounters with the island's bulls and stallions were legion. In consequence he was always getting seriously injured, he contracted several major illnesses and he had kept Squarebottle busy during his early days in the island. Hamish had told me about Archie (who, it was said, had made up his nickname). Nothing seemed to stop his incredible pace of life.

The stories about the vet were legendary; he should have been dead a dozen times. He lost an eye to a German bullet in the First World War; that nearly finished him. One night he went out to a cow that had just calved. The cow went for him, knocked him down, and rolled him over in the straw and muck. He had ruptured his spleen and had to be evacuated by air to hospital in the mainland. Then he survived a torrential bleed from bowel cancer and ten days after it was removed he was out helping lambing. Before that he had a lung taken away, presumably also for cancer, because he had smoked heavily all his life.

On another occasion a big Alsatian went for him and knocked him down. He fought the dog off, and when he managed to get up wondered what was hanging down his face, and he found it was his ear. So he ripped the lining out of his jacket and tied his ear back on his head. He was at the hospital having stitches, but was back at work the next day.

Hamish had chuckled over one episode. 'One day Archie tried to get a ewe and lamb off a ledge on the rocks up on the hill. He fell and went down headfirst about fifteen feet... must have lain unconscious for an hour or more... then he walked to the surgery, and I put fifteen stitches in his scalp. He came back as instructed a few days later. He was talking to me when he suddenly put his hand to his neck—this was about four days after the accident—and he drew his hand out and there was blood running off his fingers. "Good God," he said, "I'll have to be getting home or there'll be nothing left for the black puddens on Monday."'

Eventually Archie handed over the practice to Douglas, and within a week he was dead. Hamish said it was a combination of his various illnesses. 'Well, that's what I put on the death certificate. Actually I think he died of grief because he gave up the practice.'

It was hardly surprising that Douglas had found it difficult to follow this titanic man. At first wherever he went he was regaled with stories about the 'great Archie' till he had to confess he was heartily sick of it. All the storytellers seemed to imply that the old vet was irreplaceable and that the new youngster was a poor substitute.

'But it began to get better after there was a big scare about foot and mouth disease a couple of years after we came here. That was hard work, I can tell you. I must have been in every farm in the island. We were lucky the infection did not get here, that's one great advantage of being an island. But the farmers were all so scared they were glad to have me, even if I was not in the same league as Archie. After that, things got better.'

I added, 'Glad to hear it. I hope things will for me.'

'I wouldn't worry too much, if I were you,' said Joanna. 'From what I hear, you're the island's blue-eyed boy. You have great fans in the Chalmers family of Pitchroich. According to them, you can't do anything wrong.'

The evening was delightful and the fish was delicious. Joanna said the problem of being married to a successful trout fisherman was finding new ways to serve his catch.

'I am glad you like these, they are cooked to our favourite recipe. Douglas fillets the fish for me, then I spread mayonnaise over them, top them with a little cheese sprinkled with paprika and grill them quickly. Mind, I have to get my mother to send me the paprika from down south. The Co-op hasn't heard of things like that.'

I told them about the morning's encounter with Jack Gillespie. Douglas knew of him but had never met him, however he was well acquainted with Angus McLellan. 'Ah yes, he's one of the island's worthies, a great character and a remarkable naturalist, but like all keepers not one of these new conservationist folk... though I am sure he would not agree with me there. So much depends on what you mean by conservation. If you're in the business of conserving grouse, it's not good news for birds with hooked beaks, especially if they are hen harriers. But I'm sorry to hear he lost his dog. I knew that old Labrador well. I had to open him up a year or two back. Of all things he had swallowed the top off a champagne bottle, wire cage, cork, foil—the lot. Labs'll eat anything. Angus thought he was a goner then.'

'Hamish tells me I'll never control his diabetes till we find him another dog.'

Douglas pondered for a moment. 'Angus'll no be easily pleased, I can tell you, but I have an idea. Do you know the Partridges? They live in Port Chalmers. He's something in marine biology and they have just had a posting to the States. They're desperate about what to do with their Labrador. I know the dog: it's four years old and black. Could be the solution. But you will have difficulty with Angus, he's a sentimental old boy... he might think taking another dog so soon was being disloyal to the old one.'

Driving home, I was thoughtful. The following day, I rang Mrs Partridge and told her about Angus. She sounded relieved at the prospect of a good home for her Jason. I explained the need for tact and said I would see what could be done.

A few days later Angus was back in the surgery. He watched me test his urine, and pulled a face when the Fehling's solution turned red in the boiling test tube.

'What am I going to do with you, Angus?' I asked, and added: 'It seems your problem went out of control when your old dog died. That does make sense, you know. I bet you don't take half as much exercise now he's gone.'

The old man went very quiet and then, to my amazement, tears formed in the old rheumy eyes and ran unheeded down the tanned leather of his face.

'Aye, ye could be right, but I'll no get another like him.'

Then I told Angus about the Partridges. Perhaps I laid it on a bit thick, pointing out how they were fearful that if they could not find a good home for Jason, they might have to ask Douglas White to put him down.

'You'd be doing them a service, Angus, and you'd save a young dog's life.'

'I don't know, Doctor, I'll have to think.'

But the next time I saw Angus he had a young Labrador at his heel. Hamish was right. Within a fortnight his diabetes was controlled.

The following August, on the twelfth, I spent much of the day with Angus and that evening I found a brace of grouse on my doorstep with a quotation from Burns' 'The Twa Dogs':

> When up they gat an' shook their lugs,
> Rejoic'd they werena men but dogs;
> An' each took aff his several way,
> Resolv'd to meet some ither day.

CHAPTER 14

The Wedding

My marriage to Fiona was planned for early in June. That seemed ages away, but time passes quickly in the spring and early summer of a Scottish island. Just as Jennie had said, the spring was magnificent, the island producing carpets of primroses and anemones. The early flowers were followed by bluebells—hyacinths, as the islanders called them—and then the massed purple of orchids on the machair. The whole island seemed fecund, with lambs, foals and calves round each croft. Every animal seemed to be reproducing. It occurred to me that I alone seemed celibate, and I yearned for June to come.

The island was in its full glory. A profusion of rabbits nibbled the grass of the machair to the perfection of a fine lawn. Ringed plovers and redshank, peewits and snipe nested among the taller grasses and, later, the corncrake rasped his incessant call from nettle patches. The sea, seen from where I parked my car near the cliff edges, stretched away in blue tranquillity. The calm of the Hebridean Sea seemed almost unbelievable, especially when I remembered the raging storm I had encountered when first I visited the island.

Whenever there was time from work, I was off to fish, sometimes with Tom Chalmers or Erchie, the latter always saying, 'Come fishin' laddie, it'll be all right so long as you pay half the fine!' I never asked too much about its legality, but trusted Erchie implicitly. More often I would have a rod in the back of my car and stop for a few casts on my rounds. Work seemed idyllic. Now that the measles epidemic had subsided, it was still busy but not frenetic. Always there was the pleasure of exploring the beautiful island while doing my round of visits, watching it go green with the sudden burgeoning of spring. The moors, so dead and lifeless in winter, came to life with meadow pipits; along the cliffs the fulmars were returning to their cliff nesting sites; and in the gullies of the hills in the south of the island, the ring ouzels were pairing.

The best times were when Fiona came out with me to show me the favourite places of her childhood. Together we explored the woods and beaches of the island. With her knowledge of zoology she complemented my own love of natural history. Remembering what Jennie had told me about her idea of researching the history of the extinct species of Scotland, I asked her about this.

'Scotland must have been a wild place during the latter part of the Ice Ages,' she explained. 'It wasn't all deep freeze then. The Ice Ages lasted about a million and a half years, during which immense ice shields built up to cover Scotland. Periods of intense cold were interspersed with warmer periods when, though the ice did not melt completely, there were times when vegetation flourished sufficiently to permit mammalian life. In the last cold period, called the Devensian, that lasted from about a hundred thousand years ago until about ten thousand years ago, there were some incredible beasts in Scotland. Woolly mammoths and woolly rhinoceros, brown bears, beavers and lynxes were here. Later, in the warm wet Holocene, when the ice was finally going, there were aurochs and wolves.'

'Yes, Jennie mentioned aurochs. What were they?'

'As their scientific name of *Bos primigenius* suggests, they were the beginning of cattle; *Bos* means cattle and *primigenius* means first forbear. There are a few sketches of them among cave paintings. I think they must have looked like bigger and better hielan' coos. Anyway, it seems some of these creatures may have crossed to the islands, and I want to see if there is anything to suggest they were here in Laigersay.'

'Sounds interesting.'

Fiona laughed happily 'It may be some time till I get round to it. I seem to be rather busy with planning a certain wedding at present.'

Busy or no, in the spring she managed a day trip to Assilag. We crossed the causeway well before low tide when the water was a few inches deep and, by driving slowly, we could get through.

'That should give us about four hours before it gets impassable again,' said Fiona. 'This is my favourite place in the whole estate. Daddy has a little summer cottage here, which he has promised us for our honeymoon. I'll show it to you soon, but before that I want to show you the rip. It's the most frightening place I've ever been to. In fact, Murdo and I nearly lost our lives there. We got into terrible trouble because we took out Daddy's dinghy and got caught in the rip. Mummy was alive then and she was so angry with us. In the end she calmed down, when she realised how near she had come to being childless.'

So saying Fiona drove me up to the low cliff overlooking the island of Solan which, apart from the lighthouse at its southern end, was uninhabited.

'We wanted to go to Solan,' she said, pointing across the narrow stretch of placid water that separated us from the smaller island. 'It's a wonderful place for birds, and there was a carefully guarded secret eyrie of a pair of white-tailed eagles breeding in the cliffs there. Murdo was nineteen and I was eleven. I desperately wanted to go to Solan, and he said he'd take me. Do you see how calm the water is just now? It looks as though you could swim to Solan. It's often like that, but if you misjudge the tide this strait is one of the most dangerous places on the west coast. Only the whirlpool at Corrievrechan between Jura and Scarba is more dangerous than the rip at its worst. For about half an hour either side of high tide there is an enormous current passing through the gap between Assilag and Solan. If the wind is westerly that makes it worse.

'We were jolly lucky that day: a fisherman by the name of Alex Farquharson was in Assilag Bay, and he saw us. There is only one way to cope with the rip and that is to ride it, and that takes incredible skill. There is a mass of skerries as you near Solan, and the rip carries you down on to them. There's just one way you can get through, and you have to know the coast there very well indeed to find it. The fisherman saw what we were trying to do, and came after us. There's no doubt he saved our lives, by getting his boat alongside ours and guiding us through the gap in the reef. I am afraid he lost a lot of his fishing gear and damaged his boat. We were swept way down to Mulcaire—that's a good two miles. The coastguard came down and rescued us from there.

'Daddy was very cross with us, but he replaced Mr Farquharson's gear and we have remained friends ever since. Some years ago, there was a terrible accident, when one of the Farquharson boys had his leg torn off in a tractor accident.

Fiona turned to me, threw her arms round my neck and kissed me. 'I'm so glad I didn't die,' she said, 'or I would have never have fallen in love with you. Now, if you promise to be good and not try and anticipate, I'll show you where we will spend our honeymoon.'

She ran back to the car and stood smiling at me. The light breeze was folding her dress against her slim body, outlining her breasts. I wasn't sure that it was such a brilliant idea to be visiting the honeymoon cottage, if she really wanted me to be good.

During the Easter holidays my father visited Laigersay and was as enchanted as I was myself. He and the admiral immediately became friends and father seemed almost as much in love with Fiona as I was myself. I took him all over the island, reliving my adventures with the sea trout and my explorations of the coast. One day when Maggie McPhee was due for a visit, I took him with me for the ride. We called at the old blind woman's brother first, and I left father gossiping with Archie McPhee about their vegetables while I went on to see Maggie.

This time she was in her society hostess mode. She was expecting me and was sitting in the sun outside her house with a table laid for tea. Communication was as usual difficult. Then I had a brainwave and found that by putting my stethoscope into her ears and speaking loudly and clearly into its chestpiece she could hear me. In fact she pulled a face and protested, 'Dinna shout.'

After that, we could converse reasonably well. She wanted to know all about the plans for the wedding, and seemed remarkably well informed about my activities. She explained that when Archie went down to the Post Office at Lutheran he got all the news, and it was regularly topped up when the post van came up Glen Bradan.

'If ye dinna want to live in a goldfish bowl, ye shouldna be a country doctor,' she added, sensing my feeling of being under scrutiny. She also knew about my altercation with the Major's new keeper, the one-eyed Oleg, over the dead hen harrier.

'He comes this way most days,' she added. 'Tom Bacadh has a bothy near the wee lochan behind Ranneach Mhor. They seem to be working there a good bit. My grandfather used to tell stories about the glen between the castle and Loch Bradan. Way back, the Covenanters used to meet there for their secret worship and there were all sorts of secret places in the hills they could use as hideaways when the teuchits betrayed them to the redcoats.'

I remembered reading that the Covenanters hated the teuchits, or lapwings, because they were supposed to betray their secret conventicles by their incessant peewit calls.

'The bothy was built ower what used to be an auld mine working... there was copper in Ranneach Mhor. There was a passage leading down to Tuilleag Bay. I mind grandad taking me there when I was wee and could see. It was a spooky place, I can tell you. It's closed now, as it wasnae safe. I once lost a dog down there for a week, but we got her back.'

That reminded me of the admiral's dog and I asked her about Cuhlan.

'Aye, I bred him, in fact it was his mother that I lost in the auld mine; it was Cuhlan who found her. She was badly injured, but I nursed her back to health. Later I sold Cuhlan to the laird and when the old bitch eventually died I never had another dog.'

Had they told me in medical school that I would come to see chatting with a blind and deaf old woman—whose sanity I sometimes doubted—as part of the task of a rural doctor, I would have been amazed. Now that I understood my job better, I had learned to look at it that way, and it was why I so enjoyed my work.

Collecting my father from Archie's garden, where the two of them were now discussing beekeeping intricacies, I drove back with him through Lutheran and across the moors near Tom Bacadh. I told father about my encounter with the major's car and how Hamish had circumvented any further action, and he laughed at Erchie's story of the blood test.

'Sometimes,' I told him, 'I think it was the way you brought me up to love nature that made me take up medicine. Now I find myself studying the natural history of my own species. There's no better place to do that than as a general practitioner: it gives you a ringside seat from which to study other people's lives.'

As we neared Loch Bradan we saw the new keeper's pickup van, where the huge man was unloading gear from its back. He scowled at us with his single eye as we passed but he failed to give the usual island salutation of a wave to passers by.

I dropped father at the shops in Port Chalmers and returned to the surgery. Jennie was perturbed.

'It's been a bad day. Doctor Hamish had one of his disagreements with a patient and I had to soothe her down.'

'What happened?'

'Well he hates circumcision of little boys; he calls it surgical paederasty. Mrs McThingy came in with her wee boy to ask for him to be cut. "Why?" asks the doctor. "Because it's dirty," says she, so he points behind the bairn's ears and says, "So are these—shall I lop them off too?" She was fair affrontit, I can tell you. Likely that's another one who'll want to see you instead o' Squarebottle. Mind I rather agree with leaving what the Good Lord put there. He must have had His reasons.'

I laughed and asked if that was that all that had upset her.

'No, I'm a bit worried: I am sure there is something wrong. I don't know why, but I canna get out of my head that we've had an intruder. One or two things seem out of place since I left last night.'

'Jennie, you must be mistaken: who would want to break in? Have you checked the dangerous drug cupboard?'

'Aye, that's the first thing I thought of. With some of these visiting town folk you never know... but there's nothing wrong there.'

'Well, I'm sure it doesn't matter. There's nothing here to steal anyway.' And with that, I told her about my visit to Maggie. As there were no messages, I said that I was going up to Castle Chalmers.

Jennie brightened. 'Didn't I tell you the island's spring was a time for loving and lovers? Away wi' ye and behave yerself... if ye can.'

Fiona was waiting for me, and we walked through the castle woods talking of our wedding, now less than a month away. She told me that Angus Andersen was helping with the music. He was a great lover of Mendelssohn and was busy adapting his favourite composer for a trio of his own fiddle, a piano and timpani.

She was full of bridesmaids and their dresses. I asked about her own dress and was firmly told I was not to know, but that she was certain it would cause a great sensation in the island. As, at the admiral's request, I was to wear naval uniform, sword and all, my own appearance was determined by naval etiquette. I have to confess, my mind kept returning to quite different nuptial rites, but I enjoyed her enthusiasm for feminine affairs. In the shade of the ancient trees of the policies, we lay in each other's arms and dreamt of the future.

The droning of a light aircraft disturbed our idyll in the woods.

'That's Murdo coming home; I didn't expect him till tomorrow,' said Fiona, jumping up. She started running back to the castle with me in pursuit.

The airport formalities at Laigersay do not take long, and Murdo arrived from the little landing strip on the machair near Camus Coilleag shortly afterwards. Greeting his father, Fiona and me, he was full of his flight up from the south. The weather had been poor at first but then the skies cleared and he had an unprecedentedly calm flight over the sea.

'It was so beautiful I even wasted fuel taking in a circuit over the southern end of Laigersay looking at the islands and skerries there. An odd thing happened: a small boat, that looked as though it had come out from somewhere near Assilag, met up with a big ocean-going trawler south of Solan. There was something furtive about it. If it had been a century ago I would have thought of smuggling. Anyway it doesn't matter and it's good to be home, if only for a few days. And how are the lovers?'

'Fine,' Fiona and I answered together. And we told Murdo about the plans for our great day.

The admiral cut in: 'I just hope there'll be some fish for the wedding feast. Do you know when I was in Princes Street last week I saw Loch Bradan salmon advertised in a game dealer's window. I know nothing about our fish being sold. I meant to go in and ask them where they got it, but just didn't have the time. I wonder if that boat has anything to do with it?'

Murdo dismissed the idea: 'I can't think so, father, it would hardly be economic to poach fish here and then send it by trawler to the mainland.'

The laird pottered off to his study while the three of us settled on to the lawn to talk wedding plans over a glass of Pimms as the evening shadows lengthened. Murdo commented that we should take advantage of these mild spring west coast days before summer midges made sundowners in the garden intolerable. Then he asked, 'How is Dad? I thought he looked older. I didn't want to bother him, but I get the impression something odd is happening here.'

'I think he is all right,' I replied. 'He seems as active as usual. He walks enormous distances and is often fishing. But what do you mean, something odd?'

'I had a peculiar visitation from that chap you stayed with in London, Stanley Johnson. He seemed to want to know all about you, Rob, though I got the impression that was a pretext and that he was trying to get information about Laigersay.'

'Why would he want that?'

'I really don't know, but he asked me about Major Thistlethwaite too. Has he been playing up again?'

'He's got a new keeper, who seems an unpleasant bit of work, but there's nothing new that I know of,' I replied.

'You must get around the island a good deal, Rob. Keep your eyes and ears open. Give me a ring in London if you come across anything peculiar.'

'Murdo, you're getting paranoid; nothing disturbs the peace of "the Healing Island".'

'Maybe. I certainly hope so.'

Murdo stayed for a few days, and was away back to London. Before he left, he took me for a spin in his plane. We circled Loch Bradan while my brother-in-law-to-be searched the moors as if expecting something. Remembering Maggie McPhee's talk of the old mine, I looked for any sign of it. I soon picked up the bothy near the lochan a mile or so east of Loch Bradan. I could see a track leading from the Tom Bacadh policies across the moor to the bothy, but of the old mine works there was no trace. Then we flew over the cliffs, where the ancient lava flows of Ranneach Mhor had run into the sea, leaving basalt cliffs for a seabird nursery crammed with nesting guillemots. Again Murdo was searching but clearly failed to see what he was looking for. When, a day or two later, I saw him off from the airport at Camus Coilleag, I noticed that he flew westwards, out to sea, before banking south to take him over the same part of the island again. Something was bothering Murdo.

As our wedding day came nearer, I had some difficulty in finding someone to be my best man. My friends from student days were all either too busy or too far away. The few brother officers from my ship who were not at sea knew me but slightly and, though I asked them to form my guard of honour, I did not want any of them as my best man. There was only one man I really wanted but I was unsure if he would be acceptable. English snobbery would make my choice impossible but relationships were less formal in the island. When I sounded out Fiona, she was surprised at my doubts.

'Listen,' she said, 'it doesn't matter that he's the worst poacher in the island, nor that he drinks like a fish: Erchie saved your life and I'm very grateful to him. If you won't ask him to be your best man, then I will.'

So it was decided. The big man was speechless when I told him. Then he burst out in an unintelligible Highland whoop, and danced round me in a jig. When at last he had breath to speak he exclaimed, 'Losh, man, I'd be that honoured.'

We spent more time, trouble and money on Erchie's rig for the wedding than we ever did on mine. All I needed was a new white shirt to go with my best uniform which, made by the naval tailors, Gieves, was immaculate and still fitted me like a glove. Erchie was clad in a brand new Ericht Cameron kilt with a fine, silver-buttoned jacket. The rig was topped off with a glengarry in which he wore the lyre-shaped tail of a black cock. He was a splendid sight.

When the day came at last, Erchie and I were on time at the kirk. Angus Andersen greeted me with a hug and a blessing and said, 'This is a great day for you, but it is also a great day for Laigersay. I don't know about you but I'm so excited and I do hope you like the music. I hope it will be a special and pleasant surprise for you all.'

We waited the traditional time for the bride and suddenly the organ burst into Bach's 'Toccata and Fugue' announcing her arrival. I knew from the dress rehearsal the previous day that the admiral, in flag officer's uniform, would be standing at the porch of the kirk with my bride. The fugue ended and part of Haydn's 'Gloria' from the Nelson Mass provided music for the processional and a nicely naval touch.

I turned to look and suddenly felt a pang of fear. The admiral was resplendent, his chest emblazoned with medals and a sword by his side. But he was totally eclipsed by the incredibly beautiful girl on his arm, my Fiona, my bride.

Later I was to learn that the magnificent ivory silk wedding dress was the very dress her mother had worn on the day she had married the young naval officer who was to become the laird of Laigersay. A diamond tiara, which had been in the family for generations, and which had also held her mother's headdress, secured Fiona's veil.

I felt hopelessly inadequate and must have communicated my sudden doubt to the big man by my side, for Erchie gripped my hand and whispered:–

'Courage, laddie, she's every bit as lucky as you are.'

Angus greeted us at the altar and welcomed the congregation, which seemed to be the whole population of the Island except, predictably, the Tom Bacadh folk. So we took our vows before the people of the Island, as members of the Chalmers clan had done for centuries. Then, as man and wife, we had a surprise. My father stood up and read:–

'Let me not to the marriage of true minds
Admit impediments. Love is not love
Which alters when it alteration finds...'

So my father's reading of my favourite Shakespeare sonnet conferred parental love and blessing on us both. Then, in celebration of our Scottish idyll Angus picked up his fiddle and joined the pianist and timpanist as his own arrangement of the 'Hebridean Overture' filled the kirk with glorious sound. The swell and fall of the sea echoed round the church. Between them Mendelssohn and Angus had summed up all my love for both Laigersay and for my lovely bride.

We stepped out into brilliant sunshine to walk under the arch of swords provided by a guard of honour of naval officers. After that the reception at Castle Chalmers was an even greater ceilidh than the Hogmanay party had been. The revelry continued long after Fiona and I had left for other nuptial ceremonies.

CHAPTER 15

The Coming of Fuileach Mick

We spent our honeymoon in the peace of the admiral's summer cottage in Assilag. There we lazed and loved in the wonderful summer weather. Sitting together on thyme-spiced cliff tops, we watched the sea and discovered all the mysteries that lovers have sought in each other since Eden. In fact we might have been in that garden, so much were we in love. Together we explored the tiny island, paddling in the rock pools like children, and dining off scallops and lobsters that were left daily on our doorstep by the Assilag fishermen. Fiona decided I needed teaching about the wildflowers as we walked through drifts of orchids on the machair. I soon learned to distinguish northern marsh from pyramidal and lay with my lovely wife sniffing the sweet spicy perfume of the fragrant orchid. In a marshy part of the shore she tried to show me that most lovely wildflower of all, the grass-of-Parnassus, but it was too early and she promised it for later. Life was completely idyllic.

One evening a sudden meteor flash far above us in the heavens reminded us of that other world we seemed to have left, where cosmonauts circled the earth and increasingly hostile enemies contemplated each other and built their fallout shelters. But here, despite reminders of worldwide tensions, the sea remained halcyon and was so calm one could see fish breaking the surface a hundred and more yards from shore. However even honeymoons must end, and all too soon I was back to work in Port Chalmers.

A week after we got back, the phone jangled in the middle of the night and I grabbed it with a groan. It was the third time it had woken me on this busy night.

A calm voice with a slight edge to it announced: 'O'Flynn here, Feadag Mhor Farm. It's my wife. She's had the bairn and she's bleeding bad. You'd best get here.'

The caller rang off abruptly, but fortunately I knew the farm. Fiona stirred beside me as I sprang from bed.

'What is it this time?' she asked.

'Sounds like a post-partum haemorrhage at Feadag Mhor Farm,' I said as I pulled my slacks over pyjama trousers.

'That's Maureen O'Flynn. I didn't know she was pregnant.'

'Neither did I, but that's typical of that family.' I bent to kiss my sleepy wife. 'Bye. I'm afraid I may be some time.'

As I drove across the north road to Coilleag, I thought about the O'Flynn family. They were a sore trial to everyone in the island because of their stubborn independence. They would not accept help from anyone, so the fact that the man had called me suggested a real emergency. I knew the family slightly by repute. I knew Douglas White the vet loathed him, and Hamish had warned me that Maureen had had four children, all of whom had just appeared without his help. 'She's such a shapeless sort of wumman you'd never know if she was pregnant or not,' he had said. Now, by all accounts, she had had her fifth and she was bleeding.

I tried hard not imagine what I was going to find at the farm. Turning right at Feadag Mhor, I bumped over the rough track to the farm, which was blazing with light. At least O'Flynn had turned on all the lights to guide me. He met me at the farmhouse door.

'Too late,' he said in a sepulchral voice: 'she's gone.'

I pushed past him and ran up the stair. The bedroom door was open and I ran in. The scene before me was horrific. The partially naked woman lay across the bed; her legs straddled open across a mess of congealed blood. Amongst the blood was a complete placenta. At least that was out. She certainly looked dead, but my fingers detected a weak pulse.

'Bring me a chair,' I shouted.

In a moment O'Flynn was beside me as I lifted the foot of the bed. 'Push the chair under it,' I shouted, breathing heavily under the weight of the old-fashioned double bed and the dying woman.

Propping the bed to assist blood flow to her head helped a little. Then I felt her abdomen. It was the huge flabby mass of an obese mother of many children. I could not feel the uterus which, after delivery of the placenta, should be a tight mass, like a cricket ball. I knew it was distended with blood and still bleeding.

I had only a few minutes to stop the bleeding. Quickly I injected ergometrine to contract the uterus and at the same time massaged the woman's belly to assist uterine contraction. To my relief I felt the organ respond; the flabby womb contracted under my hand and I knew there was hope now, since that would stop further blood loss.

Behind me, O'Flynn gave a gasp as blood gushed: the books liken this flow to petrol poured from a two-gallon can.

'That's no problem,' I said, with what I hoped was reassurance. 'That's blood she's already lost. With luck the bleeding should stop now. Listen, get on the phone and ring my wife.'

The uterus was getting hard and firm under my massaging hand as I heard O'Flynn dialling.

'It's ringing,' he said, and tucked the phone under my ear and held it there as I drew up some morphine and injected Maureen's thigh.

'It's Rob,' I said. 'This is a major bleed. Get on to Hamish, quick as you can. He'll know what to do... stress utmost urgency,'

I heard Fiona say, 'OK, Rob,' and she was gone.

With the haemorrhage stopped we had hope, but the patient had lost an enormous amount of blood. I ran downstairs conscious that, like everything else in that room, I was drenched with the poor woman's blood. I found my big emergency bag and soon had a drip running into Maureen's arm. Saline was a poor substitute for blood but at least it would help her labouring heart to maintain circulation. I felt her pulse again. It was fast and thready, but at least it was still there. I began to think there might be a chance of saving her—but even if we got her through the present crisis there would be complications to worry about later.

It seemed no time before I heard a car screech into the farmyard. A moment later I heard the voice of Erchie Thomson shouting from below. He didn't sound quite sober.

'Well I'm here. Where's Auld Squarebottle?' he called from below.

A moment later I heard another voice:–

'I'm right behind you, Erchie, mind out of the way while I see what's going on.'

Then Hamish was beside me. My relief was enormous, for there is nothing more lonely or frightening than dealing with a massive haemorrhage on one's own.

Hamish noted the bloody shambles of the bed and my clothes and checked Maureen's pulse.

'Looks like you're doing well, laddie, but she needs blood. Keep on the good work.' With that he disappeared downstairs where there seemed to be a great commotion outside as more cars turned into the farmyard.

A few minutes later Hamish was back with a bottle of blood. 'Here,' he said, 'swap this with your saline drip. It will do more good, especially since it's mostly whisky.'

I changed the drip bottle while Hamish got a drip going in Maureen's other arm. 'Put the saline back on here, it'll do till I get more blood. Open the blood drip well, so it runs fast, she needs it badly. I'll have another one here in a jiffy.' And he was gone again.

I checked the pulse: it was slower, with a slightly better volume. I began to feel hopeful. Then I realised the patient's husband was in the room watching. I turned to him and said, 'We may be able to save her, but it's still touch and go. She should have had proper ante-natal care, then this sort of disaster would not occur.'

He didn't speak and I turned to see the grief-stricken man hanging his head in sorrow. Immediately I felt a brute; this was no time to chide him; that could wait till later.

'Where's the baby?' I asked, realising that in the fight to save the mother I had forgotten about the child.

O'Flynn raised his head. 'He's fine, a bonnie lad: he's in a drawer downstairs by the fire.'

For the first time since I got to the farm I smiled, remembering the island custom of bedding newborn babies in a drawer taken from the kitchen dresser.

Then Hamish was back again with two more bottles of blood. As he changed the saline he commented, 'Rob, this is a special one: it's from your wife. It'll do Maureen a power o' good to have some of the laird's own. Things are better now, so you'd best go and see her, but for God's sake change your clothes. You look more like a murderer than a doctor. I'll take over here.'

'Come with me, Doctor,' said O'Flynn. 'I'll soon fix you up with something more presentable.' He seemed glad to be able to do something helpful, and soon I was drawing a less sanguinary pair of trousers over my pyjamas and donning an old but clean sweater.

When I went downstairs an extraordinary scene was revealed. The kitchen was full of people. Jennie was rocking the newly arrived wee boy in her arms. Two unknown men were lying beside each other on the kitchen table with blood trickling from their arms through receiving sets into bottles standing on the floor. Most people seemed to be drinking tea and chatting excitedly. Fiona came up to me, hugged me and kissed me, whispering, 'Well done, Rob, even Hamish seems quite proud of you. But you must be exhausted, sit down and have some tea.'

Suddenly the adrenaline of the crisis drained from me, and I felt shattered. Only then did I notice daylight flooding through the windows and realise I had been at the farm for a couple of hours after several night calls. I had had hardly any sleep. The tea was marvellous and I slipped into an easy chair.

Fiona sat beside me and said, 'Darling, you look tired out, but let me tell you what has happened. It's been the most exciting night of my life. When you phoned your cry for help I dialled Hamish's number. I've never spoken to him at night before. The phone rang once, then there was a funny sort of growl. "Is that Dr Robertson?" I asked, and he replied: "It is so, Fiona. What's wrong?" So I told him what you said and there was a long pause. Then he said, "Have you got pencil and paper," and, when I said yes, he dictated a whole lot of names and telephone numbers. When he had checked that I had them correctly he went on, "Phone all of them now and tell them I need them at Feadag Mhor Farm as soon as they can get there. Be sure to say 'bidet' to them; they will know what it means. Now get on with it... wait... put Jennie's name on that list, I nearly forgot her. She's O negative too." Then he rang off.

'Well, I did as I was told. The first I rang was Erchie Thomson. He took ages to answer, and when he did he sounded drunk. Anyway I told him what Hamish had said and he didn't sound one bit enthusiastic. Then I said "Bidet," and he shouted, "Och wumman, why did ye no say so before?" Then he too rang off abruptly. It was the same with others. I suppose nobody likes a phone call at 4am but they all responded immediately to the word "bidet". Jennie was the last I phoned and she explained that what I thought was bidet was actually B-day, meaning blood day, the code word Hamish had coined for calling out O negative blood donors in a state of extreme emergency.

'Honestly, its effect was like that of the fiery cross calling the clans to battle. Then I remembered that I was O Rhesus negative too. So I asked Jennie to bring me as well. When we got here, Hamish was already bleeding Erchie. He was so full of whisky from a binge last night I wonder Maureen's not pickled too.'

I looked round the room at the assembled company, all of whom had small dressings in the hollow of their elbows. Beside Erchie and Jennie, there were the two men I did not know who looked like fishermen. Surprisingly, sitting in a chair, tea in hand, was the blind Jack Gillespie I had met a few weeks before on the beach. Beside him lay his 'eyes' Galla, whose name I now knew to be the Gaelic for bitch. There was Mhairi from the Charmer Inn chatting with the two men still attached to Hamish's blood receiving sets. Everyone was talking hard, when the door opened and in came Angus Andersen. He looked round in astonishment and said:–

'They told me there was an emergency and that Maureen was dying... and what do I find? Nothing but a ceilidh.'

'Aye, ye're right, minister,' Erchie boomed: 'it's naught but a ceilidh and a bloody one at that,' and suddenly everyone was laughing.

Hamish came down again and removed the receiving apparatus from the two fisherman's arms. 'She's doing well now, so I'll just pop these bottles in the fridge for later. My thanks to you all.' Turning to Fiona, he added, 'I've just told her she has some of your blood in her, and she was well enough to say it was nice to be a blood relative of the laird.'

Then he looked round the room. 'Och,' he said, 'tea is all very well and though it's traditional after blood letting, I think we all need something stronger. I've got a crate o' square bottles in the car. Come and help me, Erchie.'

The big man needed no urging and that was how at dawn began one of the most memorable parties the island has ever known. With Hamish's scotch and Angus's fiddle (also fortuitously in his car) what was to become known as *cèilidh na fala*, the party of blood, or as Erchie always called it, the 'Bloody Ceilidh', was soon in full swing. Tired as I was, I was soon dancing an improvised eightsome reel for six with Fiona, Mhairi and Jennie partnered by Erchie and Hamish. The whole affair seemed mad, but was a release of the incredible tension that had been present only a brief hour before. Everyone present was to boast in the future that they had been there. O'Flynn, somewhat tearful after a large dram, held up baby Michael, who had caused all the trouble.

'We'll never forget you, wee chap, and the night that you were born!' he said and the baby's head was well and truly wetted. Upstairs Maureen slept, well on the way to recovery. Every few minutes Hamish or I would slip up to see her and to check that the blood was running smoothly. Later, before people started to drift away to start the routine of the new day, Angus tapped his bow on his fiddle. Then he played the most haunting air I had ever heard. It was quite short and the group that, a moment before, had been dancing a riotous reel were hushed into complete silence. The air made me think of the wind in the bog cotton of the moors, the tinkle of the burns, the eagle circling on the thermals over Ranneach Mhor and above all the sea breaking softly on the white sands of the north and below the savage cliffs of the south. I had heard it said that the minister sometimes gave thanks to God with his fiddle. The silence persisted for a long moment as Angus put down his bow, then one man spoke. It was the old fisherman, Alex Farquharson; he said one word:—

'Amen.'

We transferred Maureen, now judged fit to travel, to the cottage hospital, where the staff supervised the slow transfusion of the last two pints of blood.

For ever afterwards the baby was called Fuileach Mick or just plain bloody O'Flynn.

CHAPTER 16

Aftermath

It was after seven on that fine summer day when Fiona and I left Feadag Mhor Farm. We were both exhausted by the tension of saving Maureen O'Flynn's life, and went home to get some sleep. In each other's arms we relaxed and the stress of the last few hours slipped away. As I slipped into sleep, Fiona kissed me again and said, 'Rob, I'm proud of you.'

'And I'm proud of you too,' I added, and was sound asleep. Later we calculated that was probably the night our twins were conceived.

A couple of hour's sleep and a bath worked wonders. I went to check at the cottage hospital and see that Maureen was all right, and found that she too was sleeping. So was her baby. He looked innocent enough, now that he had been transferred from the drawer of the farm dresser to a respectable cot. As I gazed at the sleeping scrap of humanity, my mind went back to the scene I had found in the farm bedroom. I hoped I would never see the like again.

Fortunately it was Hamish's turn to do morning surgery. He was just finishing as I walked into the old schoolhouse.

'My! That was an exciting night,' said Jennie by way of greeting. 'Everyone is talking about it and it has not done your standing in the island a bit of harm. You'll have to mind ye dinna get a swollen head. Sometimes heroics like that precede a disaster, so be on your guard. I'm just taking the coffee in.'

Pondering the wise woman's caution, I followed her into the consulting room, where Hamish was wrestling with the jammed drawer in his desk. 'I keep trying this damn thing... one of these days it'll shut.'

'Aye,' added Jennie dryly, 'and then you'll never get it open again, and you'll miss what's in it.'

Hamish dunked his shortbread in his coffee in reflective manner. 'A remarkable happening last night,' he said. 'You know, it's moments like that that make me love the people of this island.'

'Tell me about how you managed it,' I prompted him.

'Well, it was two or three years back, we had a succession of terrible tractor accidents. Jock Robertson from over in Tuilleag turned a tractor over, cut his femoral artery and bled to death before I could get to him. Then a week later Iain Farquharson from Lutheran—his father and brother were there last night—had an even more horrific accident. You know those appliances on tractors which have a device that rotates: they have a sort of jaw on the end that can be engaged in drills and things. Iain caught the leg of his trousers in the jaw, which was revolving at high revs. It dislocated his leg at the hip and twisted it clean off. I can't tell you how awful it was; the lad died soon after I got to him.

'Anyway, it made me think. We are far too far away here to get blood in an emergency, so I decided to set up a volunteer's blood bank. I held a meeting in Port Chalmers Town Hall as soon as I could after Iain's funeral. Practically the whole island turned out and I was inundated with volunteers. Over the next weeks I took blood from hundreds of people. The blood samples all went to the mainland and I got a list of blood groups. I was most interested in universal donors, the people with Group O Rhesus negative blood. These were the people who would be most useful in acute emergency. I keep a list of names by the phone in the surgery, the hospital and at home. As I never knew when I might need blood, the best place to keep it was in the potential donors' own blood vessels. I arranged with the O negative people that if ever they got a message from me including the code word B-day, they would come at once and give blood. Last night was the proof that the idea worked.'

Hamish paused. 'Sometimes I give up on the people here as a lot of idle good-for-nothings bent on poaching, hochmagandie and drinking. Then a thing like last night restores my faith in human nature, and I love them all. You did well, laddie, and so did that wee wifie of yours.'

Such praise from Old Squarebottle was rare. When I told him I had seen Maureen at the hospital, he went on: 'It's quiet today—you didna get much rest last night. I'll cover the practice. You take your Fiona out for lunch. Tell her I told you to and give her my thanks.'

So we went into Port Chalmers and filled ourselves with scallops and langoustine and I pushed the boat out with a bottle of Fiona's favourite Gewürztraminer from Alsace. Over lunch we talked of the people who had been at Fuileach Mick's ceilidh.

Fiona laughed at her mistake over the bidet. 'I really couldn't think what Hamish was on about, but the word certainly worked; it even sobered Erchie up enough to hurry over to the farm. He beat Hamish there, because he had to go to the hospital to collect the blood-doning gear. Then Mhairi appeared, saying she'd had to throw a crowd of late drinkers out of the inn, or she would have been first. The next to arrive were Alex and Rory Farquharson, all the way from Lutheran. They are father and brother of Iain, who had his leg torn off. It was that which started Hamish's crusade. They are both O negative. Alex responded immediately, despite it being well known he won't speak to the O'Flynns. The Farquharsons are interesting people: they live between Lutheran and the causeway to Assilag. It was Alex who rescued Murdo and me from the rip. They are inshore fishermen, taking shellfish round the islands in the south. They are very much "wee free" and hold strong, implacable opinions. They picked up your friend Jack Gillespie on their way and then Jennie brought me. While you were upstairs Jennie phoned Angus from the farm to tell him how gravely ill Maureen was and he was soon there to complete the party.

'It was an extraordinary atmosphere: everyone was anxious, excited and apprehensive at the same time. Then when it seemed things were going the right way it was Erchie, half tight as he was, who suddenly started laughing; then we were all at it and that was when the minister walked in on us. Angus is great, he sensed what was happening and was soon contributing with his fiddle. It was Jennie who led the dancing; I don't think old Alex Farquharson altogether approved, but I did notice his foot was tapping!'

After lunch, mention of Jennie recalled her history lesson about the island and I said that I would like to check something she had mentioned in the library. Fiona said she'd come too, and try and further my Scottish education.

As we walked to the library Fiona asked me if I had ever heard of the Old Statistical Account. I shook my head, feeling that I probably wouldn't want to know about something sounding so dreary.

'It's a marvellous work,' she continued. 'At the very end of the eighteenth century, Sir John Sinclair, he was one of the high-heid-yins of the church, wrote to every minister in the Church of Scotland with a long questionnaire about his parish. Astonishingly he got a hundred percent return, and these were published as the Statistical Account of Scotland; in those days statistical meant "state of" rather than its mathematical sense.'

'So what sort of questions did your "high-heid-yin" ask?'

'Well, there were a lot about the church of course, but almost everything—from agriculture and archaeology to natural history and disease—was covered. You'd love it for the records of birds, and for the picture of medicine of the time. Some of the ministers were almost as good as your beloved Gilbert White, and have left a wonderful record of the birds. Anyway, here's the library: I'll show you what I mean.'

A few minutes later we were standing before a long bookshelf displaying Scottish History. Fiona explained that the Account was in twenty volumes but that only the part of it relating to the islands was kept in Port Chalmers library.

'Laigersay is here in the Islands section along with all the Hebrides.' She took out the volume.

It was anything but dreary, and soon I was skimming through the words of the minister of Port Chalmers, patiently scribed with a quill over 160 years before.

> Laigersay is Norse, formed from the Old Norwegian *laege*, a healer or physician and the suffix *-ay*, an island. It is said that a dying Viking came to the island, where he was overcome by its beauty and peace and was restored to health. It was also once called *Seudaig*, a little Jewel. The Island is some twenty miles from north to south and 15 at its broadest. It is set by itself some five leagues from the mainland. The south is mountainous with cliffs, which rise almost perpendicular from the sea to great height, above a scatter of skerries and small isles. There are pillars to be found in the cliffs like unto those of Staffa. There is but one sizable loch abounding in fine trouts and salmons with a plenitude of eels.
>
> Climate
>
> Bathed by the sea, the climate is for the most part good but spectacular storms occur in autumn and winter when many of the islands become unreachable...

Minerals Vegetables and Animals

There is little lime for the fields but some iron and large seams of copper ore in the south of the island...

Birds

The most remarkable are on the muirs. Red and black game. Capercailzie are occasionally seen in the wooded areas but the hills are of insufficient stature to harbour tarmigans. The cuckow is frequent often 3 or 4 calling at a time and the crake or land rail too often disturbs one's sleep, for these rails are very numerous. Mouse-coloured swallows inhabit the sandbanks and water ouzels frequent the burns. Other birds include woodcocks and snipes with many geese in winter. Curlews and plovers of all sorts abound. The abundance of nature is most marked in spring when the cliffs teem with cormorants and scarts, sea ducks abound and the assilag (for which a small southern isle is named) come there to breed. This small seabird, also called a petrel, for it seems to walk on water, is so full of oil that it is used by some as light in a lanthorn. This bird is not larger than a starling. Mariners say that it follows ships in their wake for many days. The vulgar name of these birds is, Mother Carey's Chickens.

Animals

There are rabbits in small numbers with a few foxes and many otters but the commonest is the seal, which breed prodigiously in the islets and skerries of the south...

Fish

The sea has fish in plenty namely white-herring, cod, ling, mackerel, lythe, sythe and cuddy. Lobsters, partans, oysters and craw-fish abound...

Agriculture

There is but little arable land but what exists is well manured with kelp, there being some 80–100 tons of sea ware and tangle harvested for this purpose, so that yields are high...

Population & Distempers

Formerly there were some 2,500 souls but of late there has been much reduction due to migration of people to the mainland in search of better employment. Both men and women live long, many to 80, some even to 100. In former times the smallpox was most destructive but now with the acceptance of inoculation the disease is seldom known. A former minister, convinced of the success of inoculation took it upon himself to ensure all received this, even inoculating his parishioners before divine service...

People

The people are sober, regular, and industrious: They are lively, cheerful, and given to hospitality...

Antiquities

There are many traces of invading Norsemen and two or three ancient burial sites said by some to be remnants from Fingalian chieftains...

I was engrossed, and did not hear Fiona until she touched my arm. 'How are you getting on?' she asked.

'Fine, this is fascinating. Is there this sort of detail for the whole country?'

'Yes, but of course each entry is different depending on the place and the interests of the minister who was writing the account. But it's a mine of social history. And I've brought you two other books you should look at. This is by a Welsh lawyer called Pennant.'

'Oh, I know Pennant: he was one of the men Gilbert White corresponded with in *The Natural History of Selbourne*.'

'That's right, but this is his report of his tour in Scotland in 1772, with an account of a voyage to the Hebrides. He, too, has something to say about our island. This other book is even older: it is Martin Martin's *Description of the Western Islands of Scotland*, written about 1695. Look, here's Martin's account of Laigersay.'

She read aloud:–

> The name of this isle is derived from the Viking king
> Magnus who, mortally sick, came here in 1105. He
> prepared for death, but miraculously recovered and so he
> named the isle Laigersay, which in the Norse Language was
> Healing Island. The inhabitants observe that the air of this
> place is perfectly pure and there is no epidemical disease
> that occurs here. The natives are accustomed to take large
> doses of aqua-vitae and are careful to chew a piece of
> charmel root, finding it to be aromatic; especially when
> they intend to have a drinking bout, for they say this in
> some measure prevents drunkenness.'

Fiona looked up from the book with a laugh. 'Perhaps we
should tell Erchie that!'

She turned a page or two to a place she had marked and
added, 'Jennie would like this, though I expect she knows
it,' and she read again:–

> Serpents abound in several parts of this isle; there are three
> kinds of them, the first black and white spotted, which is
> the most poisonous, and if a speedy remedy be not made
> use of after the wound given, the party is in danger. The
> longest of these black serpents is from two to three, or at
> most four feet long...

'And here's another entry, which you might find
interesting:–

> The inhabitants of Laigersay are renowned for their second
> sight, or taish.

'I can't find a lot in Pennant, but you ought to have a look
at him. He's interesting about the mining that used to go
on here:–

> I visited the mines, the ore is of copper, much mixed with
> lead which occasions expense and trouble in the separation;
> the veins rise to the surface, have been worked at intervals

for ages, and probably in the time of the Norwegians, a
nation of miners. The copper ore yields 33 lbs per hundred.

'He also mentions agates at the foot of the cliffs. I
remember we used to hunt for them as children. You can
get some nice ones around Assilag Bay.'

'Tell me,' I asked, 'did you find anything on your old
cow, what was its name again?'

'The auroch. Not a lot, but I found a splendid book on
British quadrupeds of 1839 by a chap called Thomas Bell.
He must have been a VIP in his day, for he was Fellow of
the Royal Society, and of the Linnaean, Zoological and
Geographical Societies. He at least mentions *Bos primigenius*
and discusses its relationship to wild cattle in Scotland.'

Suddenly Fiona chuckled. 'You're not the only person
who has career aspirations, you know. Now that I have
spent all this time getting a first-class honours degree in
zoology, I feel I ought to do something with it. I don't
want to teach, and I know it's going to be quite a job
being Mrs GP, but I don't want to rusticate altogether. It
seems to me a nice little slow research interest would be a
good idea. I like the thought of an occasional visit back to
the zoology department at Glasgow to do some reading. I
reckon it will meld nicely with your passion for birds. If
we can find out what has made species disappear in the
past we may help to preserve the ones that are left. Just
think how the great auk and the passenger pigeon have
become extinct within the last century. There are lots
more that could go the same way.'

Unfortunately the volumes we were examining were
for reference only and were not borrowable. But I decided
to return for closer examination later. However now the
library was closing, and Fiona had promised to visit her
father at Castle Chalmers.

As we walked home, Fiona said, 'I love libraries, and
can spend hours in them tracking down bits of
information. I must ask Daddy what he's got in the

library at the castle—there's bound to be a lot there, but you don't really notice when you grow up in a place.

'Listen, I'm going to be some time with Daddy. Why don't I drop you off in Feadag Bheag and you can fish Allt Feadag, and I'll come and find you when I've finished at the castle?'

I looked at the sky. 'It's a bit bright, but it might be worth it.'

Half an hour later Fiona dropped me at the bridge over the Allt Feadag in Feadag Bheag village. The burn was low and gin clear, between clumps of stunted alder. I sat where I could see the stream and thought about what Fiona had said. I suppose the male assumption of being the career maker had distracted me from how Fiona might use her qualifications. Dazzled by her beauty, I had allowed myself to lose sight of the fact that she was a highly intelligent human being quite capable of realising a prestigious career. I made a vow to myself that I would not forget her research plans and would do my best to foster them.

As I watched from the bridge a dipper skimmed downstream, settled on a rock and bounced up and down. A common sandpiper shrilled away, calling its Scottish name of 'Kittie-die-dee', repeating it unceasingly, like an old fashioned sewing machine. As I peered over the parapet of the bridge a pair of grey wagtails pirouetted over the stream. I love these sleek and handsome grey and yellow creatures, but deplore their prosaic name. The Italians call them *'Ballerina gialla'*, the yellow ballerina, which is so much more descriptive.

The river was low and the fishing looked hopeless but, carrying my rod, I strolled downstream towards the sea at Camus Feadag. At least there might be birds to see and I walked slowly and quietly. The dipper accompanied me, and soon gave his chattery little song from a perch in midstream. Then there was a sudden electric blue flash speeding upstream. It had to be a kingfisher, which was a real surprise, for they are uncommon in Scotland and even less common in the islands. But the bird had gone as swiftly as it appeared. Watching carefully, I tiptoed along the bank, ducking through a low canopy of alder and hazel. All at once I smelt tobacco smoke, and a dozen yards ahead spotted a rod resting against a stunted oak.

As I approached, Angus Andersen's voice admonished me in little more than a whisper.

'You may think I'm very idle, young Rob, but actually I'm doing three important things at once: I'm smoking my pipe to keep the midges away, I'm not taking my eyes off the pool in front of me because there's a good fish in it, and I'm composing next Sunday's sermon. Did you see the kingfisher? That's only the second I've ever seen here. They are very rare here but I do know they have been recorded near Stornoway in Lewis. It just suits my mood. The ancients, people like Pliny, called the bird a halcyon. They believed it nested on the sea and for the three weeks it was brooding the sea remained perfectly calm. That's how we get the phrase "halcyon days" when everything is peaceful and beautiful... just like summer in Laigersay.'

Angus was sitting in a comfortable dry hollow between two rocks and, as he had said, not shifting his gaze from the pool. I told him I had indeed seen the brilliant blue flash of the kingfisher and had been following it when I came upon him.

'Just sit still and watch. He may come back, and while we are waiting we'll watch for that fish, it's either a sea trout or a grilse. Wasn't that a wonderful occasion this morning? I arrived as most of the drama had been played out but that sudden burst of gladness at the happy outcome did one's heart good. Some might think it almost sacrilegious to sing and dance after a brush with death like that, but I think that sums up this island.

'They have had some very hard times in the past. Only a century ago many died of starvation when the tatties failed, then there were the clearances, besides centuries of bloody battles. Yet despite that, they can give thanks to

God in a sudden, spontaneous exuberant outburst of joy. That's why I'm working on a sermon.'

'Talking of which,' I asked, 'what was the air you played early this morning before the ceilidh broke up?'

'Oh, it was just a piece I wrote myself. I call it "The Laigersay Lilt". You see, sometimes I pray with my fiddle. That's because it thinks more clearly than my brain and it speaks more eloquently than my voice. I think God hears my fiddle and this morning I just wanted to say "thank you". I have been much influenced by Neil Gow, the eighteenth-century fiddler from Perthshire. He wrote some marvellous music for my instrument, mostly jigs and reels, but he also wrote some very beautiful laments, some of which Robbie Burns used as settings for his verses.'

Angus paused and relit his pipe. 'You know, Rob, there are changes in the island and I am not very happy about them.'

'What sort of changes?'

'Little things, perhaps just straws in the wind. The children seem to be so much untidier than when I was wee. They leave litter all over the place: I suppose they get that from some of our visitors. It beats me how hill walkers can carry their beer bottles to the top of a mountain and then not carry the empties home with them. There are these notices saying "Keep Out" that seem to be springing up everywhere. Then there are more and more cars in the island.' The minister broke off and glanced heavenwards as we heard the throb, throb of the helicopter passing over to Tom Bacadh. 'And that damned thing is even worse!'

Suddenly the minister became alert, for the kingfisher had returned. Oblivious of us in our stillness by the rocks the little bird alighted on a twig, which stretched three inches above the shallows. The bright bird seemed to have disappeared in deep shadow, only the white flash in its throat and neck betraying its presence. It stared down into the water beneath it, then suddenly dived into the stream, to reappear a moment later with a small wriggling bar of silver in its bill. Back on its perch the kingfisher juggled the little fish till it pointed head downwards, and then it was swallowed. The halcyon had supped. I must have moved slightly, for the bird was away, leaving a memory of the deep, bright aquamarine of its back as a farewell.

'Lovely,' muttered Angus. 'It just fits my sermonising mood.' As he spoke, the surface of the still pool shattered and the sea trout jumped clear of the water. 'My, what a fish! It's like the one that nearly drowned you. There'll be no hope of him taking before dark but I'll wait on and finish my sermon. By the way, you did a good job yesterday, but I think the real credit has to go to Hamish for his foresight.'

We sat and chatted for a bit until the midges got too much for me and I went back to the bridge to find Fiona, marvelling at the character and wisdom of this minister, who was the most accomplished fiddler on the island and an expert with a fly rod. A fisher of men indeed.

CHAPTER 17

Paddy's Reform

A few days later, when it was Hamish's turn for morning surgery, I called in to see Jennie just as he was finishing, for our usual meeting over coffee. Jennie was busy in her little office dispensary brewing up the coffee.

'An odd thing happened this morning,' she told me. 'Patrick O'Flynn came in. I hardly recognised him. He'd had a bath and a shave and—would you believe it?—he was wearing a suit. I have never seen him here before. In fact, I did not know he was called Patrick—he's known to everyone simply as O'Flynn. Anyway, he's just registered as a patient, and he even apologised for not doing so before. Most odd! He even thanked me for donating blood for poor Maureen. He said she was very well, by the way, and wee Michael's doing well. I'm dying to hear what he had to say to Doctor Hamish.'

We did not have long to wait. Hamish's last patient erupted from the surgery rather red in the face and hurried from the building. 'Och, I get fed up wi' that wumman,' said my irascible colleague. 'She's fair costive in mind an' bowel and I told her so.'

I heard a terse 'tut' from Jennie, and knew she would have to do some more soothing of an upset patient, but she changed the subject and asked:–

'What did O'Flynn want?'

'Now that was a turn up,' said Hamish. 'He came to say he was sorry. He's been thinking since Maureen had that big post-partum haemorrhage. He even went over to the mainland to discuss the matter with his priest.' Turning to me, he explained, 'There aren't enough of his persuasion to employ a Roman Catholic priest in this island. So O'Flynn went to the mainland. Apparently the priest suggested that he was, as we all know, a stubborn Irishman who can't get on with his neighbours. Further, he suggested that the near loss of his wife and her virtual resurrection by a lot of heathen protestants was a message from God that he should love his neighbour a bit more. It seems to have impressed O'Flynn, for he apologised for putting us to so much trouble, thanked us all for what we did, and even said he would listen to advice more in future.'

'Quite a transformation,' I commented.

'More like a bloody miracle.'

Jennie sighed. 'I suppose everything about the O'Flynn family is forever to be qualified with that adjective.'

Hamish was planning an overnight stay in Glasgow, and was intending to take advantage of an air ambulance flight taking a patient there. It was always convenient having a free flight like that, and he seemed expert at contriving them to chime in with postgraduate meetings at the medical school. He hurried his coffee break—an unusual event—and went off to the airstrip at Camus Coilleag.

The following day, I was coping with the routine of morning consultations when Jennie came in to say there was a reverend gentleman to see me, a visitor from the south. 'He seems to be in a bit o' a state about something. He rang Angus Andersen for advice: Angus told him to come to us.'

'Okay, send him in.'

A moment later a red-faced, burly English parson came in, looking extremely uncomfortable and sweating profusely in a dark suit and a dog collar, which seemed, in a Laigersay heat wave, to be very out of place.

He introduced himself as the rector of a parish in Birmingham, who was in the island on holiday and had been recommended to me by his acquaintance, Angus Andersen.

I asked what I could do for him.

His embarrassment became even more acute. 'Er, everything is confidential here, isn't it, Doctor?'

'Of course,' I replied, wondering what was coming.

'You see, if my parishioners were ever to hear of this... I don't know what would happen. You see, I have been rather foolish...'

The poor man seemed beside himself. With an effort he pulled himself together, and continued, 'You see... it's down below, Doctor,' and his accompanying gesture indicated his crutch. I began to wonder just what this errant parson had been up to.

'I am sure it's nothing we can't deal with, Rector,' I reassured him. 'Would you like to go behind the screen and slip your things off, so I can see what's bothering you?'

When the rustling of clerical garments subsided, I went to look, but I had to withdraw immediately in order to hide my laughter, for the problem was all too obvious. On the clerical penis was a grossly engorged sheep tick. Poor man, he had obviously never encountered a tick before, but I wondered why his conscience was so guilty. Recovering my composure, I returned to his side. I clasped his hand to ease his acute embarrassment, and looked him in the eye:–

'I am terribly sorry, Rector, it will have to come off!' I said irreverently.

A moment later the arthropod was in my forceps, with its biting parts safely removed. I warned him against sitting in the heather in shorts in the warm weather, or he might get another. I do not remember ever seeing a man so relieved... but I still wondered why his conscience troubled him so!

Still chuckling, I called the next patient in. She was one of the two friends with the same name—Mary Robinson—who lived in the same village and always came to the surgery together. This was just a brief visit for a repeat prescription, and swiftly dealt with. Then the other Mary Robinson came in, and was as quickly served. It was as well that these two quickies came together, for they allowed me to catch up after the time taken by the guilty parson. Then in came Maisie Henderson, a lady I had seen several times before. Unfortunately, multiple sclerosis is common in Scotland, and it is one of those diseases which Laigersay's renowned healing qualities did not seem to help. There was nothing I could do for this charming lady in her early forties but, remembering advice from Hamish, I knew I had to give her time and attention. Her disease was quiescent for the time being but, intelligent as she was, she knew what might happen to her. Not surprisingly, she frequently got depressed at what the future was likely to bring. As I listened to her, it became obvious that her husband was frightened by her illness and rarely touched her. I guessed their sexual relations were non-existent and this sense of rejection worsened her depression.

Thirty minutes ticked by, and I realised the waiting room would be getting restive. It was then I made my mistake. One way of tactfully indicating the end of a consultation is to write a prescription. But no prescription was indicated for this lady. Then I remembered that Hamish was renowned for writing advice on a script instead of a drug. I scribbled quickly, folded the slip of paper and handed it to her. It certainly had an effect: she glanced at it, got up, walked out and slammed the door behind her. I was upset and found myself cursing Hamish; he could do that sort of thing, but when I took his advice it all blew up in my face.

Late as I now was, there was nothing to do but get on with my work. Soon I forgot about the incident, though memory of it came back to haunt me uncomfortably throughout the day.

When morning surgery was over, I did not mention the incident to Jennie, and Hamish was still in Glasgow. So I collected my list of visits and set out on my morning round. The day's list included several visits in Port Chalmers, a routine call to the Simpson sisters in Feadag Mhor, a couple in Lutheran, one in Assilag and the McPhees. I got out my tide table and saw that mid to late afternoon was best tide for the causeway to Assilag, so I decided to do Port Chalmers first, snatch a sandwich at the Charmer Inn and then work my way south to Assilag and end with Maggie and Archie McPhee.

First I called at the cottage hospital to see Maureen and Mick. Kirsty Stewart met me at the door. 'Wonders will never cease,' she said. 'O'Flynn has been here, nice as pie. The man seems transformed. Even his wife finds it hard to recognise him.'

It began to look as though Hamish's miracle really had occurred, and I commented to Kirsty, 'Perhaps the famous healing quality of Laigersay has got to him.'

'I hope so, for if anyone needed it he did!'

We discussed Maureen's case, and Kirsty said she was well and seemed none the worse for nearly perishing from blood loss. We decided to keep her in the cottage hospital as long as possible; it was the only holiday the poor woman was likely to get, and we could hardly bank on the continued reformation of O'Flynn.

The early visits were straightforward and I got to Mhairi's inn in time for a lunch break. Douglas White, the island's vet, was in the bar tucking into haggis and neeps.

'Ah, Rob,' he greeted me, 'I see you come here for a bite on your rounds, just as I do. I wanted to see you. What have you and Hamish done to O'Flynn? He's become quite civilised. Do you know he came over to see me the other day for advice about his livestock? He even apologised to me for being so thrawn and rude in the past.'

Mhairi at the bar heard this and cut in, 'That's odd. He hasn't been in here since the night of the ceilidh when Fuileach Mick was born. He used to be one of my regulars and sometimes difficult to get out. But I ran into him in the village and he was all over me with thanks for my blood.'

Munching one of Mhairi's excellent crab sandwiches, I declined a beer, mentioning that I was calling on the Simpson sisters and after the brouhaha I had had over the mongrel dog, I thought I had better not smell of beer. I told them what Hamish had said about O'Flynn's conversion and we all wondered how long it would last.

Then I went on to the sisters with a sinking heart. Hetty met me at the door. 'Oh, I'm so glad it's you, Dr Chalmers. Dr Robertson has been several times since you came and I did want to see you again. It was so funny about that awful dog. When Jennie at the surgery told me what had happened, I was mortified at having blamed you... and all the time you were blaming me. Hermione and I *did* laugh when we heard the true story. I saw the dog again: it was with some visitors from the mainland. I might have known no Laigersay dog would behave like that. Come along in, I was expecting the doctor today, and I've made one of Dr Robertson's favourite cakes.'

Though I was by now getting used to my colleague's reputation for a sweet tooth, I was surprised at the warmth of this reception. Miss Hermione was equally welcoming, and I was shown into the parlour, where tea was already laid, complete with scones and a honeycomb. I began to understand why the Simpson sisters were down for a visit on the first Tuesday of every month.

They wanted to know all about the night of the blood transfusion, and tutted over Maureen O'Flynn's brush with death. They complimented me on what they had heard of my management of the case, but were eulogistic about 'dear Dr Robertson's' foresight in setting up an emergency blood supply.

After due admiration of the cats I went on my way, reflecting again at the job of a rural doctor, part of which involved bringing company to lonely old women and flattering them by consuming innumerable cakes and scones.

Then the Lutheran calls were minor acute problems, and quickly dealt with, but on driving through the village I saw Jack Gillespie walking along with Galla beside him. The dog was wearing her harness and clearly on duty. She stopped as I drew up beside the blind man.

'Good afternoon, Jack, I trust you have had no trouble after giving blood the other day.'

'Not a bit, Doctor. I was delighted to be part of the party. How are they all? Paddy O'Flynn came over to thank me himself, and brought a leg of lamb and some eggs. I have never really spoken to him before; he had a bad reputation, but he seems a changed man. He almost begged me to call him Paddy.'

We talked of the heat wave before I drove on, marvelling of the miraculous transformation of O'Flynn to Paddy. It seemed he had sought out everyone who was at the farm that night and thanked them personally. I pulled off the road at Alex Farquharson's croft, where as usual he was sitting mending creels. He too had had a visit from Paddy.

'Ach, ye know we never saw chust eye to eye. I dinna care for popish people. But I'll say this for him, he meant kindly and even found out my fav'rite baccy and brought a great tin o't.'

I found myself warming to this difficult Irishman who suddenly seemed to have mended his ways. Like Hamish and Douglas White, I wondered for how long.

I always enjoyed going to Assilag, which is even more peaceful and relaxed than Laigersay. My visit was to Sheila Scrimgeour, a crofter's wife at the southern end of the Island. It was another case of multiple sclerosis and, with a shiver of embarrassment, I thought again of Maisie Henderson. Mrs Scrimgeour's disease seemed to have burnt out, but had left her in a wheelchair. Her husband was the island chess champion and I knew was a friend of Squarebottle's; they used to have a game together when the crofter came up to Port Chalmers for his messages. Hamish told me he looked after his wife devotedly and ran his croft immaculately. Once again my visit was anticipated and tea was laid. I began to wonder how Hamish managed on his rounds with so many teas, all specially prepared for him and to all of which he had to do justice or cause affront!

Once again this call was largely social, but in the middle of the obligatory tea and cakes there was commotion outside, and a voice shouted: 'Is the doctor there?'

I went out to investigate, and there was a very calm young lad with his alarmed mother. The boy had a fishing fly lodged in his face just below his eye. I examined the hook and saw the barb was buried deep in the flesh of his cheek.

Turning to his mother, I said, 'I'll soon have that out. Can you get me a piece of string?' She disappeared, glad to be able to do something, and I asked the boy his name.

'Tom Morrison.'

'Well, Tom, where were you fishing?' I asked.

'Down where the burn meets the sea.'

'Catch anything?' He shook his head. 'I see you like a Mallard and Claret: that's one of my favourite flies too. Did you tie it yourself?'

'Aye.'

The boy began to look apprehensive when his mother came back with a ball of cotton string. 'What are you going to do?'

'I'll show you. Just keep quite still. First I cut a piece of string about two or three feet long. You see, I am threading the string round the bend of the hook with a loose belly in it. Then I press down on the eye of the fly like this and flip the string like that.'

'Will it hurt?' he asked with a slightly trembling lip.

'I don't know, did it?' I replied, and pointed to the floor. 'There's your fly.'

'That's magic! How did you do it?'

'I'll draw you a picture. Every fisherman ought to know that trick, it's so easy when you know how, and you never know when it will be useful.'

I drew Tom a sketch of how to remove a fly. 'I tell you what, Tom, this has earned me a lot of free fishing. I once was watching a chap fish very good private water. He got a fly in his lip. When I took it out he invited me to fish his river and I caught some fine trout.'

When I had finished my picture I was not too pleased with my artistry. 'You really need a bit more belly in the string before you pull through. But the fly comes out as easily as anything. You didn't feel anything, did you? The important thing is to disengage the barb by pushing down on the eye of the fly before you pull through. I can't tell you how often I have done that by a burn. It earns a lot of gratitude too. Remember it, then one day you'll be able to take a fly out of a brother angler.'

But it was time to say goodbye to Tom, his mother and Sheila, to get back across the causeway before high tide.

When I reached Archie McPhee's house, I found him at work in his garden picking soft fruit.

'Hello, Doctor,' he greeted me. 'The rasps are marvellous this year, ye maun have a puckle to take home. We've been hearing great things aboot ye. But man, ye'll find my sister fair affrontit. She's had yon keeper o' Thistlethwaite's up to see her, trying to get her to move oot.'

I climbed out of the car, trying to sort out all this information.

'Now let me get this clear. The keeper is trying to get your sister to move. He can't do that.'

'Yon's what Maggie told him. It's her hoose, like it was faither's before her. She and I were brought up there.'

'Did he give any reason?'

'Oh aye, he said the hoose stood on the major's land and he wanted it for development. Mind, he did suggest that he was doing her a good turn, since they would re-house her in a modern house in Lutheran. But she told him what he could do wi' his modern hoose.'

'That sounds like a modern version of the clearances,' I mused. 'I wonder what he meant by development?'

'Och, I dinna ken. But I kinda sense it will be my turn next if he does get her oot. Anyway she sent him awa' wi' a flee in his lug. For a' that, I ken she's worrit.'

I chatted with Archie about his health, which was robust as ever. He had not had the gout in ages and had no need for what he called his 'crocus tablets'. At first I was puzzled by this, but remembered that colchicine, the drug used to treat gout, was derived from the autumn crocus. I collected a large punnet of raspberries before driving on to Maggie's, wondering just what was going on at Tom Bacadh.

Maggie was defiant. 'Yon one-eye'll no shift me fra ma home, even if wi' one eye he is a king in ma blind hoose,' she declared, but she had no more idea than her brother why Thistlethwaite had sent his unpleasant keeper to warn her he wanted her out. It was hard to imagine what development could take place, unless it was something to do with the short River Bradan, which in its mile and three-quarter journey to the sea was rich in salmon, and potentially a goldmine. As I listened to the old blind woman's indignation, I began, like Angus Andersen, to have an uneasy premonition of change in Laigersay.

CHAPTER 18

Grouse

There had been talk of little else during the past week. Fiona was up and down to the castle helping her father and his staff prepare for the guests who would be arriving in the island for the twelfth. Not that it was all that big a party. Since the death of his wife, the admiral had cut back on the size of the house party for the first day of grouse shooting. I heard that there were only to be four guests from the south, for most of the guns would be islanders. Mind you, the grouse shooting in Laigersay was not outstanding; a season might yield two or three hundred brace, nothing like the big moors of the mainland.

In addition Murdoch was flying up with his latest girl friend. Fiona was despairing about her brother's love life. He always had a different glamorous girl on his arm but never showed sign of settling with any of them. Throwing her arms round me in a great hug she said, 'I want my lovely brother to be as happy as I am.'

While Fiona went off to meet the flight from the mainland, I collected my bag from the car and walked to my morning surgery. Jennie now produced a list of the patients who had booked to see me. One of the first things I had done after replacing the broken examination couch was to introduce an appointment system. At first this had not worked well, but people began to see that it helped them to fit in with the bus schedule and slowly the idea was catching on. It certainly made it easier for Jennie to control the ebb and flow of patients at the surgery. Hamish, resistant to change as ever, said he did not care for it but at least he tolerated it.

This morning when I looked at the list I noticed that Maisie Henderson, the lady with multiple sclerosis, had booked another appointment. When I remembered the unusual prescription I had given her which had made her leave my consulting room so abruptly, I felt a twinge of apprehension. As I glanced down the list of appointments my heart suddenly fell. Mary Robinson's name was followed immediately by that of her namesake. At once I knew I was in trouble; I had been rushed when they last came and I suddenly had a realisation of the awful mistake I had made. For a moment panic seized me, and I wondered if I should pick up the phone and seek advice from the Medical Defence Union, the organisation that insures the profession against blunders of all sorts. Regaining a little of my composure, I asked myself what Hamish would have done, and in my mind I heard: 'Dinna fash yersel, laddie, and don't cross bridges until you get to them.' So I began the surgery.

Maisie Henderson came in with a parcel. 'I won't keep you long, Doctor, I really only came in to apologise for slamming the door when I left. Also I wanted to say thank you for the best prescription I have ever had in my life. I did what you said, and it has made all the difference at home and I feel so much better. Though I have to say I was taken aback at the time. Anyway I brought you a bottle of my husband's favourite medicine. He tells me it's rare, so I am sure you will enjoy it.'

I muttered my thanks and once again found myself respecting Hamish's wisdom. I had correctly diagnosed Maisie's deep unhappiness, which was not caused by her multiple sclerosis but by her husband's fear of her disease. But I was glad she did not take the script I wrote for her to David Ross, the chemist, for I had written on it: 'Go home and make love to your husband.'

When Maisie left, I opened the parcel and found a very special old Bunnahabhain single-malt whisky. I paused for a moment, reflecting on the very personal relationship that a doctor has with his patients, and that Hamish was right: one occasionally had to take unconventional methods to get them to take advice. I found myself smiling when I thought how Fiona would laugh when I told her about Maisie's prescription. I guessed what she would say: 'Don't let us ever get like that,' and then: 'if we ever do, be sure to give me the same medicine!'

Then I stopped dreaming, took a deep breath and called the first Mary Robinson in.

'I have a bone to pick with you, Doctor', she began, and I thought my worst fears were realised. 'Why didn't you do it before? My new pills have cured my rheumatism and I haven't felt so well for years.' Suddenly half my fears were relieved.

A few minutes later the second Mary Robinson also demanded why I had not given her this new medication earlier. That is why to this day one patient in Laigersay takes antidepressant tablets for her rheumatism and another takes antirheumatics for depression. Sometimes I wonder if it is not just the colour of the pills which affects a cure. Again, Hamish is quite correct in his belief in the greater efficacy of yellow aspirin as compared with white, and I remembered him saying the advantage of prescribing nasty medicine is that it reminds the patient of the doctor's advice three times a day.

Hamish was in fact putting into practice aspects of what was being described as 'the doctor–patient relationship' in the writings of Michael Balint, a London psychiatrist. This revolutionised the way patients were managed from the late 1950s. Baling wrote of the 'drug doctor' which was prescribed at every consultation and was taken along with the nasty medicine three times a day—and was as often as not more important than any other medication. As is so often the case when theories are published, many wise doctors realised that the theory encapsulated what they had been quietly practising for years. Jennie was right to assert that wisdom and kindness were some of the most important attributes of a good general practitioner. These were subjects untaught in any medical school at the time.

With some relief I could now turn to other pressing interests. I had been invited to the shoot, but as an inexpert shot and a bird-lover I opted to be one of the beaters. Fiona and I were invited to dinner at Castle Chalmers on the night before the season opened. I knew that all the talk would be of grouse and as a supposed 'ornithologist' I wanted to read up the subject. As soon as my visits were over I took myself to the library to study some of the experts.

'The red grouse,' I read,

> is the only species confined to Scotland, although it has been introduced to many other parts of Britain. It is closely related to the willow grouse of Europe, which is known to science as *Lagopus lagopus*. 'Lagopus' means having a foot like a hare, aptly describing the bird's feathered claw. The subspecies in Scotland is *Lagopus lagopus scoticus...*'

You cannot get more Scottish than that! I skipped down the page:–

> Grouse are generally short-lived. Nearly two out of three alive in August die within a year, irrespective of shooting... though some may live for eight years. However in the late 19th century grouse disease was responsible for many problems on the lucrative sporting estates of the North. In 1905 this became so serious that an official enquiry was set up with Dr Edward Wilson (who was later to die with Scott on the ill-fated South Polar expedition of 1912) as its principle field observer. Wilson visited every important grouse moor in Scotland and discovered that the disease was caused by a minute threadworm, which crawled up the fronds of heather and lay in the dewdrops on the ends of the young shoots on which the grouse fed.
>
> Other factors have contributed to the decline since 1900, including severe weather, when excessive rain killed many young birds, and louping ill (so called because of the peculiar gait exhibited by sheep affected with the disease). It has been known as a viral disease of sheep in Scotland

since 1807. The virus is transmitted by sheep tick and is a not uncommon affliction of sheep-workers.

I paused in my reading, remembering the unfortunate rector from Birmingham and chuckling to myself. I hoped he would not contract louping ill! Then I continued reading.

Though grouse shooting as a sport is about 200 years old it really only developed in the 19th century. Before that it was not considered a fit occupation for the aristocracy. Travel to the moors was arduous, and tramping them, bearing a heavy muzzle-loading gun, was considered plebeian, fit only for minor gentry. Two inventions changed all this; the railways provided easy access to the moors and the advent of the breech-loading shotgun in the 1850s made fast shooting at driven birds practical. From then on the twelfth became glorious indeed. The railways responded by putting on special Scottish trains, with as many as ten a day from London.

At first grouse shooting was a masculine sport. However, gradually, more ladies were in the butts potting away with their men folk. Their influence turned many rather basic bachelor shelters into comfortable and gracious homes. The 'twelfth' became increasingly fashionable, with city tailors and dress designers catering for the need of smart practical clothes for the moors and the glamorous house parties, which accompanied them. Shooting magazines in the early 1900s carried advertisements for accessories such as silver hip flasks and shooting accessories.

All this brought work and wealth to the Highlands and Islands; and the great houses of rich appeared almost overnight. Game-keeping became an important and lucrative occupation with generous tips from royal or titled sportsmen. The seasonal burning of old heather to encourage new growth to feed the birds and the construction of 'butts' provided out of season work for many. The red grouse brought prosperity to a great number of impoverished country Scots.

I sat back and thought about this. At heart I was on the side of the birds, and did not like the mass slaughter which occurred on the twelfth. However, I had to admit to ambivalence, for I certainly enjoyed eating them and, as a devoted fisherman, could not in fairness side with the growing body of anti-blood sport supporters. Then I reflected on how the grouse had affected the economy of Scotland, and that without them an army of keepers and beaters would be out of work. The hoteliers and shopkeepers also benefited from the huge influx of visitors for the season.

Turning a few more pages, I came across a list of 'vermin' destroyed on a single estate in three years in the mid nineteenth century. It included, I read, '15 golden eagles, 27 white-tailed eagles, 18 ospreys, 98 sparrow-hawks, 7 peregrine falcons, 11 hobbies, 275 kites, 5 marsh harriers, 63 goshawks, 285 common buzzards, 371 rough-legged buzzards, 3 honey buzzards, 462 kestrels, 78 merlins, 63 hen harriers, 6 gyr falcons, 9 Montagu's harriers, 1,431 hooded crows, 475 ravens, 35 horned owls, 71 nightjars, 3 barn owls and 8 magpies.'

Such murderous destruction of birds supposed to harm grouse had led to the loss of at least five species of raptor in Scotland. Why nightjars, which live on insects, were included is hard to imagine. This is an amazing list for two other reasons: firstly it is hard to understand how we have any predatory birds at all today in view of such carnage; secondly what a marvellous range of birds there was before the gamekeepers got to work.

Destruction of raptors continued after the First World War when 'there was an increase in predators and many "Vermin" clubs were formed with the object of reducing predation.' One such club in Argyllshire was 'accused of wanton destruction of interesting and beautiful wildlife in the form of peregrines, eagles, and buzzards. However, when birds, however handsome, destroy the living of human beings, which was the case with the owners and gamekeepers of Argyllshire moors, who saw their income and their wages disappear with grouse, there is only one possible outcome.'

After this reading I felt a little easier at holding my own with 'grouse talk' at dinner at Castle Chalmers. But I hoped the discussion would not become too controversial. The whole field of conservation was becoming a potential minefield and entrenched opinions ran deep.

Nowadays the parties for the twelfth were not as large as they used to be before the admiral had let the shooting for the southern part of the island to Major Thistlethwaite. But there were good moors north of Tom Bacadh where sizable bags were still to be had. The laird had invited Kirsty Stewart, matron of the cottage hospital, to act as his hostess for the evening. He and Murdoch were soon introducing me to the guests who were staying at the Castle, among them General Sir Danvers Colquhoun and Lady Carole. I was surprised to see my acquaintance from London, Stanley Johnson, and his extremely glamorous girl friend, Franceska Davidson. Murdoch also had a girl friend from London up for the party. The present lady, Helen Agnew, was an attractive young woman rumoured to be making a stir in London's publishing world.

I soon found myself in conversation with the general, who was resplendent in full highland evening dress, making my sombre dinner jacket seem rather dowdy. He informed me loudly, as he sank one glass after another of the laird's special whisky, that he was a great devotee of grouse shooting and enjoyed visiting his old friend the laird. Lady Carole was sumptuous in dress and jewellery that seemed rather out of place in a Scottish castle. I remembered an account in one of the books I had read that afternoon to the effect that titled ladies had demanded that their nouveaux riches husbands built palatial houses for their elaborate and sophisticated shooting parties. Lady Carole, I thought, in an earlier age might have insisted on just such a mansion.

Franceska, on the other hand, was delightful. She had Polish ancestry and was to be in the butts tomorrow, but not shooting, and said she would not miss it for the world. She knew Laigersay from previous trips with Stanley, and I began to sense that their relationship was of long standing. She was much younger than he, and stunning to look at in a revealing evening dress but, unlike Lady Carole, she fitted in to the setting. She spoke of catching salmon in Loch Bradan and rough shooting over the moors. 'The one thing I haven't done is to bag a stag: Stanley has, of course: he's even achieved the McNab.'

'The McNab?' I queried.

'Oh, that's a silly sporting triumph which involves catching a salmon, shooting a grouse and a stag all on the same day. It's difficult and involves a lot of organization and big tips for ghillies.'

Then Fiona joined us. She had been busy offstage helping Tetrabal Singh, who had been borrowed for the evening to supervise the kitchen. Angus Andersen led in the party of islanders. Hamish had brought Jennie Churches as his dinner partner; as former schoolteacher, Jennie was known and liked by all and had taught Fiona at the island's primary school. Angus was accompanied by his old friend Mhairi from the Charmer Inn. She was related to the laird through her marriage, and was rumoured to be an excellent shot.

Tetrabal Singh was in charge of all the arrangements and he ushered us in to dinner and showed us the seating plan.

Sir James Chalmers

Lady Carole	Jennie Churches
Dr Robert Chalmers	Angus Andersen
Mhairi Chalmers	Fiona Chalmers
Stanley Johnson	Sir Danvers Colquhoun
Franceska Davidson	Helen Agnew
Murdoch Chalmers	Hamish Robertson

Kirsty Stewart

I wondered how I would get on with the general's lady, for she seemed rather formidable. She immediately launched into tales of former 'Glorious Twelfths' and there was a certain amount of name-dropping, from royalty to senior politicians. Then she asked, 'Do you shoot a lot?'

This was embarrassing, for it could touch on my personal views on a subject I would have preferred to avoid.

'Not much,' I replied. 'I am more of an angler. In fact this is the first "twelfth" I have been to. I am out with the beaters tomorrow, because I want to see as much as possible.'

'Well, you will certainly see a lot of heather and walk a long away. I do not shoot either, but will join the party for luncheon. That will be quite enough walking for me.' Then she leant forward, and addressed her husband: 'Danvers, tell Dr Chalmers the story Douglas Home told you.'

The general was only too delighted and beamed at the mention of the prime minister's brother.

'Ah yes, that was a lovely story about a cock grouse,' and as the hors d'oeuvre of seafood was laid before us he recounted:–

'At the turn of the century there was a red grouse at Cawdor in Aberdeenshire, which the keeper had tamed. During the shooting season it would entertain guests by walking up and down the dining-room table at breakfast taking an occasional peck at a plate and calling, "Go back! Go back!" at the house party, who were just about to set off for a day's grouse driving. One year an Englishman rented the moor. He completely fell in love with the bird and succeeded in persuading its owner to part with it, for a sum. The grouse was packed in a hamper and sent by train five hundred miles south. There everything continued happily until one morning two weeks later it was discovered that the bird was missing from its pen. The new owner was desperate, but after a day or two of frantic searching he decided that a cat must have eaten it, so he wrote to the keeper at Cawdor to break the sad news.

The keeper wrote back to say the bird had beaten the Englishman's letter north by a day.'

After that, Lady Carole turned her attention to the laird and seemed to be flirting rather coquettishly with him. That left me free to chat to Mhairi. I had been pondering the eclectic selection of guests. The contrast between the women on my right and left was typical of the island, where there was less division of society than in the England of my upbringing. So Mhairi from the pub rubbed shoulders with the general's lady. Actually I liked her much more, and it was a mark of her worth that she was obviously highly respected by the minister Angus Andersen. We spoke of the night of the blood transfusion and laughed about the change in Paddy O'Flynn.

She told me of her husband, a cousin of the laird's, who had come home from the war with only one arm and had retired from farming to run the inn at Feadag as a little hotel and she had taken over on his death three years before. Now in her early sixties, she had grown up on the island and knew everyone by name and most of the dogs too. She was an accomplished fly fisherman, a great gardener and champion clay pigeon shot. She had heard all about my accident from Erchie Thompson, and said, 'You must fish that pool again and see if you can catch a really good sea trout, otherwise it will jinx you.' I confessed I had not been back to the spot where I had so nearly lost my life. 'That's what Helen from Pitchroich told me,' she said. 'I know that both she and Tom hope you'll go back.'

Then Tetrabal Singh was carving a huge saddle of lamb redolent of mint and rosemary and conversation stopped as dishes were handed. In his usual way Tet paused to quote Burns to us by way of grace:–

'The heather was blooming, the meadows were mawn
Our lads gaed a-hunting ae day at the dawn,
O'er moors and o'er mosses and mony a glen
At length they discover'd a bonnie moor-hen.'

Tet bowed and made *namaste*. 'Good sport tomorrow, ladies and gentlemen,' he said, and was gone, back to his kitchen to attend to the dessert. Angus passed the claret round and said to the general, 'I know you think the alarm call of the cock grouse is described as sounding like a shouted, "Go, go, go back, go back". But it is much better in Gaelic as: "*Cò? Cò? Cò? Mo chlaidh', mo chlaidh'*," meaning: Who? Who? My sword, my sword!'

'A thing I have never understood is why the opening day is the twelfth, when for other game it tends to be the first of the month,' I interjected.

The laird answered, 'It has been so since 1752, when an Act of George III corrected an error in the calendar. The old calendar had managed to get eleven days ahead of itself. When these days were removed in 1752, what had formerly been the first of August became the twelfth.'

Not to be outdone, the General added, 'In 1915, Lord Lovat managed to get a Bill through the House of Lords authorising the shooting of grouse from the fifth of August... the Commons rejected the Bill amid shouts of, "We want to shoot Germans not grouse"... quite right too! However, in 1940 the grouse-shooting season was advanced by Order in Council to the fifth of August, for it was essential to keep the stock within reasonable bounds in order to prevent an outbreak of disease.'

Tet concluded his delicious menu with a dish of carragheen and individual portions of Atholl Brose in sundae dishes. Though carragheen is a traditional island dessert made from seaweed, to me it is still only a bland blancmange and I much preferred the blend of whisky, honey, oatmeal and cream of the Atholl Brose.

There was less lingering over the port this evening because of the early start the next day. As the party began to break up, Murdo's girl friend, Helen Agnew, drew me aside and asked me which teaching hospital I had been at and, when I told her she said, 'My sister, Frances was a nurse there, did you know her?'

'Good lord, Frances! Why yes, I knew her well, in fact we went out together for a time. I was quite sweet on her for a while. But I think she got tired of me and found someone more interesting. In those days I was more interested in rugby, beer and work than I ever was in women.'

'Frances told me quite a lot about you,' Helen said with a slight smile.

Then the admiral was urging us all to sleep well in preparation for the glorious morrow. I bowed slightly to Helen, and wished her good night. Soon the island party left, and I warned the other castle guests of my embarrassment at getting lost in the labyrinth of the castle at the previous Hogmanay.

As I collected Fiona for the drive home, I was aware of a slight sense of foreboding.

CHAPTER 19

The Glorious Twelfth

The following morning dawned cloudless, with the promise of a sun-filled Glorious Twelfth. As soon as breakfast was over, a procession of shooting brakes arrived outside the castle. The laird still favoured the old pre-war Ford utility shooting brakes rather than what he called the newfangled but more versatile Land Rovers which Hamish and I preferred for getting round the practice. My father-in-law boasted that they had cost him under £300 when he bought them new in 1938. Two of these vehicles were for the guns and another three were crammed with beaters. Angus and Mhairi, the non-resident guns, and the beaters had arrived with the transport and the forecourt of Castle Chalmers was a bustle of people and their excited dogs.

The laird greeted each of the guests and, opening a small gold case, he offered it in turn to each gun.

'This belonged to my grandfather; it is the best way of allocating positions in the butts.'

Each gun took a sliver of ivory from the case, so determining the number of the butt he or she was to shoot from during the morning drives. I was standing by Mhairi as she selected her number; it was '7'. She explained there were seven butts, each with one gun—actually that's one person with a pair of guns—accompanied by a loader.

'I have drawn seven so, on the first drive, I am right out on the right wing, usually the poorest place.' She glanced up at the trees. 'But with this breeze it may not be so bad. Then on the second drive I move to number five, and on the third to number three. They are in the centre and reckoned to be the best. You, poor lad, will spend the day traipsing through high heather on a hot day and, because you are who you are, and volunteered, won't even get paid at the end of the day. But, I tell you this, if you listen to your ghillie, you'll know more about a grouse shoot at the end of the day than the likes o' the general will ever know. I have Erchie Thomson as my loader. He's the fastest man in the island at reloading. Last year the laird put him with the general who complained that the reason he'd bagged so few was due to Erchie's slowness. That's why he's got another ghillie to load for him this season. It will be interesting to see how he explains his poor shooting this year.'

The laird produced a map of the island, and explained: 'We will drive out to the first line of butts just west of Port Chalmers and the birds will be driven north westwards from the Tom Bacadh boundary. The keepers say there are plenty this year, so sport should be good. When we finish the first drive, the transport will take you round the back of Coille Bheag and there will be a bit of a walk through the wood. That has the advantage of screening our approach from the moor itself. The butts there back on to the woodland. There could be a few black game there but I would ask you not to shoot them, as they are getting very scarce. Years ago we even had capercaillie there but they have long since gone and we don't want the black grouse going the same way. However, there should be plenty of red grouse. The transport will have come round just west of the butts and we will lunch there before coming round by road to Milton of Bacadh, where the last drive will take place. I think you all have your allocated butts, so I wish you good, and, please, safe shooting.'

Angus McLellan came up to me, wished me a good morning and said he was delighted to be feeling very well. I had heard he had been out on the twelfth for nearly seventy years, and he certainly was not going to miss this one. He had Jason at his heel.

'How's he shaping?' I asked, looking at the keen young black Labrador.

'Ach, he's still learning but I might make something out o' him yet. Not that he'll ever be like the old dog.'

Jason knew he was spoken of and seemed delighted at this faint praise. I suppressed a smile, knowing the old keeper was devoted to the new dog that had so improved his health that he could once again face a long day on the moors.

There were three cars for the twenty or so beaters. The party consisted for the most part of village lads keen to earn a few shillings but I was glad to see two older men whom I knew, Peter McTavish, the undertaker, and Tom Chalmers from Pitchroich farm. As we set off south of Port Chalmers, Peter told me how he loved beating and always hoped people wouldn't die just before the twelfth—otherwise he might be too busy for his favourite day in the hills.

'You can keep the shooting,' he said. 'I much prefer walking them up as a beater, though the money scarcely pays to slake my thirst at the end o' the day!'

We took the road across the moors that led to Tom Bacadh and turned right along a track I did not know to an isolated farm. Here the vehicles were parked, and Angus drew all the beaters round him.

'On the first drive, we'll make a line along the burn here. Peter and Tom, you know the ropes: I want you as flankers, Peter at the west end o' the line and Tom at the east. Tom, you may be busy: many o' the birds'll veer that way wi' the wind as 'tis. You've got Mhairi opposite you on the first drive. Between the two o' you I doot few will be missed. I'll be in the middle. You youngsters' (and here he looked at me) 'must heed any orders I shout to you. Remember guns are lethal and you've got the bloody general in number four butt.'

He glanced at his watch; the first drive was to start at half past nine, in twenty minutes time. 'Get to your places. Don't start till you hear my whistle.'

I noticed as I walked beside Angus that Jason was the only dog, and I commented on this, for there had been a medley of Labradors and spaniels with the guns. 'Och, I dinna want dogs among the beaters. They put up hares and run after them and that ruins the drive. I'll no let Jason here do that.'

At precisely nine thirty, Angus blew his whistle. From the way it had been described to me, I could imagine the guns, more than half a mile ahead of us out of sight behind a rise of the moor. They would be on tenterhooks and their loaders would have the weapons ready, each standing slightly behind the marksman, the second gun ready for instant use and the next two cartridges held tightly between two fingers ready for split second reloading when the first was discharged. Behind them impatient dogs would be straining at leashes.

We started forwards, and there were certainly plenty of birds, the heather under our feet exploding with grouse like land mines, each one an almost heart-stopping experience. The cocks were indignant and shouted their furious 'Go back' calls at us as they whirred away, to drop into the moor a few hundred yards ahead. I glanced to right and left along the line of beaters, each carrying a white flag and, for a moment, thought Peter and Tom had failed to join us. I realized that the old keeper had put his most experienced beaters at the flanks, where they were probably keeping down out of sight ready to turn any errant covey back over the waiting guns concealed in the butts.

Although it was cool so early in the morning, I was soon sweating profusely, as it was hard work walking through the tall heather. The honeyed smell of the ling filled my nostrils in the warm sunshine, and as I looked round there was no sign of habitation anywhere in sight. But for my fellow beaters, I could be alone in the world. Apart from the grouse, a myriad of meadow pipits flew into the air and several mountain hares, now in their blue-grey summer pelts, lolloped away from us. Soon it would be time for them to change to white in protective winter camouflage, helping to preserve them from the eagles.

A large covey exploded into the air in front of us and wheeled downwind to the left. Two sharp whistle blasts called to Tom Chalmers on the flank. Instantly, appearing from nowhere, he turned the birds back to the centre of the drive with a wave of his white flag. The covey hesitated at the unexpected sight of a man in front and to the left of the main line of beaters, and then they turned with a mutter of complaining growls of 'Go, go, go, go' and plunged back into the heather in front of me.

By now we had to be nearing the butts and my weary legs were ready for a rest. The next covey of grouse flew fast and straight to a line of scattered stakes ahead of us and suddenly the shooting started. Birds were bursting out of the heather in scores and the guns were busy. It was noticeable that birds were falling in large numbers on my left flank, where Mhairi was on top form, blazing away as fast as her loader could keep her going.

Then suddenly it was all over; whistles blew and an eager pack of Labradors and spaniels was unleashed from quivering suspense in the butts to quarter the area in front of the butts, where the heather had been burned to make retrieval easier. The guns gathered and chattered excitedly, each reliving a particular shot at a high, fast bird. The general was most vociferous about his prowess. I glanced at his loader and wondered if I had mistaken the slight sardonic smile that flitted across his face.

The pile of dead birds in front of Mhairi was the biggest. The admiral was congratulating her. 'I think in future I will always give you the worst butt, Mhairi Chalmers, you've done it again.'

She smiled. 'Aye, I've got some birds,' she said modestly.

'I dinna think she missed a single bird,' said Erchie. 'Mind, she had a verra guid loader.'

The general was certainly making the most of the few he had, but complained the wind had taken them to his right. His loader smiled slightly again. I watched the interplay between the famous, much decorated man and the keeper. Ghillies and keepers exhibit a strange mixture of obsequiousness and arrogance. They serve great men— royalty, the nobility and politicians—and have an uncanny way of summing up a man's worth. Mostly they keep their opinions to themselves but, when in their cups, have enlightening comments on some of the contemporary great and good. It was clear that despite their subservience to him they did not like the general. I wondered what they thought of the tenant of Tom Bacadh.

The guns then walked back to where they had left the cars. They were driven back towards Port Chalmers and then west to the village of Coilleag, from where they walked through the wood to the line of butts just south of Coille Bheag, the smaller of the two forested areas near Castle Chalmers. For us beaters there was time for a rest. Our second drive was due to start from the first butts, moving further north towards the wood this time, nearly a mile away. It was good to put one's feet up while the guns were ferried to their new position. Cigarettes and pipes came out and the blue haze of tobacco smoke filled air previously tainted by the smell of powder from the shooting.

But our rest was soon cut short by another briefing from Angus McLellan. Then we strung ourselves out across the moor, waiting for the precise moment to start. This time the walk was easier as the heather was shorter, following burning in previous seasons. As we walked, there were different birds, with winchat and stonechat perching high on occasional stunted trees; and once a merlin flew past carrying a meadow pipit in its talons. A beautiful male hen harrier came bouncing over the heather in its questing, hunting flight. It made old Angus curse, for keepers do not like harriers, calling them 'murder on wings'. I think them one of the most beautiful sights of the moors. A short eared owl, the only British owl to hunt by day, also quartered the moor for short-tailed field voles. But the predominant birds were the red grouse until we neared the butts, where we put up a magnificent pair of cock black grouse. They flew away, their splendid lyre-shaped tails shapely above the white powder puffs of their under-tail coverts. These birds, my favourite of the grouse family, were the first I had seen in Laigersay and the sun glinted on the purple sheen of their glossy black plumage.

I was dreaming of other birds when I was suddenly peppered with falling shot. Then I heard the bang. I was unhurt because the shot, spent and dropping from high, bounced harmlessly off my stout tweed jacket. But it was a reminder that shotguns could kill and safety precautions were needed. Angus was very cross, and muttered: 'I bet I know who did that.'

We were now approaching the butts, and fusillade after fusillade of shots rang out from guns, which we could not yet see, over a slight rise in the moor. Again several coveys veered to the left, to be turned back by Tom waving his flag.

Then the second drive was over, and we joined the mêlée of happy dogs picking up the dead birds. Again Mhairi, shooting from one of the middle butts in the line, seemed to have done best, which clearly irritated the general.

'Don't hold with women shooting,' he muttered.

'Especially when they do so much better than you,' added Hamish, as tactless as ever.

Then the old keeper asked: 'Who fired the first shot just now?'

'I think it was from our butt,' said the general's loader.

'Yes, I shot at a high bird and winged it, but I didn't see where it fell.'

Again I saw the slight smile on the loader's face.

'Well I'm sorry to say ye winged the young doctor here. I'd be grateful, sir, if you'd be more careful and not shoot towards the beating line.'

'We want to shoot grouse, not doctors!' said Hamish, echoing the general's own words of the previous day, and not so softly that they were unheard.

The general went red in the face, and it was good that we heard less from him after that. Again I reflected on who was boss. The old keeper, who in service life might have been a sergeant major, could maintain respect and still dress down a misbehaving senior officer.

No harm had been done but, as I prised the odd spent shot from my jacket, I reflected that it could have been worse and that, for the second time in Laigersay, my life had been at risk.

The ladies had come up to join us at lunch, spread in the shade of a gnarled old oak in Coille Bheag. As I wandered away to where the beaters were sitting munching sandwiches and drinking from bottles of ale, I noticed that Fiona was deep in conversation with Helen Agnew. Once again I experienced a shiver of unease and had a conviction that they were talking of me. The admiral called me back: 'Come and join us over here, Rob, and tell us how you enjoy being a beater.'

I told him how much I enjoyed the moors and their wild life and apologised for getting in the way of the general's shot. I almost felt sorry for him after Angus had remonstrated with him as only an aging Scottish keeper can, packing more disgust than one would think possible into a few words.

Lunch, again masterminded by the enigmatic Sikh chef, was magnificent. The table under the oak was spread with a white cloth and the castle silver had been brought up to decorate it. Tet enjoyed the tradition and spectacle of the glorious lunch of the glorious twelfth. There were oysters and prawns from Port Chalmers Bay, together with lobster, salmon and caviar. For those who preferred meat, there was deliciously rare cold fillet steak. The wines were superb, with champagne for the ladies and then Chablis or claret according to choice. The general's lady graced a deck chair in elegant clothes specially created for her in Bond Street. This made Mhairi, in her rural shooting tweeds, look dowdy. She did not mind in the least and referred to the general's lady:–

'Yon's an orchid among the dandelions.'

The scene reminded me of other great social occasions such as Wimbledon, Glyndebourne and Henley, but with a background of the heather-purpled moors this was an extraordinary combination of wilderness and high sophistication. I found myself thinking that it was an anachronism and wondered, in a rapidly changing world, how long such occasions would last.

After lunch Angus called me to where the keepers were sorting the birds. 'Come and see, Doctor. You don't often get an opportunity to handle so many birds. The two drives have yielded about seventy brace; that's very good for Laigersay, but we wouldn't have done so well without Mistress Chalmers from the pub; she's a demon shot.

'Now look at these birds; the young ones are the best for eating, so we must sort them. Then we must protect them from flies in this weather. I was up here last week making wee pits in the ground where we hang them to keep cool and away frae flies. Now see this: it's a poor bird wi' a keel for a breast bone. I'm surprised it could fly at all. Likely that's one o' the general's. That's a sick bird: we'll no be keeping yon. This one's better, nice and plump but it's an old yin.'

'Gosh, they all look the same to me.'

'Not if you look closely at the two outermost primaries. See how on this young bird they are nice and pointed, but in the old bird they are worn and rounded. That makes all the difference in the eating, and so in the price the bird will fetch. Now this is a fine cock bird: he must hae led the life o' Riley, for he was important in the pecking order.'

'How can you tell?'

'Because the comb is more prominent in birds with higher social rank. He was the high-heid-yin o' the muir.'

The old keeper became reflective. 'Ye know,' he added, 'they don't pay the same respect to the grouse that they used to. I remember down south a letter in the press in the twenties reported when for the first time actually on the twelfth itself, grouse was served at luncheon at the Savoy Hotel. Some of the earliest birds shot on a well-known Yorkshire moor were taken from the butts by motorcar and transferred to an aeroplane, which reached London in the forenoon. Aye, those were the days.'

As the guns were finishing with a glass of the traditional sloe gin, and Tetrabal Singh was organizing the packing up of the silver and furniture, a policeman on a motorcycle came bouncing across the moor. Angus McLellan went to investigate. He was soon in anxious conversation with the admiral and Hamish. They came over to me.

Hamish said, 'Rob, there's been an accident on the Tom Bacadh shoot, and they are asking for a doctor urgently. Let's toss for it.'

I was not too disappointed to lose, for the two hot walks across the moor, followed by such a superb lunch, had made me disinclined for further exercise. Also I was glad of an excuse to have another look at Tom Bacadh. Hamish arranged for a message to be relayed to him at the next butts should I need help. Nobody had any information as to how severe the accident had been, but my own peppering by the general made me realise that this could be serious. I left the shoot, settling uncomfortably on to the policeman's rear pillion. As we made the journey over the rough track to the road, I thought about shotgun injuries and mentally prepared for the worst. I hoped I would not have to try out Hamish's emergency blood transfusion drill again so soon after the affair at Feadag Mhor Farm.

At the surgery I grabbed my emergency kit. I tried to get more information from Tom Bacadh but the phone was unanswered so, none the wiser, I made my way to the castle. This was only the second time I had been there since my unfortunate meeting with the major when his car went off the road. I found an under-keeper waiting for me, who informed me that the injured man was a wealthy visiting German politician named Wertheim. The accident was not as serious as it might have been, but was a near thing to being fatal. The German, an inexperienced shot, had climbed a fence but had not rendered his gun safe by breaking it. His foot had caught in the wire and tripped him. As he fell, the gun went off, narrowly missing a beater and a garron, which the estate used to bring back the shot game. Everyone was alarmed at the incident and the German visitor had dislocated his shoulder.

The under-keeper had helped him to a Tom Bacadh Land Rover and had brought him back to the castle. The patient was demanding an air ambulance to take him to an orthopaedic specialist. I looked at his shoulder. Unfortunately the injury was now several hours old and the scapular muscles were in tight spasm. That was a pity, as I could have reduced the dislocation quite easily a few hours before, just as I had done several times at rugby football matches. Now he needed a general anaesthetic.

He had eased his discomfort with a large lunch and much alcohol to relieve his pain. We would have to wait some hours before we could give him an anaesthetic. I rang the number Hamish had given me, and one of the beaters answered, taking a message for Hamish that I needed his help, but not for an hour or two. I put the patient to bed with a syringeful of pain relief, told him not to eat or drink any more, and settled down to wait for Hamish. The keeper showed me to a comfortable deck chair in the garden and I started to read a magazine. However the morning's exercise and a good lunch made me drowsy and I nodded off.

It must have been half an hour later that I woke needing the loo. I got up to explore, but the castle was silent, for everyone was doubtless out on the moor. I found a lavatory, and was just returning to the garden when my eye caught what was obviously a library, and I went to examine it. The shelves were full of books on birds and bound reports from various European ornithological societies. Perhaps the major was a more interesting person than I thought. Then I noticed beautifully laid out cases of birds' eggs and naturally went to look. There were thousands from all over the world, all clearly labelled. I began to be intrigued, and saw on the large desk a number of eggs laid in a tray labelled 'Pending'. Among these I recognised four osprey's eggs and immediately wondered if these might be the reason the ospreys on Loch Bradan had been unsuccessful at breeding this season. Among the papers was a notebook in which someone, presumably Thistlethwaite himself, had jotted '4 osprey to Wertheim £1000'. My German patient, asleep upstairs after the morphia I had given him, was here for more than the shooting.

A noise behind me made me turn. It was the young under-keeper. 'I don't think you should be in here, sir. Would you mind returning to the garden to wait until your colleague arrives?'

'Of course,' I said. 'I am interested in birds myself and could not resist looking at the major's collection.'

'He likes to keep it private, sir. I'd be obliged if you'd wait in the garden, where I will have tea brought to you.'

Recognising that I was being warned off, I returned to the garden and had a cup of tea. I was still there when the major's guests returned from their shoot, full of the day's sport.

The major saw me, and said, 'Oh, it's you, I had expected Dr Robertson. What has happened to Herr Wertheim?'

I explained that the patient had dislocated his shoulder and required a general anaesthetic to put it right, and that I was waiting for my colleague to help.

'I see. I hope it will not take long.' He gave the impression that it was all very inconvenient, and apparently had little sympathy for his guest.

'Dr Robertson should be here soon, and then it will not take many minutes.'

Major Thistlethwaite nodded curtly, and left me to contemplate the roses in his garden. At the door he turned.

'Where did you train?' he asked. When I named my medical school, he continued: 'Did you know a Dr Wishart, who must have been there about your time?'

'Wishart? I seem to remember that he was an anaesthetist. I knew him slightly, but he was considerably my senior. I think he got sick and had to give up medicine... but it's a long time ago and I can't remember.'

'I was just curious; I knew him in London.' And with that the major left me to the roses.

When Hamish arrived, enough time had passed since our patient had eaten for it to be safe to give an open ether anaesthetic. With the man asleep, the shoulder muscles relaxed enough for me to put the shoulder back and the whole procedure was over in a few minutes. With noticeably few thanks we left for home, and I told Hamish about the eggs of protected species that the major was selling to high bidders from Germany.

CHAPTER 20

The 'Howling Hottentot'

Jennie brought coffee as I was finishing a quiet morning surgery; in the late summer nobody seemed to have much need of a doctor. Jennie announced: 'There's only one message today, and that's a slightly strange one, and it doesn't sound very medical. Old Mr Farquharson, whom you met at the night of the blood transfusion, rang to say if you were out that way he'd love to take you fishing. I said I'd get you to ring back.'

There may have been little call for visits but even in Laigersay there was a lot of paperwork. There were a number of repeat prescriptions to write, a letter of referral to a specialist on the mainland to dictate and then there was a drug representative to see me. We were spared many reps on the island. This one was combining business with a fishing holiday. We spent more time discussing what fly to use than on his samples.

It was nearly midday before I phoned Farquharson. A soft accent, reminding me of the Outer Hebrides, replied, 'This is Lutheran two-four-five, Alex Farquharson speaking.'

'Ah, Mr Farquharson, it's Dr Chalmers here; we met the other night.'

'Aye, didn't we chust. I have never seen anything like it. You and Dr Robertson did very well; the island is verra fortunate to have ye both. Now I was chust wondering, they tell me you like the fishing. I chust wondered if you'd be interested in coming out with me one day when the weather is fine and the tide obliging. Perhaps your lady would come too? I mind taking her fishing with her brother when she was in her teens.'

'We'd love to, Mr Farquharson,' I replied, remembering Jennie's warning that he was a stickler for a correct style of address. 'When would be a good time?'

'Well, the weather is set for the next few days and tide will be right tomorrow and the next day. Is that too soon for ye?'

'I don't see why it would be, but I'd better check with my wife and I'll ring you back.'

To my delight, Fiona was pleased at the idea. 'I haven't been off the southern islands for ages; it's beautiful there and Alex Farquharson, despite being a dry old stick, is a great fisherman. It was he who saved Murdo and me when we got caught in the rip. I know you'd love it, and I would too: we loved sea fishing when we were kids.'

And so it was that the following afternoon we drove down to the cottage beyond Lutheran. Alex was a widower, and he and his son Rorie lived in a small cottage where the road cut through the cliff to join the causeway to the Island of Assilag, which by now I knew was an old Gaelic name for the storm petrel. I knew that Alex was a staunch member of the Wee Free church and, aware of the rather joyless and retributive reputation of that faith, I was slightly apprehensive as to how I should get on with him. I need not have worried, for he was charming, even if somewhat accepting of how life treated him. The loss of his son in the tractor accident, which had led Hamish to set up the emergency blood supply in the island, had cast bleakness over the old man's life. However his deep faith supported him for, however inscrutable it was, he saw his loss as just a manifestation of God's will.

We found the old man sitting in front of his tiny croft overlooking the cliff. He was working repairing lobster creels, and smoking his pipe.

'It's chust a grand day, is it no?' he greeted us. 'Now, I wonder if ye'd mind if we took your car across to Assilag, where I keep the boat. Rory is away in his van to Port Chalmers, and my car is in dock chust now, waiting on a spare part from the mainland.'

'Of course,' I replied. 'It's a nuisance when that happens—how long have you been waiting?'

'Och, it'll be chust six months, next week.'

I tried not to show my surprise at his patience and he must have guessed what I was thinking.

'Things tak time on the west coast,' he added, 'especially in the islands.' He laughed as he picked up another creel and started checking its binding. 'I mind a year or two back we had a Spanish professor oot here stayin' with our dominie. He came to study Gaelic, for he was keen to make comparisons with some dialect they had in Spain, which he thought had Celtic roots. Anyway he quite fell for the place. He was here most of the summer. One evening as he and the schoolmaster were taking their dram watching the sun go down over by America, the Spanish scholar said to the dominie, "We have a word *mañana* in Spanish which we use whenever we don't want to do something, and postpone it till the morrow. Now that I have been here some time, I think there must be an identical word in the Gaelic?"

'The dominie thought for a long time as the sun settled into the distant sea. Then he refilled their glasses and he said: "I love the moment when the sun goes like that. I always expect to hear an explosion of steam, as it seems to disappear into the sea... but in answer to your question: no, there is no such word in the Gaelic, for you see nothing is ever so urgent here."'

Alex was stiff with rheumatism and grunted as he stood up. I had not really noticed at the farm where he had given his blood, but he was immensely tall, erect as a guardsman and extremely thin. He looked over the cliff, his sea-washed, pale blue eyes scanning the horizon.

'Well now, we should go and see what the Lord has for us in the sea, the tide is chust coming nicely. We should fill the basket by this evening.' He disappeared inside a shed beside the cottage and returned with a pail full of bait and a large wickerwork fish basket. 'I was down there earlier to collect bait as the tide began to go out. Now, where's your automobile?'

As we went down the track leading to the causeway he glanced back at the croft, which was separated from the road by a broken-down wall. 'Och, I keep meaning to mend that dyke, but it doesnae seem to matter: there's naething to keep oot the garden. It was the ambulance that knocked it down. Now, drive canny here on the causeway, it's gey rocky. We've got a good three or four hours before the tide comes back and covers it. We maun be back then or we'll have to camp on Assilag. Turn left here along by the shore road to the village. I keep the "Hottentot" here.'

'The "Hottentot"?' I queried.

'Aye, that was Iain's name for it when he was wee, he called her the "Howlin' Hottentot". It's a good boat. I've used it weel, these ten or more years.'

Alex unlocked the padlock on a little shed. 'It's a shame I've got to lock this,' he said, 'but some visitors from the city helped themselves to my outboard a year or two back, so I've taken to locking it. For years before that I never bothered. Local people don't meddle with what isnae theirs. It's a pity other folks aren't the same.'

Slowly and methodically the old man loaded the boat with the creels he had repaired, and with a number of hand lines. Some were for mackerel, with bright coloured feather lures; some were furnished with heavy lead weights for the cod and pollack that lurked in the deep water under the cliffs.

Then he was ready, and Fiona and I were glad to help him push the boat over the shingle into the sea, for the midges were biting unmercifully. Alex seemed unperturbed, though a cloud of the tiny pestilential insects surrounded his grizzled head.

'Ach they've got tackits in their boots,' he muttered, seeing us slapping and scratching. The boat eased out to sea at the pull of oars, and immediately the biting horde was left behind.

'I'll chust take ye up under the cliff,' he said. 'I hear you're interested in birds, so I thocht I'd show you one or two.' He started the outboard and the little boat chugged out to sea, disturbing seals basking on the skerries around us.

Alex took his pipe from this mouth and spat in the sea. 'I was telling you aboot my operation,' he said. I waited. I had no memory of him saying anything about an operation, but it is the fate of doctors to hear interminable stories about people's surgery (they usually culminate in the surgeon saying it was the worst case he had ever known). Alex spoke softly, so I had to bend near him to catch what he said over the throb of the engine.

'You see I have been a verra, verra sinfu' man,' he began, as he adjusted the throttle of the outboard.

This, to say the least, was an unusual variant on the 'my operation' story. It transpired that so sinful had Alex been that the Lord visited him with a perforated peptic ulcer on the late afternoon of December 31st. Alex described the arrival of the ambulance:–

'The driver wasnae weel. He parked so close to the croft wall he knocked most of it down.' The driver and his mate were a wee bit unsteady on their feet; they dropped him twice as they carried him on a stretcher out to the ambulance. The drive to Port Chalmers was bumpy because the vehicle twice left the road, and the second time they had great difficulty getting out of the peat. When they arrived at the hospital a young doctor also had difficulty in standing. He tried to set up a drip into Alex's arm. With a cry of 'Olé!' he lunged with a needle, and at first attempt lodged it in a vein in Alex's elbow. So great was his surprise at this success that he fell backwards, causing Alex 'to say to the nurse that perhaps she'd better haud the puir mannie up'.

'Aye, it was touch and go,' said Alex. 'They were talking of opening me there and then, but fortunately they postponed surgery till after Hogmanay. I was rather poorly by then, but probably safer than being cut by that lot as they were that night. So I had my operation when they were all sober again. This was all a long time ago, before Doctor Hamish, mind, such a thing would not happen now.'

I was astonished. Anyone else would have been lodging complaints in all directions, and rightly so. To Alex, this was a manifestation of God's wrath at his sinful life. So sinful had he been that God visited him with a perforation of a peptic ulcer on the very day when He knew everybody would be drunk!

By now the little boat had travelled across Assilag Bay to the narrow strait between the island of Tuilleag and Laigersay itself. Here we were coming under the lee of the huge cliffs which dominate the sea off the south of Laigersay. At once we smelt the powerful stench of nesting seabirds. The air and sea around us were full of wings and the face of the cliff was lined with serried ranks of nesting auks, fulmars, kittiwakes and cormorants. There must have been hundreds of thousands of birds on rock ledges whitewashed with guano. As we neared them the stench grew overpowering, and the noise cacophonous. But it was exciting to see this profusion of seabirds. They each had their own sections of the rocks.

The shags and cormorants nested on the cliffs, with the former usually lower than the latter. The guillemots and razorbills were a little apart, but both perched on tiny ledges, where they stood shoulder to shoulder, either staring out to sea or at the sheer wall in front of their bills. Kittiwakes favoured rock gullies in the cliff, where their incessant cries of Kit-tee-wake added to the raucous calls of auks and cormorants.

At the top of the cliff were the favourite sites of the fulmar, and deep among the sea pinks, in burrows excavated by rabbits, were the puffins. All these birds came to the cliffs only in spring to breed; for most of the year they were out on the open sea, often scores of miles from land.

As we watched we could see their different flight patterns and hunting techniques. The gannets flew high above us; suddenly they closed their wings and turned in a steep dive, culminating in an explosive entry to the sea. I knew they dived as deep as they had dropped from the air above. Puffins, like mechanised footballs, whizzed across the water, their wings moving so fast as to be almost invisible. Those going out were unladen, but birds returning to the nest sites all had some silvery sand eels in their comical multicoloured bills.

Gulls foraged for floating goodies, while occasional storm petrels walked delicately on the water. Amidst this multitude of procreant bird life it felt quite unimportant to be human.

'God is bounteous,' remarked Alex. 'He provides for all these creatures and still has some left over for us. Let's see what we have in the creels.'

With that he started hauling his lobster pots. He only had a score of creels to lift, but they each took a few minutes. Some were empty, but most had fine partan crabs and three had lobsters, one of which was enormous.

'Mind the claws,' warned Alex as he slipped tough elastic bands over the huge blue-grey pincers. 'He's very powerful closing them, but quite weak at opening; these bands will make him safe.'

In another part of the bay Alex was bringing up fine prawns, which the restaurateurs call langoustine or Dublin Bay prawns and sell at high prices. Alex told us he got quite good money for these, his stock in trade, though he welcomed the lobsters as well.

Then he turned the 'Hottentot' away from the cliff and passed the lines with feather streamers to Fiona and me. Soon these were nearly jerked out of our hands by hungry mackerel, sometimes three or four at a time on the trace of feathers, and hard to pull in. In no time the basket was agleam with their blue and silver scintillation.

Alex was scornful of them. 'Dirty fish, I never eat them, though they're no' bad if you smoke them. I prefer haddock and lythe.'

Fiona disagreed: 'My mother used to grill them with gooseberries, and they were delicious. And Rob has a smoker, for his trout, so I don't mind taking a few home.'

'Och, well ye've plenty there. I chust gie them to ma dog,' said Alex, as another batch came in on each hand line. 'Noo, we'll chust move a bitty near the cliff. There's a hole there that usually has some good haddies. There's a fish I like well.'

The old man squinted up at some mark he knew on the cliff, and matched a distant point on Tuilleag up with a house away over on the southeastern end of Laigersay till he had the 'Hottentot' located exactly where he wanted her.

'Aye, we'll chust drop the anchor noo, and we'll be right on the spot.' The anchor cable ran out and we were bobbing on the slight swell only a dozen yards from the cliff.

'It goes down real deep here,' said Alex. 'There's all sorts of fush down there. I had a big conger eel here once but it's the haddies and codlin' and lythe I'm wantin'.'

'Has the lythe got another name?' I asked, for I was not sure what it was.

'Aye, it's called a pollack in some parts. Many people won't eat them, but I like the subtle flavour o' almond... better than your dirty old mackerel.' As he was speaking his knife was working on the mussel shells in his bait pail. He baited each of the three hooks on the paternosters and passed hand lines to us again.

'Chust let the line run out till you feel it slacken as the weight hits bottom, then lift it up about half a fathom. If we're on the spot you should feel them take at once.'

Fiona was already hauling in her line. 'I've got one,' she said, full of childish glee. In a moment three splendid haddock of about a couple of pounds each were wriggling in the bottom of the boat.

Alex pointed at them. 'If you know the Good Book you'll remember that in Matthew chapter seventeen Jesus told St Peter "to cast a hook into the sea and to take up the fish that first cometh up; and when thou hast opened his mouth, thou shalt find a shekel..." And Peter did that and to this day the stains of Saint Peter's thumb and finger marks are there on the fish you have chust caught.'

Quickly he baited the hooks again. As Fiona lowered her tackle to the depths, Alex went on:–

'Aye, they're godly fish caught on a paternoster. That means "Our Father". It comes from the prayers that fisherman said as they lowered their baits. But Doctor, why are you no' catching fish on yon side of the boat? Maybe I'm not quite on the mark.'

As he spoke, Fiona was bringing in more haddies, when suddenly I felt a very hard tug. 'Got one,' I shouted, and started hauling up the long line, which suddenly went slack in my hand.

'Oh! He's away,' I exclaimed continuing to haul. 'No, the fish is still there and it feels a big one.'

'Aye, likely that will be a dogfish. They do that, for they swim up with you as you haul them in so you think they've gone. Aye, there it is. That's what they call a spurdog. Ca' canny wi' it. It has spines chust in front o' its dorsal fins that can give a sore chag. They're pretty coarse eating, but they sell them in the shops as rock salmon. It's another fush I feed to ma dogs.' While he was saying this, Alex gaffed the dogfish and it joined Fiona's haddies in the basket in the boat.

'Ye still havena caught my favourite. Let's try the engine again, and putter along the base o' the cliff. We'll try the feathers again, but fished deep, with a very heavy lead. That's how ye get the big lythe, or pollack, as ye call them. Might pick up a codling too.'

The engine sputtered into life as Alex lifted the anchor, and soon we were making slow speed along the bottom of the cliff. This time it took longer, and we had time to look about us. Suddenly I saw a sinister triangular fin about twenty yards from us and, as I looked, a second smaller one was following behind. Trying to control my voice, I asked:–

'That almost looks like a couple of sharks... but it couldn't be, could it?'

Alex turned and said nonchalantly, 'No, it isna two sharks, it's chust one. Yon's the tail at the back, it's a' one. That's the biggest fish we get round here: they go up to thirty or forty feet long and weigh several tons. But dinna fash yersel, they're quite harmless. They feed on plankton, but they're gey big and could hurt the boat if we get too close. I've seen them leap clear o' the sea chust like a salmon does. Ye can hear the crash they make as they fall for miles. There's a fellow, up Soay way, who fishes for them with a harpoon gun for the oil in their livers. Ah, the lassie's at it again.'

Sure enough, Fiona was hauling in her line, this time with a codling of about ten pounds.

Again Alex used the gaff to get the fish into the boat. 'Commercially these are very important; most of the fish sold with chips is cod but I'd rather have lythe. Many of the codling have parasitic worms in them and you see them when you clean the fush. They don't do any harm, but they fair put me off.'

'I've got another one,' I exclaimed, 'and this really is big.'

'Oh aye, happen it's yon basking shark!' was my mentor's laconic reply.

Hand over hand I pulled the line in and soon even Alex had to admit it was a good sized fish. It was the lythe he had been hoping for, and at about a stone in weight it was the biggest he had ever taken off Assilag.

'Mind,' he added, 'it's no that big. The record for rod and line was taken in 1921 at Land's End in Cornwall. That was twenty-one pounds, a stone and a half, quite a lythe. But I'm afraid that must be the end o' today's fishing. We maun return now or we'll never cross the causeway. Bring in your lines now: I'm heading for home.'

There is a strange, atavistic pleasure in being a hunter-gatherer. We had enjoyed a day full of birds. Taught by the local expert, we had a boatful of crustaceans and several stone of fish, comprising five species. We had enjoyed some hours in the fresh sea air in lovely sunshine. It was a great day out even if, at times, a trifle pious.

And I had heard the strangest story yet of 'my operation'.

CHAPTER 21

Tragedy

That summer Hamish had his book on Scottish wildflowers published. He had been working on it for years and Tetrabal Singh told me that he was organising a party to celebrate the event. Tet was inviting several old friends from the mainland and the occasion was to be a surprise. He swore me to secrecy.

By the late summer we had found a cottage in Port Chalmers, and we moved into it in early September. Fiona introduced me to many of her friends in the little town. More and more, the island people enchanted me. There were simple crofters and there were writers, poets, sculptors and painters. One man had set up an enterprising home industry of candle-making. Some were people opting out from a society still reeling from war and from the new threat imposed by dreadful weaponry and a madcap race for superior arsenals. It all seemed very remote in Laigersay, where my daily worries were more concerned with the minor ailments of my patients. I often found myself wondering at the contrast with what my life might have been like in the bustle of a London hospital, spending my day with life and death situations. There the people would have been anonymous, unknown packages of tissue and pathology; here in Laigersay I soon knew most of them, not just by name, but also for the secrets of their lives. I decided my love of people was rather like my love of birds, and where better to observe their natural history from than a rural general practice?

Some of my patients were heroic, others timorous; some incredible in the sadness of their lives, while others were hilarious. There was Agnes Smith, an ancient cockney who had come to Laigersay during the war when her daughter married an island sailor. She was a modern Mrs Malaprop who escorted me on a tour of the surgical battleground that was her abdomen.

'This,' she said pointing to a scar in the notch between her ribs, 'was where they cured me double Ulster; this, on the right, was me gall. The one lower on the right was me benedict; the middle one was where it was all took away.' Then, with an arch look, she lowered her calico drawers to reveal a grey wisped pubis and a fine white scar in her groin. 'And that was me operation for rapture.'

Some of the islanders raised ethical problems I found difficult to resolve. Old Amos, an ancient crofter of Lutheran, posed the worst of these. When Mary, his wife, died in her late seventies Amos announced his intention of joining her in the kirkyard as soon as possible. His mind was as clear as a bell, but he took to his bed and refused to get out of it for anything. The bed slowly rotted under him and the stench was mephitic, but still he lay there in his own ordure. Neighbours grew restive and the cry 'something should be done' was muttered frequently. I visited Amos regularly, trying to persuade him to accept the cottage hospital or even the home in Port Chalmers. With smelly stoicism he always replied, 'Thank you, doctor, but I'll just wait here till it's time to join my Mary.'

Neighbours who took in meals grew rebellious and threatened to stop, and when the malodorous trickle that led from the old man's downstairs bedroom reached the main street of the village there was uproar. My conviction was that here was a sane man who elected to behave in a way which, though most considered it unacceptable, was what he wanted. That was no reason to force him into compliance with the majority. To me, the demand of the villagers that he should be put away recalled the anti-Semitism of Nazi Germany, recently brought back to everyone's memory by the trial and execution of Adolf Eichmann.

At last I could stand public pressure no longer and discovered a section of the Public Health Act which allowed compulsory admission to a place of safety for anyone who offered a public health threat to society. It was a complex business and required the signing of documents by a specialist from the mainland, a Writer to the Signet and a senior social worker. That took a deal of organisation, and by the time I arranged it there was open revolt in the village. The documents were duly signed and the ambulance man wrapped poor frail old Amos up in a blanket, put him on his shoulder and carried him to the vehicle.

'It's not right. I don't want to go,' screamed Amos at the top of his voice, beating on the ambulance driver's back with his fists.

I turned to the lawyer and said: 'I feel as if I had a swastika on my arm.'

'Me too,' he replied, 'but what else could we do?'

I waited three days before I had courage to visit Amos in the home, where I was greeted by a very angry old man.

'Why the hell didn't you send me here before?' he demanded.

How difficult ethical decisions may sometimes be!

Messages came to the surgery in many ways. Most were by phone, others by word of mouth from friends and neighbours, others by handwritten notes. One lad denied a certificate excusing him from school left a cherished message that I was a 'nity ole quack'. Another letter tucked into a tiny blue envelope, which bore the inscription 'DOCTOR ROBERTSON IN PORTANT', read:–

'For my wife medison she is very much condpasted'.

Hamish and I had many a laugh over the things patients did and said. There were times when laughter was the only consolation in the face of tragedy. Once a fishing boat was lost in a storm off Assilag, which left three young widows. On another occasion an outbreak of meningitis at Port Chalmers School lost the community a ten-year-old boy and crippled two others. But the worst disaster was nearer at home and came out of the blue.

It started, almost as farce, with a message from Archie McPhee, which, after passing through many intermediaries grew like a Chinese whisper. By the time the word arrived at the surgery it was a peremptory demand for immediate assistance for his sister Maggie. I abandoned a full evening surgery, leaving Jeanie to reschedule the patients, and hurried through Port Chalmers so fast that a police car was soon on my tail. Winding down the window, I waved my stethoscope to indicate I was on urgent medical business. Nothing happened for a moment, then to my horror I saw the flashing blue lights go on as the police accelerated. As they overtook me a grinning policeman shook a pair of handcuffs were out of his window. The local bobbies had their own way of getting a message across.

Smiling to myself, I broke all speed limits on my way to Maggie's house. Archie flagged me down as I passed his house.

'It was the coo,' he said. 'She didnae let it oot, so I thocht it best to let you know. I couldnae go mysel' for my gout's come back.'

I stared at the old man in disbelief. Had I abandoned a whole surgery of patients, alarmed the police and driven helter-skelter through the island because a cow was late out of its byre? I was about to erupt, in some fury, when I saw the old man was genuinely concerned.

'Hop in,' I said, 'and we'll see what's amiss with the coo.'

Maggie was fine, but so perturbed that she had simply forgotten about her cow. She seemed rather disturbed in her mind, addressed me again as the laird and kept saying something terrible was about to happen. I could make no sense out of her, but she seemed physically well. I gave her a mild sedative and told her to take it, though knowing Maggie's attitude to conventional medicine, I doubted that she would.

Then, after explaining to Archie about the importance of accurate messages, I promised to send out some more 'crocus tablets' and started for home. It was a beautiful summer evening. Maggie's 'emergency' had virtually given me an evening off, as I knew Jennie had sent all the other patients home. I was in one of my favourite parts of the island and I sauntered home, enjoying the evening and watching the eagles that had an eyrie by Ranneach Mhor.

A breeze from the sea brought the drone of an aircraft and I soon spotted Murdo's plane coming from the south. I stopped the car and got out to watch. I hadn't seen him since the wedding, but had heard he was busy in London. Fiona had said she expected him, and it would be nice to have him home for a bit. As I watched I saw him alter course, and then he descended, flying low over the moors. The plane turned this way and that as though the pilot was following something. Then—as I watched—the plane seemed to go out of control. For a moment it fluttered in the air like an injured bird, and then dived straight into the flank of Ranneach Mhor. For a second there was no sign of the plane, and then a violent explosion shot flames high into the air.

There was no road, and I had to run through often waist-high heather for at least a mile to reach the wreck. The violence of the explosion suggested I would be able to do nothing when I arrived. Panting and cursing, I topped a rise, and could see the smoke coming from the wreck. For a moment I thought I saw a figure in the smoke and ran on, half hoping that Murdo might yet be alive. But it was not to be. He had been thrown free of the plane by the impact. His neck lay at an unnatural angle. It was clear that he was dead. Sadly, I closed his sightless eyes and returned to my car to fetch help.

I got to the nearest telephone in Lutheran and phoned Hamish, asking him to go to the castle and break the news to the laird. Then I spoke to the police in Port Chalmers and, staving off banter about speeding doctors, reported what had happened. Then it was their turn to speed. I waited by the road to guide the rescue team to the crash, for by now dusk was falling and the smoke from the wreck was less obvious.

When the police arrived, they had found out that local air traffic control had actually been in contact with Murdo when the aircraft went out of control. I asked them if that helped to explain events, and the constable said: 'They think it might, but they were cagey and said it was too early to tell.' Then they were busy taking a statement from me, and there was no further chance to ask them what Murdo's last words might have been.

The days that followed were some of my blackest in Laigersay. The admiral was so shocked I feared for him. The loss of her much loved brother also devastated Fiona.

Worst was to come when the inquest was adjourned; official secretiveness seemed to cloak the whole affair. In the middle of this, who should arrive in Port Chalmers but the enigmatic Stanley Johnson, whom I had last seen at the opening of the grouse season.

He greeted me as a long lost friend and told me he was in the island for Hamish's secret party, but had come a little early to do some fishing. He was unusually interested in the plane crash and listened intently as I described what I had seen.

'Did you hear anything unusual?' he asked.

'Unusual? What sort of unusual?'

'Oh, I don't know, perhaps a shot?'

I stared at him. 'No, but there was an onshore stiff breeze. Anyway I might not have noticed; everyone has a gun here, and the sound of a shot is commonplace. But why do you ask?'

'Murdo's plane had been struck by a rifle bullet before he crashed. His last words were that someone was shooting at him. The police do not seem to know whether the crash may have resulted. Take your mind back—was there anything at all that you saw when you went to the crash?'

I was back there, remembering running through the high heather, and I remembered getting up after a fall. 'I thought Murdo was all right. For a moment I thought I saw him moving on the other side of the flame and smoke, but he must have died instantaneously.'

Stanley was watching me carefully.

'Uh huh,' he said. 'That makes sense. You see Murdo was actually speaking to air traffic control. He said he was watching someone he thought was Oleg Karkovski, then he suddenly exclaimed: "The blighter has fired a shot at me." That was the last thing air traffic control heard from him.'

The funeral was held a few days later. It struck me as incredible that I had attended four family occasions at the castle: the wonderful Hogmanay party, my own wedding, the grouse shoot—and now Murdo's funeral. Each was a traditional affair full of highland ceremony.

Just as at the wedding, almost the whole island packed into the kirk at Port Chalmers. Angus was a tremendous support to his old friend the admiral, who had aged considerably at the death of his son. The mystery and suspicion that surrounded the crash worsened the old man's health and he looked a shadow of his former self. Fiona, herself distraught, was greatly concerned for her father, and Hamish and I had had our work cut out to support them at the funeral.

The event was very moving. The coffin was carried into the kirk covered in a great and obviously ancient Cameron plaid. With great solemnity, Angus Andersen removed the plaid and carefully folded it before passing it to the admiral. I had the feeling that this plaid was used only for the funerary rites of clan chiefs. Watching the laird as he took the plaid from the minister I felt sure that it would be stored away until the admiral needed it for his own obsequies.

Angus spoke of the young man's life, recalling the youth he had known well when he first arrived as minister at Port Chalmers. He eulogised Murdo's university career and the national service record that had led to his love of flying. He spoke of the career he was forging in publishing, mourned the loss of the laird elect and, as one of the laird's closest friends, offered prayers for the family.

Erchie Thomson, the best piper in Laigersay, played the lament as the congregation filed out to the private mausoleum in the kirkyard where generations of Chalmers lairds had been interred.

There followed a reception attended by many of the islanders. It was an ordeal for the family as one by one the laird's tenants offered their condolences. At last it was clear that he could take this no longer and I spoke out:–

'As Sir James' doctor, I think he should rest now, but I know he is most appreciative of everyone's kindness.' With that I led the old man out of the reception.

'Thank you, Rob. I have to confess I have had enough of everyone's sympathy. I could do with a little bit of Scapa. Bring the decanter to the study, with a glass for yourself.'

A moment later I found myself pouring the old man his dram.

'Rob,' he said, 'I have been talking with my legal adviser. I am not sure how much longer I may have to live, and certain things have to be settled. I have instructed the Writer to the Signet to draw up the necessary documents to confer upon you the lairdship of

Castle Chalmers.' He raised his glass. 'Lang may your lum reek,' he added with a smile.

So the episode that began with a message from Maggie McPhee ended with the fulfilment of her prophesy.

Chapter 22

Suspicion

For some days after the funeral, life slowly returned to normal. Fiona was a sad girl who needed much of my support. Hamish seemed to understand this, and often suggested I went home during the day. I was having a difficult time. Fiona seemed to have become rather irrational after her brother's death. At first she had been plunged into denial, refusing to accept that Murdo was dead. She spoke of him all the time as though he had flown back to London and might return at any moment. As the days passed, her attitude changed; she was plunged into grief and I spent hours holding her sobbing body.

Then, as suddenly, her mood changed again to one of anger. It must be someone's fault that death had taken her beloved brother. She recalled the time when they had nearly died together in their father's dinghy in the tide race between Assilag and Solan. 'Why didn't we die together then?' she demanded of me. Then she turned her rage on Stanley Johnson, the sinister man whose presence in the island seemed to her to be suspicious in the extreme. Then it was entirely my fault, for if I hadn't brought Johnson to Laigersay none of this would have happened. I began to despair, for where, in this tumult, was the lovely rational girl I had married only a few weeks before? She seemed to be slipping away from me and I was in danger of becoming as distraught as she.

Fiona announced that she wanted to go to her father for a few days. It was something of a relief to take her to the castle and to immerse myself in work. The next day Jennie came in with her usual coffee and shortbread as the last of the morning's patients left.

'It was a terrible thing about the young laird,' she said. 'How's your puir wife taking it?'

'She is absolutely shattered, Jennie. I do what I can, but she is taking her brother's loss very hard. At first she simply would not believe he was dead, even when I told her I had seen him at the crash. He broke his neck, you know. He was thrown out of the aircraft as it hit the ground. I found him several yards from the crash—just as well, for it was a mass of flames,'

'Puir soul, he couldnae ha' known much aboot it.'

'Well I am not sure about that. You see, he was actually talking to air traffic control as it happened. He said he had made a detour to watch someone on the ground, who was behaving suspiciously with a rifle. Then he said he thought it was Karkovski. Anyway, whoever it was took a pot shot at the aircraft. But we don't actually know that it was Oleg. We'll just have to wait and see. Anyway Fiona has moved on in her grieving; from disbelief she's become very angry. I haven't dared to tell her what we know about the shot. I think she suspects I'm holding something back, because a lot of her anger is directed at me.'

'But you had nothing to do wi' it!'

'Of course not, but she is blindly angry. She seems to think it has something to do with Stanley Johnson, the man I stayed with when I was down in London. For some reason she has got it into her head that he is involved in whatever is going on in Laigersay and it's all my fault for bringing him here.'

'Did you?'

'No, of course not, I hardly know the man. But he certainly seems surrounded by mystery, and he keeps turning up. Even Murdo himself mentioned having met him in London, when he was asking questions about the island. He seemed interested in what I was doing here, and kept questioning Murdo about Thistlethwaite.'

'Well, it seems things may be getting a bit clearer. The mysterious Mr Johnson rang while you were consulting and asked if you could ring him back. He gave me the number.'

'I wonder what's going on... if I can find anything to make Fiona listen to reason and to stop blaming me, I shall be very glad.' So saying, I dialled the number Jennie had given me. At once the ring was answered.

'Stanley Johnson,' a familiar voice announced.

'Dr Chalmers here. I believe you rang?'

'Ah yes, I wondered if you could spare me a few moments. I rather want to talk to you on a matter of some importance.'

'By all means. Why not look into the surgery?'

'If it's all the same with you, I'd prefer a place where there is no chance of anyone overhearing. The best place would be out on the moor somewhere—would that be all right?'

'You make it sound rather sinister.'

Johnson laughed. 'No, not really, but it is important and concerns Murdoch Chalmers, you and your wife. I suggest we meet as soon as possible. It needn't take very long. I am staying in Lutheran. Suppose we meet at the Charmer Inn in about an hour's time. We could walk on the moor, where there is no chance we would be overheard or watched.'

'This all sounds very cloak and dagger. Can't you tell me what is going on?'

'That's precisely what I intend to do. I'll see you in an hour at the inn.' And then the phone went dead.

I immediately redialled, but all I got was an engaged signal. I guessed that Johnson had deliberately left his receiver off the hook.

After I had dealt with a small pile of paperwork, I set out for the Charmer Inn and, with some misgiving, drove across the island to Feadag. Now I was beginning to share Fiona's feelings about Stanley Johnson. I had had my doubts about the shadowy figure since I had first met him in London. I did not much like the way he seemed to recur in island matters and his secrecy about himself was almost paranoid.

I found him sitting on a bench outside the Charmer Inn talking to Mhairi, who had obviously just brought him a pint of her special ale. He looked up as I parked the car in front of the pub.

'I am sure I can tempt Dr Chalmers to a beer?' he said, looking at me with a raised eyebrow.

'Thank you,' I replied and Johnson beamed at Mhairi, who bustled off to get it. A moment later she was back. 'I haven't seen you since the twelfth,' she said to me. 'You should have been in. I had some great grouse pasties. I could hardly keep the minister off them. He's a great one for eating here.'

'Yes, I think Angus has a soft spot for you, Mhairi,' I teased her.

'It's nothing but cupboard love. But then, poor chap, living as he does—I doubt that he gets adequately fed at the manse.'

'Is it Mr Andersen you speak of?' asked Johnson

'Aye, the minister at Port Chalmers. He's an old bachelor who has a housekeeper at the manse, but she's not much of a cook. So he likes to come over here for his lunch two or three times a week. Mind you, he's abstemious, though I will say he does like a drop o' my special ale.'

So saying she bustled back into the bar in response to a jangled bell announcing someone else's thirst.

'I am not surprised the minister comes here,' added Johnson. 'The bar food is really excellent and she makes so much of local fish and game.'

'I think Erchie Thomson may have something to do with that,' I grinned. 'I don't think Mhairi asks too many questions about provenance. But I hear the fishing has been poor.'

'Yes. That touches on what I want to talk to you about, but elsewhere. Have you been after that big sea trout again? You have an account to settle with that fish.'

'Aye, I have,' I agreed and, suppressing my curiosity, my mind went back to that day almost a year before when I had so nearly lost my life in the Pitchroich sea pool. My referring to Erchie Thomson brought the incident back with crystal clarity. Much as I wanted to clarify the mystery surrounding Johnson, I felt like playing his own game. So I spoke of fish and fishing, and recounted the splendid day Fiona and I had spent with Alex Farquharson in the 'Howling Hottentot'.

Johnson listened intently as he supped his ale. I found myself thinking of this enigmatic man that he was a great listener. It was almost as though he were recording every word in his memory. When I finished the tale of the basking shark he spoke:–

'Yes, I have seen them down there. Tell me, does Mr Farquharson keep his boat on Assilag, by the cottages there?'

'Yes, he has a bothy there where he keeps his outboard.'

'Always under lock and key, I suppose?'

'Yes, he mentioned he'd taken to locking it; he said some visitors had helped themselves and he was cross about it.'

'Well, I think it's time we took our walk. Let's go up by Milton of Bacadh; that should be deserted enough for us.'

'Okay, but we should probably watch out for snakes, there are plenty of adders over there. It's a getting a bit late in the season, but there may still be some about.'

'There seem to be a number of unpleasant creatures in Laigersay just now,' he commented, 'but I don't think those reptiles need concern us.'

We drove up in my car, leaving Johnson's Land Rover by the pub. He was silent as we drove along the track to the old mill buildings and then, as we drew up, he said:

'I sometimes think this island is the most beautiful place in the world. And on a late summer day like this, it is quite superb.'

He got out of the car and sat on a low parapet beside the leat, which in former days had carried the water to the mill wheel. He seemed to be in no hurry to tell me why he had asked me to this out-of-the-way place.

'Wonderful places, these old mills. They were all over the Highlands and Islands at one time. We think all the power we get from water is new, but this has been here a long time; it's just that instead of getting electricity from generators, it used to be direct from the water, by means of an iron wheel and complex gears. It was enough to grind all the corn and work the flax. Have you noticed that these old mills always seem to have grey wagtails nesting nearby? There is supposed to be some mythical association between the bird and the mill, but I forget what it is.'

Johnson pulled out a pipe and started filling it. 'I owe you an apology, Dr Chalmers, in that for a long time I have mistrusted your motivation in coming to Laigersay. I have to confess that I have not been entirely honest with you.'

'Now you tell me,' I said in a tone of some irritation.

'Yes, I can understand your attitude, but if you will bear with me I think you will understand why I have been somewhat opaque in my dealings with you. Firstly, let me tell you I work at the Home Office in a relatively newly established department. I am particularly interested in drug trafficking...'

'Drugs? That is surely not much of a problem in Britain, and I really can't see what it could have to do with Laigersay. Chicago or New York, perhaps, but hardly Port Chalmers.'

Johnson drew on his pipe. 'I am afraid that is not quite right,' he said. 'Of course, like many things, it was earlier and more obvious in America. But it started to become clear as early as 1921 that some of the drugs entering New York were coming from Europe. Cocaine, heroin and synthetic drugs probably originating in the Far East were arriving there from Germany via London. By the mid twenties British doctors were expressing concern that many young people were resorting to drugs to relieve the stress of their fast lives. In 1927 cocaine from Hong Kong, it was called *fujitsura* then, was entering Britain: some 8,000 ounces of it were seized; and heroin was arriving from the same source. By 1936 it was estimated that there were about 30,000 drug addicts in Britain. Bizarrely, Hitler saved this deteriorating situation. War disrupted supplies of everything, including drugs, with the result that the drug problem virtually disappeared in the forties. When it came back in the early fifties, it was not so much hard drugs as marijuana that was the problem.

'Now we come to the time when you were a student. I wonder if you remember a Dr Wishart, who was an anaesthetist at your teaching hospital?'

I was startled at this reference to a doctor only a few years older than myself. It was the second time recently that someone had mentioned his name. 'Yes, I knew him slightly. He was ill and, as far as I can remember, retired on health grounds... what of him?'

'He was a pethidine addict. His addiction only came to light when it was noticed that patients failed to get pain relief after injections of the drug. Wishart had substituted distilled water in the rubber-capped bottles in which pethidine was supplied to the wards. He was so successful at this that it was six months before he was discovered. He was struck off the Register for his pains.'

'Oh dear, many people must have suffered as a result.'

'That was only part of the problem. In 1954 a young trafficker was arrested who had received a large amount of heroin from a hospital pharmacy. The pharmacists marked some of the morphine dispensed for use in the wards with a dye and this was discovered in drugs being sold in Soho. The theft was traced to students working at your teaching hospital. The culprit was never discovered but must have been aware that the hospital authorities were on his track because the leak stopped, and never restarted.'

As I listened, I began to be aware of an unpleasant sensation of anxiety. My mind went back to my student days and I found myself mentally checking my friends. We were all very short of cash and I had heard that one or two in my year sought funding in very unethical ways.

Johnson interrupted my reverie, adding:–

'As you may have guessed, you were in the group of students who were suspected. At the time you were suspected, but because of your outstanding academic career the hospital authorities looked elsewhere, and you were exonerated.'

'Good God, you can't believe I was involved in drugs?'

'Well, we have evidence that you experimented with marijuana, to be precise, at a party one December about two years before you qualified.'

I looked at him in astonishment. 'I know exactly when you mean. I was very ill after that party, but I had no idea it was due to drugs... but how the hell do you know all this, anyway?'

Johnson examined the bowl of his pipe. 'As I said, I owe you an apology. When you came up here, I found myself wondering why a young doctor of your ability should want to bury himself in such a remote place. When I met you in London, it was quite clear that you had high ambitions. I knew your professor slightly, and I met him, and heard things about you of which you should be proud. These related to your potential as a leader in your profession. I spoke to your prof just after you had written to him declining the post as his registrar. He was an angry man; he said your coming here was a waste. So it was then that I started making enquiries about you— because, by that time, I was also getting very interested in what was happening in Laigersay.'

'But you surely can't mean to suggest that Laigersay is actually implicated in drug trafficking'

'I am afraid that is just what I do believe, and hope to be able to prove. But let me return to your original point about the state of drug addiction in Britain. In the late fifties we hardly had any hard drug problem, such as there was occurred almost entirely among a small group of doctors who abused their ease of access to opiates. But things were changing. An Interdepartmental Committee on Drugs was set up under Lord Brain. They made their first report in 1961. That report was very reassuring and concluded that the incidence of addiction to dangerous drugs was small, and there seemed no reason to suspect that an increase was occurring. That was fine, but even before the report was set in type the situation changed so dramatically that it could not be ignored, and it was obvious that an American pattern of addiction was emerging. A research worker computed that the number of heroin addicts had increased in a geometric curve, doubling at roughly eighteen-month intervals since 1955. One reason for this has been an influx of Canadian addicts coming to Britain to avoid Canada's new penal drug code, which was introduced in 1958.

'So you see, there is a problem and it is increasing at a terrifying rate.'

'But where does Laigersay come in?'

'Ah yes, that brings us to our mutual acquaintance John Thistlethwaite. He is no major, by the way, and little more than a petty criminal who has suddenly hit the big time. He first cropped up as an accomplished confidence trickster in London about ten years ago. Then he was a Mr Peregrine Talbot, posing as an antique dealer. Before that he was involved in a fraud involving tobacco shares but we were never able to get enough evidence for a conviction. He travelled the length of the country swindling folk out of their heirlooms and selling them at high prices.

'Eventually things got too hot for him and he disappeared, only to reappear as the second laird of Laigersay, as he described himself, under the name Major

John Thistlethwaite. At first he was reasonably law-abiding but could not resist selling off Admiral Chalmers' salmon, which he was poaching on a large scale. That was quite a lucrative business, but he found a more profitable sideline: a trade in endangered species, particularly birds. This began to attract the attention of a very rich German egg collector.'

'This wouldn't be a guy called Wertheim, by any chance?'

'Yes, I believe you met him and, if I may put it that way, twisted his arm.'

'That's an unusual way of describing reduction of a dislocated shoulder, but yes, that was how I met him. I suspect he was over here to purchase a batch of osprey eggs, some of which came from Loch Bradan. The rest were possibly stolen on the mainland.'

'You probably noticed that there has been a helicopter about the island during this last summer. That is Wertheim's preferred method of travel, which conveniently drops him in Britain without troubling immigration and customs authorities. The key to all this is the source of Wertheim's wealth—drug smuggling. I suspect Wertheim has little respect for Thistlethwaite, whom he must know to be little more than a fairly petty criminal. That is why he brought in his minder Oleg Karkovski, ostensibly as a gamekeeper, but really to protect his interests and keep the major under control.'

'We have all suspected Oleg... he's a very easy man to dislike. Is he, as we're told, a Finn?'

'No, he's a Russian, who emigrated to New York before the war. He is well known to the FBI, and is wanted on numerous drug charges. He left New York in a hurry after a particularly nasty drug-related murder.'

'Was he involved in Murdo's death?

'Almost certainly. He is known to have been in the vicinity at the time, he had a suitable weapon and, of course, we have the evidence of Murdo's own voice naming him as the man who fired the shot that brought the plane down.'

'I have to tell you that my wife is incredibly distressed about her brother's death. She believes that you, because of the secrecy which has surrounded you, are implicated in it as well as Oleg. She blames me for bringing you here to the island.'

'I am sorry about that. I understand she is a very spirited young lady. You don't think she might take matters into her own hands, do you?'

'What do you mean?'

'Not sure that I know, but I would not like her anywhere near Tom Bacadh. I don't like women around potentially violent criminals. I think you should keep all of what I have told you under your hat until I have definite proof. I worry that your wife may hold the major responsible and take some action of her own. Let me know if she says anything about having it out with him.'

'I don't think that is very likely... anyway, what do you intend to do about all this?'

'There are one or two details I need to sort out, but in due course, when I have all the evidence I need, we will close in on them. But that may not be for a few days yet.'

After that, Johnson got up from the parapet he had been sitting on. 'Well, that concludes everything I have to say. I hope you will accept my apologies, and I will let you know if I think you can help us sort the matter out.'

With much to think about, I drove him back to his car. He chatted about fishing to keep the conversation away from drugs. Despite attempts at questioning I got nothing more out of him.

CHAPTER 23

Letter from a Friend

After my talk with Stanley Johnson, though things were certainly much clearer, I cannot say I liked him any more. It is certainly very unpleasant to find that one has been a suspect in drug abuse, and the idea of the man's nosing about into my past was detestable. I had nothing serious to hide, and my association with the anaesthetist who stole pethidine from sick patients was nothing but chance. All my contemporaries were just as much associated with him as I had been. But the thought that I had been considered capable of stealing drugs from the hospital, for sale in the street, disgusted me.

With these memories of my past, I suddenly again experienced that unease I had felt when talking to Helen Agnew. My mind went back to her sister. Certainly I had been fond of her, and for a time had even nursed romantic ideas about her. I was lonely and depressed much of my time at medical school, and always pressurised by work. It seemed then as though my teachers expected superhuman ability of me.

I had to learn the contents of so many books that they seemed to be weighed in tons. Frances had been affectionate and fun, but our relationship never progressed for, despite my hopes, any sort of long-term relationship was impossible. Eventually she just drifted away. A year or so after that, I heard she had been ill and had left nursing. I had not heard of her again until the chance meeting with her sister, at the dinner before the grouse shoot.

I was now in a difficult position with Fiona, since I had promised Stanley Johnson not to repeat the story of the Laigersay drug scandal. But fortunately her mood seemed to have eased. She had returned from the castle to our home, was contrite at having blamed me for her brother's death and even said with a laugh, 'You should have given me Maisie Henderson's prescription.'

It was a relief that Fiona was nearly her old self. We had a lot of walks together; she liked taking me to places she had enjoyed in childhood with her brother. I was not sure how helpful this was, but went with her whenever I could, allowing her to come to terms with her grief as she thought fit. Once she took me to a marshy area near Pitchroich.

'We always came here in September,' she told me. 'It was a favourite place, and one of the few sites in Laigersay where we could find the grass-of-Parnassus. That was Murdo's favourite wild flower and I think it's mine too.' Then she pointed out the exquisite white blooms, standing proud above the boggy ground like a shower of stars. Each flower was delicately veined in green.

'I think they are lovely,' she said. 'Murdo would be glad I have shown them to you. Hamish loves them too: in fact they are on the cover of his new book.'

That reminded me of the surprise party that Tetrabal Singh was planning for Old Squarebottle.

Hamish was going about his daily routine as usual seemingly unaware of the proposed celebration.

One day there was an unusual case of poisoning. Hamish had been called to see an elderly aristocratic lady who lived just outside Port Chalmers. She was a great gardener and her home was surrounded by a riot of colour. Despite failing sight she did most of the work herself, but had the help of an even older gardener, whose sight was little better than hers. He looked after the vegetables while she managed the flowers. She was complaining of giddiness, and when Hamish took her pulse it was extremely and abnormally slow. When he asked what she was eating she mentioned that she was very fond of spinach, which the gardener brought her from the garden. Hamish found the gardener in the potting shed and asked to be shown the spinach. It was, as he already suspected, foxglove, and the lady was suffering from acute digitalis poisoning. Proud of his detective work, he came back to the surgery to tell Jennie and me about his diagnosis.

Jennie became very quiet and then disappeared back into her little dispensary. Soon she was back looking anxious, and said:–

'Do you remember, a while back I thought we had had an intruder, but I couldn't find anything missing? Dr Hamish talking about poisoning gave me an idea. Some of the cyanide has gone—come and see.'

Sure enough, several of the blue bottles had been replaced with empties, which were carefully hidden at the back behind those that still held the highly toxic crystals. But why on earth should someone go to the trouble of breaking in to steal cyanide? Jennie, who was a devotee of crime fiction, was appalled at the implication.

'What should we do?' she wailed. 'We never should have had the beastly stuff here in the first place. Though I suppose it was safer here than in an old farm steading or a garden shed. Now there's enough of it gone to murder half of Laigersay.'

'It's some time since it went, and nothing's happened,' I tried to reassure her. 'Perhaps we should just keep quiet about it.'

Hamish was angry. 'Until someone dies? How irresponsible can you get? I'm going to the Polis.'

And so he did. The questioning was endless, first from local officers, and then from a senior officer sent over from the mainland. Where had we got the stuff? What was it for? What were we going to do with it?

Each interview left Hamish and I feeling as though we had committed some awful crime, as indeed one officer hinted we had, for the poison had been stored with inadequate security. Eventually they got tired of asking questions, and the matter seemed to go away. Except for Special Constable Erchie Thomson, who started, as he put it, nosing around.

But then the crisis at home, which had eased so suddenly, broke out again. I went home to find Fiona blazingly angry. She was brandishing a letter. 'You had better read this!' she shouted.

I took the letter and glanced at the signature. It was from Helen Agnew.

'Dear Fiona,' it read,

'I have been pondering for some time how to write to you. You see I know what it is to lose an adored sibling. My sympathy for you at the loss of your brother Murdoch brought back the loss of my sister Frances. I fear that what I have to tell you may make things worse at present, but it is my earnest desire to prevent pain for you in the future.

'My sister Frances told me of the affair she had with your husband when he was a medical student. He spoke of marriage and at the time she seemed very happy. Then he jilted her. She came to me and told me all this when she was about three months pregnant. She was distraught and in her despair had started taking drugs. She had an abortion but the drug problem increased and she was taking large amounts of heroin intravenously. Though I have no proof, Robert Chalmers was suspected at the time of being implicated in drugs and I believe that it was he who was supplying Frances.

'Eventually she contracted hepatitis and she died four years ago.

'All this came to mind when I was in Laigersay with Murdo for the Twelfth.

'My dear I am truly sorry to inflict more grief on you at this present time. I too am suffering from the loss of Murdo, a fine man who had spoken to me of marriage. Had his death not supervened we might have been as sisters. It is in such a relationship that I have decided to write this letter. I hope in time you will be able to forgive me and see that I was right to do so.

I was very distressed to hear of Murdo's death when I was in New York on business and much regretted that I was unable to attend his funeral.

'Yours very sincerely

'Helen Agnew.'

I sat down in a chair and looked at Fiona.

'What am I to tell you?' I asked. 'I cannot say it is all lies because some of it is true, but at the same time I am quite innocent of this accusation. I don't know where to begin, except to say that my relationship with Frances was quite proper. We went to parties together for quite a time. I never knew about her drug taking. But now I have read this, I do remember she once gave me something at a party that made me very ill. I never knew what it was. Eventually she walked out on me. I was cut up about it at the time, and then I never saw her again. I was certainly not the father of her child, and I knew nothing of the abortion. Oh Fiona! you must believe me: we have too much at stake.'

My wife stared at me angrily, but at least she spoke rationally. 'Rob, I want to believe you, but it seems to me there are too many things I do not understand going on here at present. I know I am not myself since Murdo died, and I am going to move back to the castle with my father until I can see things more clearly. I spoke to Daddy about it last week, and he promised me asylum there until I feel better.'

That was how, within weeks of our marriage, we came to separate for the second time. For once, Laigersay's famed healing powers seemed too weak to help. I was plunged into a state of abject misery because a chain of events involving other people had contrived to put me in such bad light. One thing was now crystal clear: there had been far more drugs being used by my contemporaries than, in my innocence, I had appreciated at the time. I would probably never know exactly what happened to

Frances. When she stopped seeing me, she had complained how dull I had become, and that she wanted more fun and action. Poor lass, it sounded as though she found it.

With Fiona away, I was plunged back into a dreary bachelor existence. For the first time since my return to Laigersay, I found myself regretting my decision to turn down the registrarship in London. There was nothing for it but to throw myself into the anodyne of my work.

The next day Erchie called at the surgery with an explanation of the cyanide mystery. Stanley Johnson, ostensibly in the island for the fishing, had mentioned to him that some of the burns in the south of the island seemed lifeless; there were no fish to be caught, or even seen. Erchie went to inspect the burns and found numbers of small dead trout in the estuary. His suspicions were aroused, and he took to patrolling some of the island's rivers at night. He had heard of the use of cyanide for poaching. The cyanide, dissolved in weak solution, was put into pools holding salmon. The poison, diluted in the large volume of water, killed everything in the pool. This was an effective means of poaching but totally destructive of all animal life for some distance downstream.

One night he spotted two men working by the pool where I had lost my big sea trout. He disturbed them and they ran, but they left behind a blue glass bottle, which was identified by Jennie as one that had contained some of the missing cyanide. I was horrified at the tale, and asked if by selling the fish they were not at risk of poisoning people.

'Apparently not usually. I've been reading aboot it,' Erchie told me. 'Though there was a big case o' fish poisoning in Wales some years back, when quantities o' poisoned fish went on the black market. Nobody died, but it took several seasons before the river recovered. It's ma guess that there is an organised ring o' poachers in the island.'

'That fits,' I said. 'The laird thought he saw his salmon on sale in Edinburgh.'

'Aye, an' I've a shrewd idea who they are. It was dark, mind, but one o' thae poachers looked like the underkeeper frae Tombaca.'

Erchie and I, debating the possibilities, remembered that Murdo had said he had seen a small boat going out to a trawler off Assilag Island. Then I told Erchie about the old copper mine, and what I had read, and what Maggie had said about it.

'Aye, I mind that well. I went there when I was a bairn. But it's a' closed up now.'

'Maggie says she lost a dog down there, so there must still be a way in. Can you remember where the mine led?'

'Och, it was just a maze of caverns and branches. The main one ran way up into the hills, and the other way came down to the shore under the cliffs in Assilag Bay. Years ago, I believe, there was a jetty for loading the ore. It was in a little cove of shingle surrounded by high cliffs. You could only get to it by boat. But ye're right, it would make a fine route for smuggling fish, or anything else for that matter. I'll take a look and let you know.'

Erchie was back next day with a long face. 'It's no good, laddie. I went over there in a boat. At the seaward end there's a ramshackle auld boathouse which blocks where the shaft came oot below the cliff. It's falling down, but for all that has a new looking padlock on the door. I went up to the bothy but I couldnae see onything there. Ye're in wi' Maggie McPhee, go and ask her how the dog got in.'

It was time to see the blind old lady again anyway. I was pleased to find her better than on the day she had had the pre-vision of Murdo's crash.

'Gie me your tubes,' she said. 'Wi' them in ma lugs I can hear just fine.'

I gave her my stethoscope and she put the instrument in her ears. She was cock-a-hoop that I had been appointed as the successor to the laird, just as she had foretold. When I asked her if there had been any repercussions after Oleg Karkovski's talk of eviction she shook her head.

'Though my brother says old One-eye has been nosing around here a good deal. But he doesnae speak to either o' us.'

On the subject of the mine, she was reticent. However, she said she thought her brother might help.

'Of course,' she added, 'the one who really knows is Cuhlan; it was he who found his mother when she fell in.' Maggie thought for a bit, and then said: 'Why not borrow the dog from the laird, and we'll all go and see what we can see.'

Though by now I was used to her speaking of 'seeing', I never knew whether she was referring to her blind eyes or her special gift of second sight, or 'taish' as it was called in the Island. Three days later, Erchie and I borrowed the laird's wolfhound and drove up to meet Archie and Maggie McPhee. Luckily Archie's gout was better, for we bumped about going over the rough road to the bothy. Maggie was cramped in the back with the great dog. She caressed him and spoke to him in Gaelic, and he responded with great wet licks to her blind face. It was a great reunion of old friends.

As soon as I stopped by the bothy, Cuhlan bounded out of the car and stood sniffing the air of the hills and, seeming to know what was expected of him, ambled off uphill beyond the bothy, scaring meadow pipits from the heather as he went. A wolfhound's gentle trot is fast, and we had a job to keep up, especially Archie, who was guiding his sister. I broke into a run as Cuhlan disappeared over a ridge, and was just in time to see him vanish into the ground.

The dog had led us to an unfenced hole leading downwards. The hole was big enough to crawl through, and looked as though a subterranean tunnel had collapsed. Calling to the others, I crawled after Cuhlan and found myself sitting on a pile of rock near the roof of a large chamber. As my eyes grew accustomed to the gloom, I saw a slope leading down at about 30° in front of me and knew I was in a branch of the mine. Shouting to Cuhlan to follow me, I crawled out and joined the others.

'You're brilliant, Maggie,' I said, 'and so is Cuhlan,' and I told them about the entrance to the mine.

'We're over a mile from the bothy here,' said Erchie, squinting south-westwards into the sun, the way we had come. 'The workings must be very extensive.'

'Aye,' added Archie, 'the mine was shut down in the late twenties as it was no longer profitable, but they reopened it when copper was scarce in the war. I heard tell they had made a great new extension to the old workings. This'll be it.'

We decided that once they had helped with the discovery of the entrance, the elderly brother and sister should leave Erchie and I to do a bit of exploring.

'Och, we'll just walk home,' said Maggie.

'But it's a couple of miles at least,' I protested.

I did not know the blind could give a withering look, but that is what the old woman turned on me.

'We do that distance all the time,' Archie commented. 'Good luck with your exploring.' And they set off with Cuhlan to tramp across the moor.

Finding torches from our rucksacks, Erchie and I crawled back into the mine. The slope of rocks was a difficult scramble, but in a minute or two we were down to what had been the floor of the chamber and could see a nearly horizontal shaft leading from it. The floor was reasonably smooth where mine vehicles had travelled along a rough road. Here and there, fallen rocks littered the old road surface, and a greenish tinge showed where traces of copper had coloured the rock face. Most of the copper-bearing ore had been extracted, and we could see how excavation had followed the seams through syncline and anticline, leaving a sinuous cavity twisting and turning as it followed the folds in the earth's crust. But the tunnel was well engineered, although sometimes partially obstructed by rock falls. It was clear that this had been one of the main routes for removal of the mineral.

After a few hundred yards, our way was blocked by a huge rock fall similar to the one by which we had entered. This seemed to fill the whole of the tunnel, but Erchie, shining his torch beam at the roof, thought there might be a small gap between the mass of fallen rock and the roof of the workings. He put his torch out to save the battery, and we sat in the dark on the rock pile to discuss plans.

I was for going back, but Erchie wanted to climb up to the roof in case there was a way through to the main part of the mine. As we debated, Erchie suddenly hushed me and whispered, 'Listen.'

At first I could hear nothing, and then I became aware of the sound of a motor a long way off. It grew louder, and seemed to be beyond the rock fall. Erchie whispered again, 'Look up,' and, doing so, I saw a faint glim of light coming from beyond the rock pile. Then both light and noise faded as what must have been some sort of truck passed on down another tunnel on the far side of the rock fall.

We waited until all noise had gone. Then Erchie spoke again. 'Laddie, that proves it; the mine's still in use and forbye there is a way through, for if light can pass, then so can we.'

So saying, the big man started clambering up the slope of the rock fall. It was not easy to find the small gap between the fallen rock and the roof of the tunnel, and we were careful not to show too much light, in case whoever was on the other side came back. Eventually, some thirty feet above the floor of the tunnel, where ore had been extracted high into an anticlinal mineral fold, we found a small gap, through which our torchlight showed the other side of the rock fall and the main tunnel behind it.

I squeezed through behind Erchie. The new tunnel was different. It ran at right angles to the passage we had explored and was clearly in current use, because the floor had been roughly cleared of debris, presumably to allow a small vehicle to drive through the tunnel. It must have been this that we had heard, and whose headlights had betrayed the presence of the way in.

We scrambled down and ran along the roadway in the base of the tunnel. Torn between wanting to discover as much as we could and anxiety lest the vehicle we had heard should return, we moved quickly. The tunnel led us to a flight of steps, which climbed to a large wooden trap door. Erchie tried it gently and it opened over his caber-tossing shoulders.

Whispering 'Wait a mo',' he slipped through the gap. In a moment he was back and he said: 'We're right below Tom Bacadh Castle. There's a flight of stairs leading into what must've been the old dungeon. Laddie, I think we know all we want here. Let's get back before our friend returns. Something tells me it may be 'Orrible Oleg, and I don't think he'll be pleased to see us.'

There was no argument, and we hurried back to the rock fall. We were only just in time, as we could hear the motor of the truck on its return journey. We wriggled through the gap at the top of the rock fall and turned to watch. The small truck drove past below us and we could see from the bulk of the driver that Erchie's guess was right; the only other man on the Island as big Erchie was Oleg.

It was easier to find our way back, and soon we were out in the bright sunshine again, bedraggled in mud-stained clothing. It was getting late and I had an early evening surgery before the party for Hamish. We hurried back to Port Chalmers, where I was surprised to see a familiar red face. At my request Erchie stopped, and I hailed Peter Kidd, the man who had caused me to be so drunk when I first met Fiona. 'How are you, Rob?' he enquired. 'When last I saw you, you were in trouble with broken ribs.'

'Fine now, thanks, but when you last saw me I had more trouble with your Islay malt than my ribs! What are you doing here?'

'Tetrabal Singh asked me to Hamish's party. He and Stanley Johnson have something or other planned, and I'm supposed to be part o't.'

Promising to see him later, I rushed to change out of muddy clothes before surgery.

CHAPTER 24

The Battle of Tom Bacadh

The party was a small affair; I had expected something more lavish. When I arrived a little late after a longer than usual evening surgery, the guests were present: the admiral, Stanley Johnson, Peter Kidd and Tet himself. Otherwise there was only me in addition to Hamish. As soon as I arrived, Peter Kidd thrust a large scotch into my hand, adding, 'Make it last, laddie, you'll need a clear head tonight.'

Then Stanley was on his feet to propose Hamish's health, and we all raised our glasses and congratulated him on his wildflower book.

'Actually,' Stanley continued, 'it's my fault we are all here. I asked Tet to arrange this party as a pretext because I wanted an ostensible reason for being here, and at the same time to ensure the presence of Peter Kidd and Dr Chalmers.' He turned to me and continued, 'As you are the future laird of the island, Sir James felt you should be in on the affair, and after our chat the other day you dispelled my admittedly very slight doubts about you.

Sir James has known about what is happening at Tom Bacadh since the death of his son. He suggested you should be brought into the plan, as he is feeling his years. That is largely why I spoke to you as I did on the moors.'

Then the Admiral interrupted: 'Yes, Rob, such a serious affair in Laigersay has to involve you, and anyway I am too slow to be much use if it comes to a fight.'

I stared from one to the other, beginning to understand that the problems of Laigersay were approaching crisis, and I told them of that afternoon's findings in the mine works.

Stanley was interested. 'You know, Dr Chalmers, that my work is involved with detecting drug trafficking. Peter Kidd works in my Glasgow department, and of course we have our old friends Tetrabal Singh and Hamish here in Laigersay.

'For some time we have been aware of a cartel in London which is importing drugs from Latin America and relaying them to Europe. For a long time we could not find where the drugs were entering the country. I had heard of Thistlethwaite when he was in London, though he was not, as far as I am aware, involved with narcotics then. We have been watching him for some time, and when Murdo Chalmers told me of unusual activity here in Laigersay we began to look more closely at what was happening in the island. Murdo knew about my work, and kept me informed about activities here in Laigersay.

'The salmon poaching you discovered was really only a cover, though I have no doubt that Thistlethwaite and Oleg Karkovski made a good deal out of it: and they probably did even better with their sales of rare eggs. We had also been watching Karkovski in London and when he decided to come here in the guise of gamekeeper we began to think that Laigersay might conceivably be the port of entry for drugs bound for London and Europe. We were only partly right, for the heroin and cocaine, which were arriving here by small ship, were not destined for Britain: the market in this country is still too small, thank God, for it to be sufficiently profitable. The drugs go on to Holland. Wertheim owned a helicopter and this proved an excellent way of transporting their merchandise over there without attracting attention.

'Murdo was always looking out for poachers when he was flying over Laigersay. That was how he spotted Oleg on the moor and, though we have no proof, I am pretty sure it was Oleg who fired the shot that led to Murdo's crash. Firing a rifle at a plane is unlikely to cause much damage but by unlucky chance the bullet cut the fuel pipe and stopped Murdo's engine. In my view, that was murder but it might be difficult to get that charge to stick in a court of law.

'We have been watching the ship that is delivering the drugs here. She sails out of Jamaica and has been shadowed by the Royal Navy. She should be off Laigersay late tonight, and we think Thistlethwaite and Karkovski are expecting a big consignment of narcotics. We want to stop them inconspicuously, if possible red-handed, and that is why I have gathered you together. Any questions so far?'

There was a general shaking of heads.

But Stanley Johnson's tale had left me astonished that so much skulduggery was being enacted within the peaceful surroundings of Laigersay. 'What exactly are you planning?' I asked.

Stanley looked round the room. 'Oh, it's quite simple: we will just go to Tom Bacadh and arrest them. In fact we will leave here in a few minutes time. Some police reinforcements from the mainland arrived in the Island this afternoon. Only the senior officer is in on the story; the others believe they are breaking a poaching syndicate. We will also explain about the illegal sale of eggs. We want to keep it as quiet as possible for security reasons. There are other drug runners involved and this is just part of an international operation.

'The laird, Hamish and I will go to the front door of the castle and try and make a formal arrest. As back-up, I want Peter and Tet to be at the rear of the castle in case they make a run for it. Rob, I suggest you enlist the support of Erchie Thomson and come up through the mine on the route you found this afternoon.'

I looked at my father-in-law. 'May I take Cuhlan? He seems to be able to see in the dark.'

'Of course, but I don't know where he is.'

'Oh sorry, I completely forgot. He's up with Maggie McPhee. We'll pick him up en route.'

Stanley went on: 'I think they might well use your passage as an escape route. After all, it leads down to the sea, where they probably expect the trawler. They may be armed. I shall have a revolver, and I know Peter has his. Hamish?'

'Aye, I still have a wartime pistol. I'll bring it with me, and Tet, as I remember, is handier with a sword. Do you still have it?'

The Sikh nodded gravely.

'That leaves you and Erchie unarmed, I am afraid,' said Stanley.

'I don't mind. I have never handled a handgun and I'd be useless with it anyway.' And I added: 'If I've got Erchie and Cuhlan with me I don't think there'll be too much to worry about.'

So, like in a wartime film, we synchronised watches and agreed to be in place at precisely 11 pm.

I found Erchie at home and quickly explained what was happening.

'Aye, I always had m' doots about the poaching. It seemed ower elaborate and, as Murdo said himself, hardly economic.'

Laigersay was looking magnificent in the light of a rising full moon as we drove south through Lutheran. As we crossed the machair a barn owl quartered the ground for voles to feed its brood of youngsters in the steading beside the crumbling shell of a house by the road. Erchie started laughing, and then told me of the old couple who used to live there.

'I mind a story Doctor Hamish told me about them. He was called out there when the old wifey thocht her man had gone. Sure enough, when Hamish got there he was sure the old fellow was deid... I 'spect it's sometimes no easy to tell?'

I nodded. 'It can be very difficult.'

'Anyroad, Hamish told the old girl he'd gone. Then the old man sat up and said, "Doctor, I'm no deid yet," whereupon his wife said: "Wheesht, John, the doctor kens best!"'

We were still laughing when we picked up Cuhlan from the McPhees, who were supping tea together at Archie's. We explained as much of what was planned as we thought we could. Maggie took my hand and said in her prophetic way, 'Tak care. I see death tonight. Stay with Erchie and you'll be all right.'

As we curled the wolfhound into the car, Erchie commented: 'Och, I ken you like her, but yon *cailleach* fair gives me the creeps... though I like the dogs she raised.' As if knowing he was being spoken of, Cuhlan made two eloquent thumps with his tail, raising dust from the back seat of the car.

We sped over the track to the bothy, and parked the car out of sight, near Cuhlan's entrance to the old mine. Now that we knew the way, it was no time before we reached the rock fall and climbed to the space near the roof from where we could look down into the main tunnel. With Cuhlan lying between us, Erchie and I watched and waited to see if there was any activity below.

All was quiet, so we slid down the rock fall and were soon hurrying towards Tom Bacadh. Erchie walked ahead, using his torch as little as possible to save the battery. Cuhlan was beside me as we walked through the dark tunnel. I had my hand on his collar; he was better than any torch. Once he stopped, and I knew from his bent back and sudden smell that he was busy leaving his mark on the mine. A minute later he stopped again, and I felt him stiffen, and turn his head back the way we had come. I tapped Erchie's shoulder, and the three of us stood still, listening. A long way behind us we could hear the faint drone of the little truck we had seen that afternoon. As we listened, the sound grew louder: it was coming towards us.

We hurried on, searching the featureless walls of the tunnel for somewhere to hide. If, as we guessed, it were Oleg in the truck, he would rouse the castle if he found us. Then, as we were nearing the stairs to the castle, Cuhlan stopped, and turned into a narrow alley off the main tunnel. We squeezed after him and found ourselves in another chamber littered with old machinery. This must have been a workshop of some sort, as the beam of the torch showed benches and an anvil. There we hid, just in time, as the truck was catching up with us.

As it passed I could see, in the dim light of its cabin, the huge figure of Oleg hunched over the steering wheel. Then he was past; once again Cuhlan had saved our skin. I stooped to pat him as thanks. In doing so, I knocked a piece of ironwork off a bench beside me. The crash was deafening and we froze, listening. Had Oleg heard us? The engine of the truck cut out and we heard the driver get out. A torch beam shone down the main tunnel, but the man seemed satisfied and he clambered up the steps to a trap door, opened it and disappeared through it. We waited, listening open-mouthed, but all seemed quiet.

'Sorry about that, Erchie,' I whispered.

'Och, I don't think he heard it... even if he did, the old mine must be full of things falling aboot. It didnae fash him, any road. Come on, it's nearly eleven o'clock.'

We paused to examine the little truck. It was rather a homemade affair, based on a Volkswagen beetle chassis. Its open back smelt strongly of fish. The keys were in the ignition. It occurred to me that it would be a good idea to remove them, and I slipped them into my pocket.

We climbed the stair and opened the trap. Cuhlan bounded in and then we were all in the basement of Tom

Bacadh Castle. It was a gloomy place with two cells placed on either side of a great chamber. The dungeons looked as though they had not been altered in centuries, and unpleasant ceiling hooks conjured up horrible ideas of how the rooms might have been used in bygone times. But the chamber was deserted, and there was only a minute or two until eleven. We tiptoed up a stone staircase which led to a great iron studded door, clearly designed originally to ensure prisoners could not escape. The door led into a passageway. Oleg had left it slightly ajar, and through it we could hear the distant sound of raised voices. Straining our ears, we heard Oleg's voice.

'Something's wrong, I tell you. There's fresh dogshit in the mine, and I heard noises. I say we should get out while the going is good.'

Then Thistlethwaite was speaking: 'Calm yourself Oleg, you're getting very twitchy. I assure you all is well. I think you may have overlooked that we have a lady with us, and I expect Herr Wertheim any time now. He's flying in from his home near the Dutch coast. In fact, that sounds like him now.'

Straining our ears, we too could hear the helicopter's engines. It must have landed, for we heard the motor stop. Glancing at my watch, I realised it was now past eleven o'clock. I guessed that the surprise arrival of the helicopter had delayed Stanley's plan.

Then we heard doors slamming, and a new sound: I recognised my former patient's voice.

'*Guten Abend, meine Freunde. Ach,* I am glad to be here. The North Sea was very windy. I thought I might run out of fuel before I reached here; as it is, the tank is virtually empty. I see you have guests—may I ask why?'

Thistlethwaite greeted Wertheim, and added, 'My visitor will be leaving shortly. She came here rather unexpectedly earlier this evening.'

A banging on the front door of the castle interrupted his voice. Then we heard a mumble of voices; we moved silently through the great door which led from the dungeons, and waited listening. We could hear more clearly now.

The words grew louder, and we heard Stanley's urbane voice: 'Major Thistlethwaite, I have a warrant for your arrest. The castle is surrounded. I suggest you come quietly with us.'

Then there was confused shouting and a shot. Oleg burst into the passageway where we were hiding. As he ran by, Erchie thrust out his foot and the big man tripped with a curse. Turning as he fell, Oleg drew a gun and aimed at Erchie. But Cuhlan was quicker and the wolfhound's jaws closed on Oleg's forearm. The man dropped the gun with a scream, kicked Cuhlan off him and ran for the door. Erchie was after him, but too late to stop the great door closing. Between us, Erchie and I forced the huge door open, and the dog came through it with us. Oleg was well ahead of us and we saw him disappear through the hatch to the mineshaft below. As we reached the hatch we heard a bolt slam into place from below and the trap door was firmly locked. Then Peter and Tet were with us. Tet drew his short sword and started cutting at the ancient woodwork of the trap door. While he did so, Peter told us that they had come in through the back, and saw Erchie and me follow Oleg into the dungeon.

At first Tet's efforts seemed hopeless, then one plank, more rotten than the rest, gave a little, and the Sikh redoubled his efforts till part of the bolt could be seen.

'Out the way, Tet, let me do it now,' said Peter. Placing the muzzle of his revolver against the bolt, he shot it away. Then the trap opened easily to reveal the passage below. There was no sign of Oleg, but Cuhlan knew where he had gone. The dog leapt down the stairs and raced down the mineshaft.

'He's got the scent,' said Peter and made to follow him. Snatching the key from my pocket, I shouted: 'Get into the car,' and all four of us were soon careering along the passage of the mine. A distant bark told us that Cuhlan was running well ahead of us, but of Oleg there was as yet no sign. Soon we passed the side turning where we had entered—we were now in a part of the mine I had not seen before and I guessed we were descending to the sea.

Sure enough, ahead of us we could see the faint glim of moonlight to the west; Oleg had left the boathouse doors at the seaward end of the tunnel open. We jumped out of the truck onto the shingled shore searching in the dim light for a sign of our quarry. Then stones rattled down from the hillside above us. Straining his eyes Erchie spotted Cuhlan racing up the precipitous cliff, and way above him was Oleg. The big man was climbing slowly on a narrow, exposed ledge topped with an overhang. As Cuhlan closed the gap between them, Oleg found a hold and began to haul himself over the overhang.

Then Cuhlan jumped into space, catching the big man's foot and, hanging from him with all his weight, he pulled the man off balance. Then they both fell. Oleg arched backwards into space to crash on to rock fifty feet below. The dog fell on his back onto the narrow, downward-sloping ledge just beneath him. For a split second he lay there and we watched, knowing that at any moment the hound must fall to his death, as the man had done.

Cuhlan seemed to summon every sinew in his body, he righted himself, stood on the ledge and then, as if nothing had happened, turned and ran down the cliff face to join us round Oleg's body.

Though I had disliked Oleg intensely, there is always sadness at death. The four of us stood in silence round the dead man, and I found myself dealing with mixed emotions. There was triumph at our success in the chase, tinged with horror at having brought about the big man's death. Even Cuhlan gave a soft whine. Then another sound caught my ear. We all glanced up at the night sky above the cliff.

'The helicopter—it's making for Assilag,' said Tet.

'I doot they'll no get far: that Kraut said he was almost out o' juice, and they'll no have got any in Laigersay the nicht.' Erchie, too, had heard the approaching helicopter.

'They must have given Stanley the slip somehow. My guess is they are making for the incoming trawler.' As I spoke, the helicopter passed overhead, and we could see its lights as it descended on to Assilag.

'Come on,' I shouted, 'jump in the truck. The only way we can get there is back through the tunnel. I hope there's a vehicle at Tom Bacadh we can commandeer.' Without clearly knowing what I was doing, I started the engine and we went bouncing over the shingle back into the tunnel.

Erchie was hanging on for dear life, and the wolfhound had bounded into the back as I started.

CHAPTER 25

The Causeway

We made the journey back through the tunnel at breakneck speed. We clambered back through the broken trapdoor into the dungeon of the castle. Above us we could hear murmured voices, which grew louder as we as we passed through the iron studded door. Bursting into the room whence Oleg had emerged only twenty minutes or so before, we were greeted by a strange sight. The admiral and Hamish were tied to chairs, and the latter was trying to free the laird. Stanley Johnson was propped against Thistlethwaite's desk trying to staunch bleeding from his leg. As we entered, the admiral wriggled free from his bonds and started to free Hamish.

I ran to Stanley, while Tet freed Hamish. 'What happened?'

'That bugger Oleg shot me, got me in the leg. I think it's only a flesh wound, but it's bleeding hard and I can't stand.'

'Let me look,' I said, taking out my pocketknife and cutting away the material of Stanley's trousers. 'Hmm, looks like the bleeding has stopped, but by the look of things you've lost a fair bit. Fortunately the bullet missed the femoral artery, but it looks as though there could be some nerve damage.'

'I'm sure I'll live. But listen, Rob, Thistlethwaite and Wertheim have got Fiona...'

'Fiona? What did you bring her for?'

'Wait, let me tell you. She was here when we got here. she seemed to have come of her own free will. We were just about to enter at eleven pm as planned, when Wertheim arrived in his helicopter. So we delayed until he came into the castle.'

'Yes we heard him arrive, but go on.'

'When we came in, Oleg let off a shot, hitting me, and bolted.'

I nodded. 'But what about Fiona?'

Wertheim had a gun in her back and said he would kill her if we tried anything. Thistlethwaite tied Hamish and the admiral to chairs, while Wertheim kept Fiona covered as a hostage. They didn't bother about me. I had fainted and I think they thought me dead. Then they left, taking Fiona with them. A moment later I came to, and heard the chopper start up again.

Hamish came and took over tending to Stanley's leg. I told them about the chopper being short of fuel, but that we had seen them managing to get as far as Assilag.

'Then they'll be heading for the trawler that's making a delivery tonight—somewhere off the south of the island. My Land Rover is hidden behind the shrubbery near the rear of the castle. Take it, here's the keys... see if you can stop them. We three can look after ourselves here.'

Calling to Erchie, Tet and Peter that we must hurry, I ran to the door.

'Sorry about Fiona, Rob, I had an idea she was plotting something,' Stanley called out after me.

We found the Land Rover and were soon speeding across the moor.

'What on earth induced Fiona to go to Tom Bacadh by herself?' I asked aloud.

'Perhaps she wanted to sort Thistlethwaite out,' suggested Tet. 'She was beside herself with anger and wanted to tell him what she thought of him. She'd be quite capable of that.'

'Madness,' I said braking to swerve round a group of sheep huddled in the road, and then accelerating so wildly that we were bouncing in the car.

'Take it easy, man, for you'll no save your wife by putting us all in the ditch.'

Of course Erchie was right. I drove more carefully after that, but still as fast as I dared.

Soon we were approaching the causeway and bumping over shingle. Suddenly a man in waders carrying rope and fishing gear appeared in the headlights. He waved frantically. I slewed to halt beside him and saw it was the fisherman, Alex Farquharson.

'Ye're too late,' he shouted. 'The tide's turned, you'll no get across the causeway.'

'I've got to,' I shouted back. 'Fiona's been abducted and she's in danger over there.'

Alex dropped the gear he was carrying, opened the rear door and squeezed in beside Tet and Peter dragging his coiled rope after him. 'Then I'm coming too,' he said. 'If anyone can get ye across I can; but I'm thinking you may have to swim.'

'Okay, tell me where to go.'

'Watch for the marker poles, Erchie, count them aloud as we go; there are twenty-three of them. There's a tricky bit at the ninth pole and the deepest spot is between eleven and twelve. If we get to twelve we should get through. There's the first pole.'

'Number one,' intoned Erchie. The poles were set about ten yards apart, and the tide was running from right to left in a gathering current a few inches deep.

'Number two.'

'You're lucky to be in a four-wheel drive with high clearance like this,' said Alex. 'Ye might even make it.'

'Three.'

'Keep in low gear and steer on the left o' the track here. It's a wee bitty high ower there.'

'Four.'

'That's fine, steady as ye go.'

'Five.'

'Now come to the centre o' the line between the poles, the sea's undercut the left side o' the road here.'

'Six.'

'Ye could go a touch faster, keep the revs up, we dinna want to stall.'

'Seven.'

'All richt, keep going, ye're doing fine.'

'Eight.'

'Fingers crossed, everyone.'

'Nine.'

'Right. Now steer as if ye wanted to hit that left-hand pole. There's a muckle great hole just close to your offside front wheel. If ye go in that we may all drown. Easy now, you've got half of your offside wheel ower the edge, keep as close to the left as ye can. Erchie, ye'll need to push the pole away as ye pass or it'll snag the mirror. Well done, we're through. But I'm doubtful about the eleventh.'

'Ten,' called Erchie, and we noticed water sloshing at our feet within the cab. Then, suddenly, the engine coughed and died.

'Chentlemen, from here we walk. If ye're lucky ye may be able to salvage your vehicle in the morn. Now listen carefully: there's a strong tide running from right to left. It's at its deepest by the twelfth pole; it'll be up to your waist and a strong force. If ye go over the edge of the causeway there's nothing to stop ye between here and Tuilleag. Now I'll lead, each o' you tie on to this line behind me. Make sure ye're fast, for all oor lives depend on't. Follow the path I take, and if anyone falls, turn to face the current and everyone hold on for dear life.'

Tying the rope to his belt, Alex stepped out into the dark rushing water. 'Noo, if the Indian chentleman comes next.' He helped Tet out of the car and stood him by the Land Rover.

'Goodness gracious, it's cold,' muttered Tet as the water reached his waist.

'Now the other chentleman from the back.'

Alec checked Peter's lifeline.

'Now the young laird, and lastly you, Erchie. It's a guid thing ye're the last, Erchie, a man your size'll be our anchor. Are ye ready? Wait till the line straightens after the man in front o' you, and follow me across.'

I watched as the small figure of Tetrabal Singh followed the old fisherman. I could see how the water pressure was buffeting the slight Indian's body, but he was making progress, crabbing sideways, taking short steps. The water seemed to be lapping higher, almost to his chest.

Then I saw Peter start to follow. He seemed to do better with his greater height.

Then it was my turn. As I left the reassuring but shuddering body of the Land Rover, I was amazed at the sheer pressure of water tearing at me. As Tet had said, it was cold, and the force seemed hungry to drag me down. Suddenly my feet slipped, and I was deep in tumbling water. I fought hard to surface and felt the rope at my waist tighten, and then it broke.

This then was death. I had a vision of my body being washed up on Tuilleag. Then a hand grabbed my hair and another was round my waist. The great strength of Erchie heaved me up spluttering across his shoulder, and he strode through the tumult of the waves.

A few moments later, we were out of the current and with each step the water level dropped. Erchie stood me on my feet in about a foot of seawater.

'Och, I think ye're destined to be hanged,' Erchie grumbled. 'Drooning's obviously too guid for ye!'

I struggled the last few yards to the shore, and sat on a rock to cough and get my breath.

For a moment we all sat and shivered at the Assilag end of the causeway. Then Erchie spoke again: 'Well, ye've got us here. What do we do now we're here?'

Again it was Alex Farquharson who answered. 'These folk who took Fiona, what would they be planning to do. D'ye jalouse?'

For a moment I did not understand, but Erchie replied: 'Guid thinking, Alex. We reckon they are drug smugglers and they have a rendezvous with a ship o' some sort off the coast here.'

'Have they indeed? There's been a foreign-looking, ocean-going trawler aboot offshore all afternoon.'

Alex scanned the horizon, which was dimly lit by bright moonlight.

'If I'm no mistaken,' he said, 'that's her ower to the south there, a mile or so off the tip o' Mulcaire. Now, these smugglers, they wouldn't be anything to do with that one-eyed keeper frae Tom Bacadh, would they?'

'Yes,' I almost shouted, jumping up from my sodden rocky seat. 'Do you know where they keep their boat?'

'Oh, aye,' Alec replied slowly and deliberately. 'It's in Village Cove on the west coast o' Assilag aboot half way along the island.'

I found myself wanting to shake the old man. God only knew what might be happening to Fiona, and Alec was apparently quite unconcerned and unhurried. His next question was surprising.

'Chust what time is it the noo?' he enquired.

'A few minutes to midnight,' said Erchie. 'It must be soon now.'

'Aye, that's what I'm thinking, Erchie. High tide tonight is at nine minutes afore 1 am.'

'Will somebody tell me what's going on?' I demanded with some irritation.

'The rip will start in about twenty minutes,' Erchie explained. 'If Wertheim and Co are to reach their trawler from Village Cove before dawn, they should have started by now. That means that when they round the south point of Assilag, they'll go straight into the rip. How much nearer to the trawler are we here, Alex?'

'At least a couple o' miles. That's why we're no in any hurry. But we need to think very carefully. We could go oot there in the "Hottentot", and wait in the lee o' Assilag to see if they come oot. If they do, as soon as they round the point they will be beyond help. The rip will take them on to the skerries by Tuilleag. There's only one way of escape. Fiona has been there, but it was ten or twelve years ago, she may not remember. In any case her captors may not let her steer their boat. But perhaps she will be able to convince them that's their only hope. Mind, it's a slim one.'

'Can't we do anything?' I interjected with increasing alarm.

The old fisherman scratched his head. 'That's what I'm saying. There's chust a chance if we follow them down the rip that we could save life. Mind you, it's a big gamble.' He paused, and then added: 'Aye, gey risky.'

'I'll try anything,' I said.

'Well, I'll need one man wi' me. I was thinking o' Erchie. It doesnae seem right to put the laird's life at risk.'

'I can't believe what I'm hearing!' I exclaimed, astonished at what appeared to be a flashback to the politics of the clans. 'Dammit all, she's my wife.'

Alex looked at Erchie, who said: 'I'll come, maybe a bit o' brawn might be useful.'

'I think the laird's right, Erchie. On second thoughts ye'd be like to whummle the "Hottentot". I'll tak the doctor. Noo, we still hae time on oor side.' Turning to

Peter and Tet, he went on: 'Do you two chentlemen go up to the village and tell them what we are doing. We need the coastguard informed. An' while you're there ye might get some dry clothing sent over to my bothy.' He looked at me, and added: 'We might at least start oot warm, even if we don't end up that way.'

With that, Alex Farquharson turned and walked off into the moonlight in the direction of the bothy near the mooring for the 'Howling Hottentot'.

When we reached the bothy there were other people congregated there. Someone was bearing warm clothes and, even more welcome, hot soup in a Thermos. I was handed a mug full of broth, which had a good shot of whisky in it. When I had drunk it, I was bundled unceremoniously into dry clothes and began to feel something of a man again.

Then I began to think about what Fiona had told me about the rip. I knew that it had claimed many lives. Deliberately to sail into it was courting death. I had survived two near drownings. Would the sea claim me this third time?

As if he knew what I was thinking, Erchie was grinning at me: 'Ye'll be all right,' he said. 'Just mind what I said aboot hanging.'

CHAPTER 26

The Rip

Alex seemed to be even slower as he checked the 'Hottentot'. He went over the little boat's superstructure, meticulously tightening fixtures and lashings. He bailed out what little water was in her, and took a spanner to all the bolts holding the outboard to its transom. He took out the emergency flares and put new ones in place. Then he filled the engine with fuel. After that, he stood quietly by his boat. When I went to speak to him, I saw from his moving lips that he was praying. He knew he was taking a huge risk. I doubt if he was afraid for his own life; he was a man of such profound faith he was sure death would be but a temporary inconvenience before his afterlife. But he was more anxious about his responsibility for the lives of Fiona and me. He was asking for skills greater than his own to guide us. Also I suspected he was anxious for his beloved boat.

A moment later, his orisons over, he spoke aloud. 'All right, Doctor, let's see what we can do for this puir lass o' yours. Here, put on a life chacket.'

Amid cries of good luck from all around, we pushed the 'Hottentot' off and rowed a few yards to deep water. The engine started at the first pull, and we puttered quite sedately into Assilag Bay. It was now quite easy to see the trawler, though she was probably still hidden to watchers in the boat coming along the far coast of Assilag.

To my surprise, Alex passed me a hand line with a spinner on it. 'Chust stream that oot ahint the boat. It'll gie ye something to do till the action starts. Ye might pick up the odd sea trout.' In view of what we were about to face, it seemed trivial to be fishing. Nevertheless I did as I was bidden.

'Noo, we'll just slowly potter up the coast o' Assilag. It will be quite quiet and sheltered along there, and we can watch the point to see if they come oot. Wi' luck they'll have thought better o' it, an' all oor plans will hae gangit agley.'

'Robbie Burns has a line for every occasion,' I said with a laugh, and quoted aloud:–

> 'Wee sleekit, cowrin tim'rous beastie,
> O, what a panic's in thy breastie!
> Thou need na start awa sae hasty,
> Wi' bickering brattle!
> I wad be laith to rin an' chase thee
> Wi' murd'ring pattle! '

'Well done! I see ye know the Scots poet well enough. I wonder if ye can tell me whaur these lines come frae?' Assuming an English voice he quoted: 'Now would I give a thousand furlongs of sea for an acre of barren ground,— long heath, broom, furze, any thing. The wills above be done, but I would fain die a dry death'.

'*Touché*, Alex! You cap my Burns with your Shakespeare. I happen to know those very appropriate lines. They are from the first scene of *The Tempest*, my father's favourite play. But how do you know Shakespeare?'

'Och, I read him a lot. He and Rabbie Burns aye had a telling phrase for ilka occasion.'

'I've got one,' I exclaimed, and started pulling in my line.

As I did so, I burst out laughing. 'Here we are, the two of us about to embark on a very dangerous task and what are we doing? Quoting poetry and fishing!'

'I canna think o' better, unless it be praying, an' I've already said my piece to the Lord. Let's see what you have. Oh aye, a fine sea trout o' about a couple o' pounds. I chust hope you'll enchoy it for breakfast with Fiona. But I see we have business to attend to; there's a wee boat chust come round the south point o' Assilag. I'm thinking that will be your lady.'

Alex eased his throttle open a little and the 'Hottentot' turned to the south.

'We need to time oorsels verra carefully; we want to enter the rip just astern o' them and we have the much shorter distance to go. When we get into the rip we must run the engine as fast as she'll go. We need to be faster than the current under us, so we have steerage, otherwise the current will slew us broadside on, and we'll be lost. The rip's fast itself, and we'll be faster, so ye maun hang on for dear life. As a precaution, clip this line on to your belt. It might chust save ye if ye go overboard.'

So saying, Alex handed me a karabiner attached to a coiled line fastened to a stanchion, and he clipped another on to his own belt. All the time he was watching the other boat, judging its speed and course.

'When they enter the rip on their present course, they are likely to capsize almost at once. If they've any sense they will realise what is happening and hand the tiller to Fiona. She's guid in a boat, and at least she's been in the rip before. Now here's what we'll do. I'll approach the fastest part o' the rip from the side, and try to bring the "Hottentot" as close to them as possible, so as to guide them through the spout.'

'What's the spout?' I interjected.

'It's the point where the rip hits the skerries. There's a gap about twenty feet wide in more than a hundred yards o' jagged rocks; the water pours through in a torrent and its like the spout o' an enormous chug. If we can get through that, we're safe. Trouble is, the spout is a mass of spray, and ye canna see. Do you feel how the "Hottentot"is speeding up? She's beginning to feel the rip under her keel.'

The distance between Thistlethwaite's launch and the 'Hottentot' was shortening now. I could see three people crouched in her stern. There seemed to be some argument going on, with a lot of waving and pointing. Then I saw Fiona quite clearly; she must have made them understand the plight they were in, and had taken over steering. Alex saw this too.

'Aye, they've seen sense chust in time. Fiona's got the helm. They're committed to the rip now. Ah, good lass, she's opened her throttle and she knows to let her boat go with the flow. They're through the first danger. Hang on, Dr Chalmers, we're going after her.'

I felt the 'Hottentot' surge under me as Alex threw the little boat's throttle wide open and put the helm over. We were in the rip. We were speeding through the water faster than I have ever moved at sea. The rip was eerily and smoothly calm here in the deep water. We were gaining on the launch and I could see Fiona struggling to hold her on course. Wertheim was beside her, helping to hold the wheel. She glanced back and saw the 'Hottentot' closing on her. I guessed she was reliving her memory of being here before with Murdo.

'She's too far left,' shouted Alex, and he waved his arm frantically trying to signal to the launch to move right. At first, she seemed to understand, for the launch altered course marginally as the speeding boats rocketed towards the skerries.

Alex was shouting again: 'Look ahead.'

A few hundred yards ahead of us, a wall of spray was shooting up into the air. 'That's where the rip meets the Skerries. D'ye see the one point where there is less spray? That's where we maun go.'

We were now close behind the launch, but with our bow cutting the torrent slightly to her right. Fiona glanced back and even gave a little wave, but immediately clutched the wheel again. I waved back, wondering as I did so if this might be the last communication that ever passed between us.

The wall of water thrown into the air by the force of the rip hitting the skerries seemed to be racing towards us. For a moment I could see the gap. Alex, by sheer dint of skill, had brought us almost in line with it. I could see Fiona was still too far left. Then there was such confusion of spray that I could not see the gap for the mass of water and spume that filled the air.

The launch struck the skerries and was thrown high. It somersaulted into the sky. I saw two people fall from it into the boiling seas. The next thing I knew the 'Hottentot' must have touched the rocks, for I too was thrown out.

Once again I was in the sea. For a split second all was black. I felt a huge wrench at my left arm and waist as the line tightened—I knew the 'Hottentot' had to be afloat still, dragging me through the cold, salty water. I trod water, trying to keep my head high enough to breathe.

There was spray all around me, and I could hardly see anything. Suddenly I hit something. It was not a rock, but it was something solid floating in the water, and I clutched at it. Wreckage of the launch, I thought. Then I realised it was the body of my wife.

Alex's prediction had been accurate: once we were through the gap, the sea was comparatively calm compared to the fury we had experienced. Bobbing along in the water, towed by my lifeline and buoyed by my lifejacket, I held Fiona's body in my arms. Alex hauled us back to the 'Hottentot'. He seized Fiona first, and left me in the sea holding on to the boat's taffrail.

At first I tried to scramble in myself, but I seemed to have every last bit of strength drained from me. The loss of my lovely, lively wife suddenly hit me, and I let go of the 'Hottentot'. I wanted to join Fiona. I tried to undo my lifejacket so that I might sink to an easy death.

Then Alex was heaving me in. 'She's no deid, Doctor. I've started artificial respiration. You carry on while I see to the "Hottentot".'

Alex was right: there was a trace of colour in Fiona's face. Kneeling beside her, I pressed firmly on her chest counting my thrusts. When I got to five, I tried to control my shivering and bent over the mouth that I had kissed so many times. Pinching her nostrils, I breathed a lungful of air into her twice, then went back to my rhythmic thrusting on her chest.

'Come on, come on, Fiona. Don't die,' I muttered. There was a flutter at her throat and I could feel a slight pulse. I forced two more lungfuls of air from my body into hers. The flickering pulse was stronger. My hands were on her breasts, as I thrust again, urging her heart to resume its own rhythm. Again I kissed her and breathed into her; colour was coming to her face.

Suddenly the sexuality of my actions struck me. Fiona and I had played such games before in love. Now she was nearly dying and my heart was breaking.

'How is the lass?' I heard Alex ask in my ear. 'Dinna stave her chest in, Doctor, like Erchie did yourn. She's going to make it. Leave her be, but get her into this life-chacket. The "Hottentot" is holed below water and she's sinking. The prop went when we touched the rock. We're still afloat, but only chust. And us half a mile from the southern tip o' Tuilleag.'

I could not take in all he said, but sure enough Fiona's eyes flickered and opened. She was only half conscious, but was going to live. I carried her under the half deck and threw a blanket over her.

'Dinna mess wi' that,' Archie shouted again. 'Get a chacket on her. We'll no' be afloat many more minutes, and we're in for a long swim.'

I could see he was right; the water level was rising in the boat. Fiona seemed to realise what was needed and struggled into the lifejacket while I tied its tapes behind her. Alex was setting flares off.

'Wi' ony luck they got the coastguard out and he'll need to know where we are.' There was a whoosh as the maroons took off, then suddenly the bright moonlight was dulled by the brilliance of the red flares.'

'If the coastguard's oot as I asked, he'll see that,' said Alex. 'But it's high time for us to go. The "Hottentot" will no last another minute. Help the lass ower the side and then you go in to support her. I shanna be long.'

We bobbed in each other's arms. Fiona was barely conscious but, buoyed by her lifejacket, her head was safely above water. It was astonishing how calm the water was here, after the tumult of the rip. But I began to feel the intense cold seeping into my legs, and wondered just how long we could survive in the cold sea. I hoped the coastguard had seen Alex's distress signal. The old man was still in the 'Hottentot'; I guessed he was saying goodbye to the little boat that had been his companion and his livelihood for so many years. Then with a gentle wave to her, he lowered himself into the sea and swam over to us.

'We maun keep together,' he said, 'and hope the coastguard is not too long.'

The 'Hottentot' slid silently out of sight.

CHAPTER 27

Epilogue

The coastguard, warned by Alex's friends on Assilag, had turned the Lutheran lifeboat out and she had made full speed round the Solan lighthouse, passing clear of the rip. Fortunately she had just rounded Solan point when Alex set off his maroons and they got a bearing on where we were. The setting moon still provided some light, but even so it was nearly an hour before they picked us up. We were all alive but intensely cold. Fiona had gone into hypothermia and seemed unrouseable. My core temperature must have been very low too, for I was no longer shivering. The lifeboat crew were used to chilled people from the sea, and soon had us stripped of our wet clothes and wrapped in blankets. Alex and I were able to accept a cup of cocoa and I could feel life returning. But I was desperately worried about Fiona, who seemed deeply unconscious. Now we were in the light I could see a wound over her left eye.

The journey back to Lutheran was accomplished speedily, and all three of us were stretchered into a waiting ambulance. Among the many voices giving instructions I heard the familiar growl of Old Squarebottle.

'Eh, laddie, ye're a sore trial to me.' Then I felt a jag as he slipped a needle into my arm.

The next thing I knew was waking in a bed. For a few moments I was confused—and then I realised I had been in this very bed nearly a year before. I was in the cottage hospital. Gradually the memory of the ordeal at sea came back to me. I tried to get up but my legs seemed like jelly, and I was surprised to find my arm encased in plaster of Paris. I tried to work out what had happened, but had no memory of hurting my arm. The second attempt to get up was easier, and I struggled to my feet.

Then the door opened, and the nurse Morag Finlayson burst in. 'What're ye doin' out o' bed?' she demanded, and guided me back.

'Fiona?' I asked.

'She's just fine; but she'll no be very pleased to hear ye're out of bed.'

'You mean she's all right?'

'Aye, she bounced back quicker than you did. Now, if you'll just be a sensible man and get back to bed, I'll let her in to see you.'

I did as I was told, and in a moment Fiona was by my bedside.

'How are you, Rob?' she asked, and threw her arms round me. As we kissed, I had a moment's vision of that last kiss we had shared, when she seemed to be dying in my arms.

Fiona had recovered completely, apart from a prize black eye sustained when the launch she was steering exploded under her as it hit the skerries. I was thrown out of the 'Hottentot' at almost the same instant. She must have been incredibly lucky to be thrown almost into my arms.

I remembered the savage pull on my arm and waist as the line connecting me to Alex's boat tightened. That must have been when I broke my arm, yet I had never been aware of pain even when I was trying to resuscitate Fiona.

Hamish came and examined me. 'Och, ye'll do,' he said. 'Ye seem to be a remarkably difficult man to kill. I think Erchie's right: ye're destined for the hangman's rope. I never knew anyone who escaped drowning three times.' He told me I had fractured the ulna and radius in my left forearm and not for the first time I wondered at the way pain is abolished at moments of intense threat.

'Och,' said Hamish, 'I've seen similar things in soldiers wounded while fighting for their lives in war.'

A day or two later I was allowed to go home with Fiona. She insisted on my going straight to bed and when I protested that I was quite fit now, she added, 'Don't worry, I'm coming too, we have some serious loving to do.'

And so we had. Our bodies came together with tenderness followed by intense passion such as we had never experienced together before. So the tension of our ordeal was released. At its height I remembered the strangely inappropriate sexual experience of kissing the breath of life into her, as I thought she was on the point of death, and my thrusting action in trying to make her breathe. Love making between us would forever afterwards be a celebration of our joint survival from the sea.

There was a lot to sort out. I told Fiona of the death of Oleg and how he had shot Stanley Johnson in the leg. Hamish had told us that Stanley was still recovering in the cottage hospital. 'But what I really want to know,' I asked Fiona, 'is why you were at Tom Bacadh?'

Fiona gave a heavy sigh. 'Rob, I got all mixed up. I was so distressed about Murdo, and I thought you were lying to me about Frances Agnew. I thought the only person who could shed any light on Murdo's death was Thistlethwaite. So I decided to go and see him.'

'But...' I began to say.

'Don't interrupt. Just listen to my whole story, then you'll perhaps understand.'

I nodded.

'Thistlethwaite was charming: he invited me into his study and offered me a drink. He was very sympathetic about Murdo. Then he started talking about you. He seemed to know a great deal about you. He mentioned a mutual acquaintance that he shared with you, a Dr Wishart.'

'Good God, that name keeps coming up.'

'You remember him? Anyway, Thistlethwaite was keen to show you in a very bad light. He told me you had been implicated in drug thefts from your hospital. He even knew all about Frances Agnew. Then he turned to Murdo's death. He told me that his keeper Oleg had been on the moor, and that he had told him that it was you who had fired the shot that brought Murdo's plane down.'

'You can't have believed that.'

'Rob, he was so convincing and he seemed to confirm all my suspicions. God forgive me, I did believe him. You have no idea how convincing he was.'

'The man used to be a confidence trickster. I suppose it all fits.'

'Then things started happening very quickly. Oleg came in. He seemed very anxious about something being wrong. Thistlethwaite told him to calm down. Then we heard the helicopter and that odious German man came in. Then there was uproar. Stanley, Hamish and Daddy came in and tried to make an arrest. Oleg drew a gun, shot Stanley and fled. I thought Stanley was dead. Hamish and Daddy had their revolvers on Thistlethwaite. Then Wertheim stuck his automatic pistol in my back and said he would shoot me if they did not put their guns down. When they did so, Thistlethwaite tied Daddy and Hamish to chairs, and he and Wertheim dragged me out to the helicopter. We took off immediately, but Wertheim said we could not go far because he was out of fuel. They decided to make for Assilag, where they had a launch, which would take them out to a trawler that was waiting at sea. You can imagine that by that time I was getting to grips with the situation, and I realised that Thistlethwaite had been lying all the time in order to put blame for everything on to you.'

Fiona stopped for a moment. 'Oh Rob, I'm so sorry I doubted you; but you must see that the story fitted so well with what Helen Agnew had said.'

'He was a cunning devil. What happened to him?'

'Hamish says they were found washed up on Mulcaire. Both Wertheim and Thistlethwaite must have drowned when I hit the skerries.'

I took Fiona in my arms again. 'Look,' I said, 'I did go out with Helen's sister but our relationship was never sexual. I did know Dr Wishart, who, it later transpired, was a drug addict. Presumably he was one of Thistlethwaite's clients, and Wishart was the source of these rumours about me. I am afraid I'm just a simple GP trying to do his job and love his wife.'

After that life returned to normal. Stanley Johnson came out of hospital with nothing but a slight limp from the neurological damage caused by Oleg's bullet. In a strange episode at sea, a Royal Navy destroyer intercepted a Latin American trawler. Laigersay once again exerted its healing quality by helping to suppress an international drug cartel. It also blessed Fiona and myself with peace again in our marriage

In the fullness of time Fiona presented her father with twin grandsons. Not long afterwards the old man died, full of years and wisdom, happy in the knowledge that his heirs would continue to be lairds of Laigersay and to live in Castle Chalmers. Erchie stopped poaching, and settled as factor at the castle. Hamish retired partly from medicine and lived a reclusive life, writing on the natural history of Laigersay. Tetrabal Singh set up one of the most famous Indian restaurants in Scotland.

Cuhlan moved back to live with Maggie McPhee and they both passed into the mythology of Laigersay. Alex Farquharson got a new boat and in a gesture to me called her 'The Ornithologist'.

And Fiona and me? Why, we just went on loving in the island that loved to be loved.